Order this book online at www.trafford.com
or email orders@trafford.com

Edited by: Nic Hayes

Art Consultant: Randy Hayes

Senior Content Editor/Transcriptionist: Camille Brazell

Most Trafford titles are also available at major online book retailers.

Printed in Victoria, BC, Canada.

ISBN: 978-1-4251-7317-3 (sc)

ISBN: 978-1-4251-7318-0 (e-book)

*Our mission is to efficiently provide the world's finest, most comprehensive book publishing
service, enabling every author to experience success. To find out how to publish your book, your
way, and have it available worldwide, visit us online at www.trafford.com*

Trafford rev. 04/23/2010

 www.trafford.com

North America & international
toll-free: 1 888 232 4444 (USA & Canada)
phone: 250 383 6864 ♦ fax: 812 355 4082

Dedication

This book is dedicated to my best friend Mark and his family: Erin, McKaden, Ben, and Chloe. May their lives be long and happy.

Acknowledgements

Nic Hayes- Editing: I wrote it, but he put it all together.

Jake Hayes – Assistant Editor

Camille Brazell – Content Editor/ Transcriptionist

Randy Hayes – Artistic Consultant

Finally for my Father Martin and my Grandfather Milton, both of whom encouraged my love of reading and writing.

FORWARD

The following is an excerpt from Vice-Admiral Donald Higgin's book, The Protectorate: A Comprehensive History of the Making of an Empire published in 2519. Admiral Higgins is considered to be the leading authority on Protectorate history, and his works on the subject are required reading for all Protectorate students at the college level.

The Protectorate: A Comprehensive 0History of the Making of an Empire. Appendix A: Time line of Major Events in Protectorate History:

2032: The Chinese-Russian War begins. The Chinese, whose population has risen to over two billion, attacks Russia's southern grain belt. The United States under President Phillip Fitzpatrick takes no action for fear of provoking a nuclear engagement.

2035: After three years the war shows no sign of ending. Both the Russians and Chinese have taken severe casualties: 47 and 63 million respectively. In an attempt to cease hostilities, President Fitzpatrick offers to mediate a settlement. Meanwhile, the United States is suffering from problems of its own. Due to the availability of inexpensive labor in other nations, America's industrial base is sorely weakened and unemployment rises to an extremely high 13%. Also, a myriad of social difficulties begins to rot the infrastructure of American society, not the least of which is illegal immigration from Mexico which reaches an all time high.

2036: An agreement is reached that ends the Chinese-Russian War. Although the treaty is negotiated by the American ambassador, credit is generally given to Colonel Alexander Kinkaid, a young and extremely gifted army officer attached to the ambassador's staff as a military advisor. For his outstanding work on the treaty, Colonel Kinkaid is promoted to Brigadier General and is regarded as a hero in the U.S. President Fitzpatrick wins re-election.

2037: President Fitzpatrick and the U.S. Congress authorize a massive aid package for both war-torn China and Russia. This legislation is not well received by the American public who have continued to grow uneasy over internal problems. General Kinkaid is assigned to the United Nations peace-keeping force in China.

2038: Russia, still harboring deep resentment for the Chinese and unhappy over certain treaty stipulations, abrogates the agreement and initiates a surprise attack on China. Russian forces penetrate deeply into Chinese territory. The United States declares war on Russia. General Kinkaid is placed in temporary command of U.S. forces in China until the American army can be mobilized.

June 9: At the Battle of the Wall, General Kinkaid's small UN force badly mauls a much larger Russian contingency. Kinkaid is promoted to Major General shortly thereafter.

July 6: American reinforcements begin to arrive in China.

July 23: General Kinkaid wins another major battle forcing Russian troops from northwest China.

Sept.: Now a Lieutenant General, Kinkaid begins a counteroffensive that drives the Russians out of China.

President Fitzpatrick orders Kinkaid not to cross the Russian border for fear of nuclear reprisals.

Oct.: General Kinkaid reinforces his position at the Russian border. Both he and his troops believe that a forceful strike into Russia would end the war, but President Fitzpatrick will not allow the army to move.

Dec.: Alexander Kinkaid is promoted to 4-Star General. The Russians, unable to break through the China-America line, begin to negotiate

January 2039: President Fitzpatrick agrees to allow the Russians to return to their prewar state without penalties. General Kinkaid, his army, and the American people are incensed with this decision.

March: General Kinkaid returns to the U.S. and receives a hero's welcome. Unknown to the civilian leadership at the time, the general begins to speak to other high ranking military officials about the possibility of a coup d' état. Meanwhile, unemployment has risen to 18%, violent crime reaches epidemic proportions and the problem with illegal immigration continues to increase. The number of persons on welfare in the U.S. reaches an all-time high.

April: General Kinkaid stages a complete military take-over of the United States. The President, Vice-president, and Supreme Court are arrested for "failure to serve the American people." Congress is ruled inoperative and is disbanded. Martial law is declared in all U.S. cities. Major roadways and other travel arteries fall into military hands.

14th: The general places his eight chief lieutenants on his ruling council. This body would come to be known as the "Council of Nine." Kinkaid announces that the United States shall be known as the Protectorate and shall be ruled as an "intellectual oligarchy." The Council orders all Protectorate borders closed. Mobilized infantry and armored divisions are ordered to the Mexican border with orders to "cease illegal immigration by whatever means necessary." The Council of Nine orders that the United States Constitution is suspended indefinitely.

15th: The Council decrees that welfare be terminated. All persons that were unemployed and able to work as of this date are placed in government work camps. Those persons and their families were fed, clothed, and given shelter. In return, a huge labor force was created Under this program, people were put to work building highways, reopening factories that eventually became Protectorate armament centers, and placed in other public-works programs.

The Council enacts the Protectorate Citizenship Law. This states that all persons in the Protectorate illegally as of this date shall be forcibly deported within six months. Illegals are given the opportunity to surrender within this time. After the 6-month period, any person within Protectorate borders illegally shall be terminated.

16th: The Council passes the "Draconian Code." The following crimes became punishable by death: Murder, rape, child molestation, severe child abuse, severe animal cruelty, drug trafficking and treason. All other crimes were assigned severe penalties. For example, first offense "driving under the influence" with no bodily harm was punished by five years hard labor. All persons not committing a capital crime were permitted to serve their sentences and be reintegrated into society. Any second offense of any kind was punished by death. Trial by jury is maintained, however, professional juries are selected by government exam. In the ten years following the enactment of this justice code, crime would drop by 97%.

The Protectorate withdraws from the United Nations.

May: The Council orders a huge military build-up. Obsolete equipment is placed on the Mexican border for impending action against that nation. General Kinkaid orders that plans be drawn up for the invasion of Mexico.

July: With Protectorate industry on the rise, the Council orders a trade embargo against most nations. This action cripples the economy of many countries, especially Japan. The Protectorate orders that all debts to other nations are null and void. To stabilize the Middle-East, the Council invites Israel to join the Protectorate. Israel assents on the 26th of July.

Aug.: Protectorate forces invade Mexico. Most resistance is crushed by the middle of the month. Mexico is absorbed into the Protectorate by the 23rd. Many nations file protests against the Protectorate which are ignored. Protectorate factories and shipyards begin production at levels not seen since World War II.

Dec.: The "North-West Hemisphere Defense Zone" is secured. Protectorate territory now includes Canada and all lands up to and including the Panama Canal. Further social change continues internally. By this time the "Religious Tolerance Act" has been adopted. Protectorate citizens may believe in anything they choose, in the privacy of their own homes, however all organized religions are ruled illegal. This act eventually breaks Judeo-Christian religions worldwide by the year 2150.

January 2040: Using Israel as a jumping off point, the Protectorate seizes most of the Middle-East. The Protectorate now controlled 75% of the world's petroleum supplies. General Kinkaid, in a master stroke of strategic planning, signs a non-aggression pact with the European Community, China and Russia. The general agrees not to attack these nations and further agrees to lift trade sanctions. This treaty allows the Protectorate to absorb Japan, Australia, and most of the African continent over the next three years.

2042: The Protectorate begins a very aggressive scientific and space program. Ten-percent of Protectorate funds is pumped into various research programs, not the least of which is the "Cold Fusion Development Project."

2043: All nations not on the Eur-Asian continent are considered Protectorate territory. General Kinkaid begins a secret plan to invade Europe.

May: Protectorate forces attack the European Continent from the Atlantic Ocean and Mediterranean Sea. The European community puts up stout resistance, but is ultimately unable to stop the advance. In an ironic twist, the Russians and Chinese sign a mutual protection pact. Fortunately for the Protectorate, the Chinese and Russians are simply not strong enough alone to halt the advance. A unified Earth is only a matter of time at this point.

April 2044: The Russo-Chinese coalition surrenders to the Protectorate. For the first time in human history, all of mankind shares in a united globe. The Council of Nine enacts a rigorous clean up program that begins to heal the scars man had inflicted on the planet.

Dec.: Dr. Candace Brazell discovers cold-fusion. This monumental achievement gives the citizens of the Protectorate nearly unlimited clean power. The Council of Nine orders immediate research into how this power may be used for propulsion. The eyes of mankind turn to see the solar system in its grasp.

2046: Fusion engines are used for the first time. The P.I.V. (Protectorate Interplanetary Vessel) Wanderlust reaches a speed of .22c. Plans are made for the colonization of the Moon and Mars. Probes are outfitted with fusion engines to explore the remainder of the solar-system.

2048: The first permanent Protectorate colony is established on the Moon. The P.I.V. Dauntless visits the Jovian System.

2049: The first permanent Protectorate colony is established on Mars. The P.I.V. Argos reaches a speed of .31c and becomes the first manned spaceship to leave the solar system.

2053: The Moon now supports four major colonies and two additional mining settlements. New Phoenix on Mars boasts a population of over five thousand. The Protectorate possesses 26 interplanetary craft.

2054: The Fusion Assisted Laser (FAL) is invented by Dr. Nicolas Hayes. This device is used in industrial, mining, and military applications.

2056: Alexander Kinkaid celebrates his fiftieth birthday. The Council of Nine rules that due to the new makeup of the military, i.e., the building of a space fleet, all military rank shall use naval nomenclature. Kinkaid becomes the first Protectorate Fleet Admiral.

2059: The Council of Nine devises a new way to choose the leader of the Protectorate. It is ruled that the Fleet Admiral shall be the chair of a council consisting of 23 Admirals, one for each Protectorate Fleet. The Fleet Admiral shall be elected by all officers holding the rank of Commodore and higher with a 75% majority. Each Admiral shall have a number of votes equal to the number of stars in his/her rank, i.e., a vice-admiral's vote would count three times. The position of Fleet Admiral shall be a lifetime position unless the 23 Council Admirals vote unanimously for removal. This election process is still in effect today.

The Council of Nine disbands in favor of the new system with Fleet Admiral Kinkaid in command.

2061: In what is still regarded today as the largest freak of discovery in scientific history, Dr. Lorans Newman invents the Einsteinian Dampener. This device effectively negates the relativistic characteristics of near-light speeds. Using fusion power and this device, the P.I.V. Star Chaser achieves a speed of .8c. The solar system opens to Protectorate mining and colonizing efforts.

Protectorate military forces consist of 23 fleets of 12 vessels each. In addition there are some 175 fusion powered ships owned and operated by private corporations.

Protectorate colonies are established on Titan, a moon of Saturn and Ceres in the Asteroid Belt.

By the end of the 2060's, Protectorate scientists have found cures for cancer, multiple sclerosis, and diabetes in addition to a myriad of other diseases. As profit was no longer the sole motivator to pharmaceutical companies, these diseases were eradicated easily.

2070: Fleet Admiral Kinkaid is diagnosed with Baray's Syndrome, a degenerative disease of the liver and kidneys. He shares this information with only his closest advisors. He tells this circle to support Vice-Admiral Hirochi Nagama for Fleet Admiral after his death.

2073: Fleet Admiral Kinkaid dies at the age of sixty-seven, mourned by the entire planet and her colonies. A week of grieving is declared by Admiral Sirra of the 4th Fleet.

After this period, the Council of Admirals convenes to select a new Fleet Admiral. Vice-Admiral Nagama receives 69% of the vote, but this is insufficient to raise him to the post. Several factions begin to develop. By rule, a new election cannot occur until the following year. The Admirals of the 23 Protectorate fleets begin to jockey for position.

2077: After four years of infighting and near civil war, Admiral Nagama is selected as the new Fleet Admiral. He immediately consolidates the Protectorate under one banner, firing the seven Admirals who opposed him.

2078: Anti-matter is produced and stored safely in large quantities for the first time. Protectorate scientists are excited over the propulsion and weapons possibilities.

2081: An anti-matter warhead is test detonated on the Moon. Anti-matter missiles are incorporated into the weapons packages of most Protectorate warships.

2103: The P.I.V. Fearless explodes with the loss of all hands. This marks the fifth-failed attempt by man to break the light barrier.

A disheartened Fleet Admiral Nagama retires in December after a relatively successful reign. The Protectorate now possesses 37 extra-terran colonies and space stations, but the inability to exceed the speed of light haunts the retired Admiral. A new election is set for the following year.

2104: Commodore Kyle Lesniak is selected to be the next Fleet Admiral. Lesniak becomes the first and only Commodore to ascend to that august rank. He devotes massive resources to the Faster Than Light Program, and promises the barrier will be broken before 2120.

2118: Dr. Matthew Winters discovers the key to FTL travel. His invention, referred to as the Displacement Drive, is tested on an unmanned probe. The probe becomes the first man-made object to break the light barrier. It is believed that the probe reaches a speed of 96c before telemetry is lost.

2119: The P.I.V. Mercury becomes the first manned ship to accelerate beyond the speed of light. This breakthrough opens tremendous new vistas to human endeavor. A new age of exploration begins.

P.I.V. is changed to read: Protectorate Interstellar Vessel.

January 2125: Protectorate vessels are capable of a maximum speed of approximately 160c. Fleet Admiral Lesniak annexes all space within a 100-light-year globe around the solar system for the Protectorate. Twelve vessels of the 14th Fleet are ordered to map this area. The 14th Fleet becomes the traditional exploratory arm of the Protectorate.

November 2125: The P.I.V. Pandora encounters an extraterrestrial scout ship. The vessel contains members of a race called the Nari. The Protectorate learns that the Nari are at war with their parent planet; these people are referred to as the Nor-Nari. The Protectorate and the Nari begin a massive cultural exchange. The Nari request the Protectorate's aid in their war. Fleet Admiral Lesniak agrees. In exchange, the Nari agree to join the Protectorate. In doing so, the Protectorate greatly improves their displacement drive by incorporating Nari technology. Protectorate ships increase their maximum speed to about 750c.

July 2126: The Protectorate and Nor-Nari meet in battle for the first time; the 14th and 22nd Fleets are outnumbered, but Protectorate weapons technology is superior. Losses on both sides are about even and both forces withdraw in good order.

August: A small Nari contingency is ambushed by Nor-Nari forces. The Nari fight well, but are soon overwhelmed. The Protectorate unleashes a counterattack on three sides of the Nor-Nari fleet, nearly obliterating four Nor-Nari defense cohorts. This battle paves the way for the siege of the Nor-Nari home world.

2128: After two years of war the Nor-Nari surrender to the Protectorate. The Nari inform the Council of Admirals of several other extraterrestrial races that they have contact with. The Nari and Nor-Nari are granted Protectorate citizenship and both planets are welcomed into the fold. Protectorate scientific development begins to mushroom with Nari cooperation.

2132: The Protectorate flag now flies over five star systems: Sol, Nari, Jarasta (the home star of the Nor-Nari world), Plaxi, and Phygia. Plaxi IV is an Earth-like, but uninhabited world where the Protectorate colony New Boston is established. Phygia VII is the home world of the Synestians, a humanoid race with rudimentary FTL capabilities. The Synestians agreed to join the Protectorate after the 12th, 15th 22nd and 23rd fleets "show the flag." The Synestian race is a unique one in that their skin pigmentation consists of chlorophyll instead of melanin. In this way the Synestians can produce their own sustenance to a limited degree.

2140: Fleet Admiral Lesniak dies at the age of 80. His reign is considered one of the most productive in Protectorate history. At the time of his death the Protectorate consists of: 40 solar system colonies, three extra-solar colonies, and four alien races. Protectorate vessels are capable of 1000c. The 23 Protectorate Fleets contain a combined force of nearly 600 ships.

2141: Vice-Admiral Sheridan Lin is elected Fleet Admiral. This marks the first female to attain the rank. Protectorate vessels contain crew compliments of Human, Nari, Synestian, and Pologian representatives.

2150: Dr. Matthew Fitzgerald invents the Nova-Cannon. This massively destructive weapon is mounted on vessels of Heavy Cruiser class or larger.

2172: The Great Crisis begins. The Protectorate is attacked by the Galvanian Alliance. This war would exact a heavy toll on Protectorate citizens before its conclusion.

2181: The Great Crisis ends. After nine years of war, the Protectorate defeats the Galvanians. Eighty-two million Protectorate casualties are reported. As the Protectorate mourns its dead, a huge gain in territory and resources is realized because of this conflict.

2205: The Great Expansion begins. This 100-year period is marked by fantastic gains in territory, scientific development, and fleet enlargement by the Protectorate.

2205: Fleet Admiral Sheridan Lin dies at the age of 105. She ruled well until her death, although it is well established that Admiral Maximilian Tovah of the 3rd Fleet was assisting her in the final decade of her reign. Admiral Tovah is elected Fleet Admiral the following year.

2218: Fleet Admiral Tovah is killed in a border skirmish with the Valdanians. The Admiral was on an inspection tour when the Valdanians staged a surprise attack. In retaliation, the Protectorate annihilates the Valdanian home world. Other possibly hostile races rethink their plans after viewing the ferocity of Protectorate reprisals.

2224: After six years, Rear Admiral Veshi Chaloota is elected Fleet Admiral. Chaloota, a Nari, becomes the first nonhuman to assume Protectorate leadership.

2230: Protectorate territory is defined as a globe one thousand light years in diameter around the Sol system.

2237: The P.I.V. Swiftsure breaks the 1500c barrier. This is the first major advancement in Displacement Drive Technology since the Nari merger in 2125.

2241: Fleet Admiral Chaloota begins to display some strange mental symptoms. He becomes moody and tends to lash out at subordinates for no reason. At the time he was nearly 89 years old, only middle-age for a Nari.

2244: Chaloota's mental breakdown grows worse. He orders ridiculous ship placements and troop dispersions. He allocates funds to bureaus that no longer exist. In addition, he becomes completely irrational, calm one minute, raving the next. The Council of Admirals meets to discuss the situation.

2245: For the first time in Protectorate history a Fleet Admiral is removed by unanimous vote of the Council of Admirals. It is learned that the unfortunate Chaloota was suffering from Scosian Neurofibritis, an extremely rare disorder of the Nari brain and nervous system. The hapless admiral would die the following year.

2246: Admiral Jackynth Jackynth becomes Fleet Admiral, the first Pyrolite to assume the post.

2288: Fleet Admiral Jackynth orders a large increase in new ship construction. He further orders that older and obsolete vessels be retired. It is his hope to have a 3000-ship navy by 2290.

2290: The Fleet Admiral's dream is realized. The 23 Protectorate fleets contain 3019 vessels, all of which are state of the art for the time.

2300: The Great Expansion ends. The Protectorate has again expanded its boundaries to include space as far as two thousand light years from Earth. Thirty-two alien races call the Protectorate home.

2319: Fleet Admiral Jackynth dies at the age of 159. His reign made possible the large navy of present day.

2320: Vice-Admiral Phillip Collen is elected Fleet Admiral.

2337: The Pollux Collective is conquered after only three months of campaigning. This brilliant victory is generally credited to Admiral Smythington Ross, Commander 4th Protectorate Fleet.

2340: The Balba join the Protectorate.

2342: Fleet Admiral Collen retires after a relatively short 22 year reign.

2343: Admiral Ross is elected Fleet Admiral by the largest margin in Protectorate history. Ross receives 93% of the vote, largely due to his Pollux victories.

2350: Fleet Admiral Ross orders yet another shake down of Protectorate Fleets. He increases the size of the navy to over five thousand vessels. In addition, ships are ordered to be refitted, regardless of type or class, every five years. This action insures that Protectorate vessels shall be state of the art at all times. This practice is still in effect today.

2365: Dr. Mark Kirchener of the New Earth Council of Medicine publishes a directory of all races in the Protectorate. This ever expanding work contains all pertinent anatomical and physiological traits of all Protectorate citizens. His work inspires Dr. Kirchener to develop drugs that are effective across species lines. This revolutionizes biochemistry and the era of full-spectrum pharmaceuticals is born. Dr. Kirchener wins the Nobel Protectorate Prize for his work a year later.

2373: Fleet Admiral Ross orders that five new Protectorate War Colleges be opened. This relieves the burden on the existing Colleges as enrollment soars to record levels.

2385: The Craxton Booster is employed on Protectorate ships for the first time. The P.I.V. Colossus attains a speed of 2137c. The Pologian scientist Sy Craxta is credited with the invention.

2390: Fleet Admiral Ross dies at the age of 99.

2397: Admiral Calpatia Zee of Tulari is elected Fleet Admiral.

2400: Fleet Admiral Zee is assassinated on her home world by Tulari separatists, marking the first stirring of rebellion in the Protectorate in over 259 years. The 3rd, 9th, and 11th fleets are dispatched to deal with the separatists who are subsequently overwhelmed and destroyed. Fleet presence is increased in possible "trouble spots" as a security measure.

2405: After five years there are no further signs of dissent. Rear-Admiral Adam Cooper is elected Fleet Admiral.

2419: The Treaty of Gola is signed by the Protectorate and the P'ora'synth Collective.

2421: The Treaty of Balboa IX is ratified. The Creeots are welcomed into the Protectorate.

2427: In 22 years, Fleet Admiral Cooper has acquired huge amounts of territory without firing a shot. His crowning achievement comes with the absorption of the Priette Cluster. Fleet Admiral Cooper is considered to be the greatest diplomatic leader in Protectorate history.

2430: Fleet Admiral Cooper orders all Protectorate expansion halted for 25 years. He feels that the large quantities of new Protectorate territory need to be mapped, explored, and controlled thoroughly before more outward movement can be realized. He orders the navy to be enlarged as well to properly patrol the new star systems.

2455: The "Cooper Acquisition Zone" is brought under Protectorate control. The 23 fleets now consist of more than sixty-two hundred ships. Fleet Admiral Cooper retires a contented man at the age of 96.

2457: Admiral Bria Endoorasarkasis is elected Fleet Admiral.

2460: Following her predecessor's plan, Fleet Admiral Endoorasarkasis continues to firm-up Protectorate defenses. She also begins a vast internal improvement program.

2472: Fleet Admiral Endoorasarkasis claims territory beyond the Cooper Acquisition Zone. She orders that this area will begin being explored at the turn of the century.

2500: After another flurry of building activity, the Protectorate Fleets contain more than sixty-seven hundred ships. Fleet Admiral Endoorasarkasis retires after ordering the 14th Exploratory Fleet into position near her territorial annex.

2501: Admiral Benjamin Raihem is elected Fleet Admiral, the first of mixed parentage - the new Fleet Admiral is half Human, half Nari.

2507: Fleet Admiral Raihem retires after only six years. He was not a young man when elected.

2519: As of the date of publication, a new Fleet Admiral has not been selected, nor is one likely to be in the near future. The author can only wonder what lies in store for all Protectorate citizens.

Donald Higgins, Vice-Admiral
1st Protectorate Fleet

Chapter I: Lieutenant (Junior Grade)
October 08, 2519
P.I.V. Vasco de Gamma, 107 light years beyond the "Cooper Acquisition Zone."

Lt. (j.g.) Martin Gammage sat alone at a table in the officers' mess. He was, as usual, early for his daily breakfast gathering with his fellow junior officers. As Martin watched the multi-species crew file into the compartment, he caught the glint of his rank tabs and smiled. He had made j.g. only six months after graduating from the Protectorate War College, an unusually rapid advancement for a history major. His promotion had won him a position on the Alpha shift as weapons officer.

A message cube slammed down in front of Martin, breaking his revelry. "Have you seen this?" Exclaimed the owner of the cube.

Martin looked up and grinned wryly. "And a good morning to you too, Edward," he replied.

Edward Longly was a tall sandy haired ensign who had graduated with Martin's class. He was a remarkable engineer with a fiery temper that exploded quickly, but cooled just as fast. As a matter of fact, Martin knew the contents of the cube. He had received a communiqué from his father, a retired Rear Admiral the day before, but decided to give Edward his lead hoping to diffuse him before their other friends arrived.

Edward glared at Martin for a moment before launching into his daily tirade.

"They did it again! What are those idiots thinking? Someone should fly back to Earth and tell those morons to vote for Admiral Connoly for pity's sake! It's been twelve years! Twelve years, how long does it take? If you ask me . . ."

"No one's asking you, Eddie." Martin saw his best friend Marcus Slivnova approaching from the food dispensers. Marcus' comment had broken Edward's speech off in mid-tantrum. Not a good idea in Martin's estimation.

Edward turned on Marcus, "Oh, you have a different opinion?"

"No, I have no opinion. I just had no desire to hear yours. Besides, Admiral Connoly didn't have a chance this year, anyway. Really Eddie, if you're going to make pronouncements, you should at least try to back a winning horse."

"I'll buy that. Good morning boys, good morning Admiral." The three men were joined by Ensign Jaspa Shindessa, a gorgeous Nari whom Martin had a severe crush on during his college years. He was over her now, or so he kept telling himself. Her last comment was directed toward Martin whose college nickname had been "Admiral." He thought this a good sign, as Stonewall Jackson's West Point nickname had been "General."

As the willowy sensor specialist sat down, the group was joined by its final member, Ryndock Calplygia, a huge Pologian. Ryndock's bulk eclipsed everything and provided Martin with a welcome distraction; he was staring at Jaspa again.

"Hey Ryn, does this morning find you well?" Martin inquired in Pologian.

Ryndock smiled down at the group, or at least Martin thought he was smiling; it was hard to tell with the Pologian.

"Your accent is improving Martin, but you used a formal phrase with an informal greeting."

"Sorry Ryn, I'll try to be more careful."

Edward, seeing that he was no longer the center of attention chimed in, "Now that the customary greetings and cultural exchanges are over, can we view the message?" His words dripped with sarcasm as he tapped the message cube with his forefinger.

"Sure Eddie, let's see what's got you so excited . . . this time" replied Martin.

Edward favored the group with a condescending sneer before tapping the top of the cube three times. Even though Martin knew the contents of the communiqué, he was interested in seeing how the media handled it, and more important, he wanted to gauge his friends' reactions.

A small holographic globe appeared above the table containing the Protectorate Information Bureau Seal. The picture then dissolved into the face of the announcer. Martin smiled a bit as he remembered a lecture from one of his history classes. He wondered if this was anything like seeing the news at what humans used to call the movies. "Hello Protectorate citizens," the announcer began, "on October 2, 2519 the Council of Admirals gathered for their annual meeting in Phoenix, North American Continent, Earth, to choose a Fleet Admiral. The votes were again badly split this year with Vice Admiral Voosar receiving 41%, the largest percentage this voting session. As you know, this figure is nowhere near the 75% majority necessary for ratification. Turning now to the world of sports, Nari Paddleball champions . . ." The announcer's voice was cut off as Edward shut down the cube.

"Hey, I wanted to see that!" Exclaimed Jaspa.

"What the hell difference does paddleball make when our own so-called leaders can't get their heads out of their asses long enough to choose a Fleet Admiral?" Edward shot back.

Marcus gave Edward a big toothy grin; "You won't have to worry about it for much longer after the fleet cashiers you for gross insubordination."

Jaspa gazed at Martin for a moment before asking him what he thought of all this.

Martin cleared his throat slightly before diving in. "I don't really know what to make of the Council's vote, except to say that I don't see anyone achieving a clear cut majority anytime soon. This year it was Voosar, last year Connoly, Jetta the year before and none of them was even close to 75%. I would wager it's going to be like this until some of the new Commodores come up, that's how Admiral Lesniak was elected."

"But that was over 400 years ago, and no Commodore has been elected since," replied Jaspa.

"I am aware of that, but until the Council gets some fresh blood, I don't see any of the recent contenders winning."

Marcus took advantage of the break in the action to speak up; "I have to agree with Martin, the situation as it stands now is untenable. No one has a clear power base now."

"Oh, you always agree with Martin," replied Edward.

"Do I always agree with you Martin?" Asked Marcus innocently.

Martin smiled at his friend, "I don't know, but you know what they say, great minds think alike."

Ryn replied with an exasperated sigh, "I think that politics gives me indigestion. Either they'll pick a Fleet Admiral, or they won't. I'm just an ensign along with the rest of you, except for our precocious friend of course," Ryn concluded with a nod at Martin.

The rumbling of the Pologian's voice seemed to quash any further discussion on the topic. The silence that followed seemed to sum up the mood at the table. It seemed unlikely that the next ruler of the Protectorate would be chosen any time soon, but the junior officers and friends in the galley were powerless to do anything about it.

"Well," Martin broke the silence while glancing at his chronometer, "it's 0745, think I'll be heading up to the bridge."

"You always do this," Jaspa replied. "How long does it take you to get to the bridge, about one minute?"

"I have to compensate for dealing with you before I leave" Martin shot back.

Jaspa gave Martin a smile that destroyed his resolve. He felt himself melting back into his seat.

"Besides," continued Jaspa, "Delta shift never leaves before 0755, so you just wind up standing around anyway."

"Well, things might heat up today," Marcus added. As an assistant operations officer, he knew that several star systems would be in scanning range before the end of Alpha shift.

"I could do with some excitement, all we've done in engineering the last few days is drill and run diagnostics."

"Be careful what you wish for Eddie, you may get it," returned Martin. He turned his gaze on Jaspa; "May we leave now your Highness?"

"All right, but let's at least walk to the lift together."

They all stood and headed for the door. The galley was a central compartment on this deck so they walked the hundred or so feet to the travel tube. The Verrazano Class heavy cruiser, of which the Vasco de Gamma was a part, was built without much regard for aesthetics. These exploratory vessels were designed to take punishment and bring their crews home alive. Martin knew this, but he sometimes wished for a splash of color here or there.

They approached the tube doors as Ryn smashed the call control with a meaty palm. "Hey," Edward exclaimed, "if you break that, who do you think they're going to send to fix it?"

"Someone has to keep you busy," came the glib reply.

The travel tube arrived, disgorging several crewmembers on their way to secondary posts. The band of friends embarked and pressed controls for their various duty stations. Jaspa and Martin to the bridge, Marcus to operations on deck four, Edward to engineering, and Ryn to a cargo bay below decks. The big Pologian rumbled as he selected his deck, "this is no way to treat a Protectorate War College graduate. I'm a glorified clerk taking inventory."

Marcus looked up and replied, "We can't all have the glory jobs like the bridge twins here." He made a sweeping gesture toward Martin and Jaspa.

The Nari favored Marcus with one of her knee buckling smiles. "Jealous," was all she said.

Martin and Jaspa said good-bye to their other ship mates and made the trip to the bridge. They stepped out of the lift as the view screen chronometer changed to 0759. A tall, middle-aged woman in the command well turned at the sound of the doors opening.

"Good morning, Ensign, Lieutenant," came the customary greeting from Commander Jane McMurphy, the ship's first officer. She always took the time to acknowledge the crew's junior officers which made her an endearing figure onboard ship. "You may take your posts," she continued, "standard Plan of the Day, but keep sharp. We have reason to believe that a contact will be made today. Sensor analysis from the previous shift indicates a signal of unknown origin in our vicinity. The Captain has ordered an investigation."

"Aye Commander," came the reply from the two younger officers. Finally, thought Martin, maybe a chance for some action.

"Captain on the bridge," cried Lieutenant Koor from the life support systems monitor. She was Dyrillian and tended to get excited under the most trivial of circumstances. She was rock solid under real pressure, however.

"Good morning all," came the smooth reply from Captain Aaron Prescott. He was a grey haired, good looking man of about fifty-five. Prescott was a seasoned explorer and commanding officer, a sure bet for promotion to Commodore on his next evaluation. He took a few moments to survey his domain before settling in the command well. Martin liked his no-nonsense approach to command. Prescott also came highly recommended from Gammage's father; the two had met when the elder Gammage had a ship command.

Prescott turned to McMurphy, "Report please."

"We have altered course to system 39Q to investigate the anomalous signal as per your orders. Our speed is 1500c, and our E.T.A. at system boundary is two hours, 15 minutes."

"Very well. Continue scans at maximum, Ensign Shindessa. Commander McMurphy, coordinate with Lieutenants Gammage and Shil for a battle simulation while we have the time." A chorus of "Aye sirs" greeted the new list of orders.

The prescribed drill kept Martin busy for the better part of the next hour. Prescott was very much the taskmaster and would not put up with sub-par performance. The ship's score for the drill was 93 of 100, with Martin's personal score of 97. He was of course pleased with his results, he just believed it was all smoke in the wind and longed for a chance to prove himself.

"Captain, sensor analysis complete for system 38S," Jaspa called from her post. They were passing close to this star on their way to the ship's ultimate destination.

"What have you got?" Asked the captain.

"System 38S. Orange K-type star, seven planets. Analysis indicates the presence of a possible mineral rich crust on planet three. No life forms, or planets capable of supporting life detected." Martin smiled as he listened to the report, confident that Jaspa would be promoted soon indeed.

"Very well, ensign. Log the system for a further geographical survey and return to your duties."

"Aye sir," came her crisp reply.

Martin leaned forward in his chair and began a diagnosis on the weapons systems. He began to wonder if explorers before him felt the way that he did now; excited, scared, and intensely curious all at the same time. He looked up at the view screen and watched as the mystery of deep space unfolded before his eyes. This is what he went to the War College for; not only to study history, but also to make it. He chuckled nervously to himself as he remembered how many of those early exploratory ships never made it back.

At that moment the lift doors at the rear of the bridge opened to reveal Ryn. Martin could not imagine what Ryn was doing up here until he noticed the electronic notepad under the big Pologian's arm. Ryn handed the pad to Captain Prescott who looked it over briefly before pushing the I.D. pad with his thumb. Prescott thanked Ryn and dismissed him. The Pologian retrieved the pad and winked at Martin before leaving the bridge. The pad must have contained a supplies report, but Martin did not know why Ryn brought it up personally. For the first time in many months, Martin was starting to get over the feelings of guilt he was having. He had asked his father to pull some strings to get himself and his group of friends assigned to the same ship. Seeing Ryn perform the trivial task made Martin calm a bit; he was glad his friends were here sharing the new experiences with him.

A loud beep from the communications board broke Martin's train of thought. Petty Officer Lyon made his report to the Captain, "Message coming in from the P.I.V. Concord."

"Let's hear it crewman."

"Message is as follows: P.I.V. Concord, Captain Lo Jin to P.I.V. Vasco de Gamma Captain Aaron Prescott. We have been ordered to sector 29A to investigate a stellar nursery discovered in that area. Be advised that this puts us out of direct contact range of your vessel. Further fleet orders should arrive at your location in approximately nine hours. Good luck, Aaron. Concord out."

Prescott grimaced a bit upon hearing the news. The message basically meant that if the de Gamma got into trouble, it would be more than one week before any help could be expected. Martin wondered why Fleet bothered to pair up ships if they constantly ordered one or the other off on some stupid mission that a probe could easily handle. His nervousness jumped a notch as he realized that they were all alone. He looked over at Jaspa who just shrugged and smiled back.

The ship sailed on toward whatever awaited it in system 39Q. Martin tried to lose himself in the thrum of the displacement drive. He tried running another diagnostic for the umpteenth time. He tried to visualize his next shore leave, but nothing worked. The chronometer showed that he was only an hour and 34 minutes into his shift. This meant that he had to kill at least another half hour until the ship was at system boundary. Now he knew what one of his professors at the College had meant when she said that exploration was long periods of boredom punctuated by a few moments of terror, and if one was extremely lucky, the glory of discovery. Martin had had enough of the boredom; he was ready for some glory.

Jaspa looked up sharply from her sensor controls, "Captain, I have a contact at extreme range moving at faster than light speeds."

"What do you make of it ensign?" the Captain inquired.

"Hard to say at this distance sir. Contact is definitely F.T.L. and of significant mass for me to be reading it from so far away. Range is about 36 light days bearing 142 mark 7."

"Do you think they've seen us?" Asked Commander McMurphy.

"They have not changed course toward us or made any other moves thus far, ma'am."

The Captain leaned back in his chair and announced, "This is what we're here for boys and girls. Helm, alter course to intercept and increase to flank speed. Communications, get the linguistics officer up here on the double. Good eyes Ensign Shindessa."

Jaspa flushed with pleasure as the Captain continued, "Helm, time to intercept?"

The helmsman examined his controls before saying, "twenty five minutes, fifty-five seconds present speed."

The Vasco de Gamma shot off at a space eating pace. At flank speed, she was doing well over 2700c, an impressive velocity by any standard. Martin felt himself being caught up in the seemingly living pulse being produced by the inanimate ship. He wondered what Eddie was feeling down in the engineering spaces as matter and anti-matter annihilated each other, producing the massive quantities of power necessary to drive the vessel.

Lt. Commander Robert Fynch arrived as Martin watched the stars blur past on the view screen. As senior linguistics officer, Fynch was an invaluable member of the crew. This was fortunate, as Fynch was not very well liked among the officers; his condescending manner tended to get on everyone's nerves.

The gangly linguist sauntered down into the command well, "Lt. Commander Fynch reporting as ordered sir."

The Captain favored him with a brief glance. "Report to your station; we may have some work for you soon, Bob."

"Aye sir." The thin man practically sniffed as he headed for the language and cultural computer at the rear of the bridge. Martin thought the only thing saving the snooty commander was the fact that he was good at his job.

After twenty or so minutes, Jaspa turned toward the command well; "I can switch to a short range scan now Captain."

"Please do so ensign. Can you determine if the contact has seen us?"

Jaspa turned back to her board, "if it has, it's not making any indication. Contact is still on its previous course. Speed: 550c. Mass . . ."

The pause was unusual for Jaspa who always seemed to be on top of everything. "Is there a problem, ensign?" Asked Captain Prescott.

"No sir. Sorry sir. Mass: 382,000 metric tonnes."

A collective gasp went up from the bridge personnel. The ship they were chasing was huge. The de Gamma, a heavy cruiser, was only about 240,000 metric tonnes. If this alien vessel proved to be hostile, the ship could be in real trouble.

"Let's calm down folks," the Captain intervened before the situation could escalate. "Size doesn't necessarily mean anything. Continue ensign."

"The vessel is constructed of standard space worthy materials. I'm detecting anti-matter in the rear of the ship and in small quantities forward. This could indicate anti-matter weapons. I am also detecting energy weapons ports, but these do not appear to be armed in any manner I am familiar with. They also do not seem to have any defense fields in place."

The helmsman turned to give his report, "Closing on target sir; four minutes present speed."

The Captain wrinkled his brow in thought. A new alien race always brought with it new and complex challenges. Prescott was at his best in these types of situations.

"Very well. Commander McMurphy sound General Quarters."

The GQ alarm rang out over the bridge speakers. Martin envisioned the crew scurrying for battle stations on every deck. The Captain turned his attention toward the young Lieutenant, "Gammage arm FAL's and missiles. Raise defense fields."

Martin turned to look at this commanding officer, "Sir, should I also ready the Nova Cannon?" The Nova Cannon was the most powerful weapon in the Protectorate arsenal. No alien race yet encountered could long resist its onslaught.

"Negative Lieutenant" the Captain answered, "If we do engage, I want to try to take this ship at least partially intact. And Lieutenant, don't anticipate."

Martin swallowed slightly, "Aye sir. Weapons armed, defense fields charged." Martin's console came alive as he rapidly input the commands that made the de Gamma a fighting ship. He marveled at the destructive power at his fingertips.

"All systems nominal" came a voice over the comm that Martin did not recognize, "Engineering standing by."

"Intership," the Captain said to the communications crewman.

"Intership on."

"Attention all crewmembers. In a moment I am going to attempt contact with the alien vessel we are approaching.

There is an element of danger in any new situation, but I could not have asked for a better crew behind me. You all know your jobs, so let's do them. Captain out."

Prescott settled back in his command chair and waited a few more seconds. Martin quickly surveyed the bridge. All hands stood at their stations in nervous anticipation. Martin's gaze finally rested on Jaspa who took a moment to glance up from her panel and wink at him. History turned on moments like these and no one knew that better than Martin.

"Range to target?" The Captain inquired of the helmsman.

"Three minutes, seven seconds present speed." Came the response.

"Target status?" This was directed at Jaspa.

"No change Captain."

"Very well; Communications send this on all bands: This is Captain Aaron Prescott of the Protectorate Interstellar Vessel Vasco de Gamma. We are on an exploratory mission in this sector. Please identify yourselves and respond on any universal channel."

Five seconds passed, then ten, then thirty. After a full minute, Petty Officer Lyon at communications broke the silence, "No response sir, however I believe they heard us."

The Captain turned his chair to face Lyon, "What makes you think so?"

Lyon consulted his board one more time before responding, "I believe I saw a flicker on what appears to be an F.T.L. communications array on the centerline of their ship."

"Two minutes to intercept" the helmsman interjected.

"I see," said the Captain, "Let's try again. Send this: This is Captain Aaron Prescott. We are awaiting a reply to our previous message. Please respond in any manner with which you are comfortable."

Lt. Commander Fynch turned toward the command well, "Sir, we don't even know if they can understand us, much less how they communicate."

The Captain cast an annoyed look back toward Fynch "I am well aware of that, but what do you suggest I do, lean out and drop leaflets on them?"

Fynch turned toward his board without another word.

"One minute to intercept, Captain" the helmsman announced. "I think I can get a visual for you now sir."

"Okay, let's see them."

The view screen rippled for a moment as it went to full magnification. The alien vessel was roughly ovoid with three projections in the rear that Martin thought must house their F.T.L. drive. At this distance, little detail could be seen, but Martin thought the ship looked decidedly menacing.

"Prepare to drop to sub-light helmsman," the Captain ordered.

"Captain!" Came the excited quip from Jaspa, "Target is moving to intercept. I am still not reading any armed weapons or defense fields of any kind."

"Confirmed" agreed the helmsman.

"Captain, I am receiving a signal now," Lyon at the communications board announced.

"Look sharp everyone," Prescott intoned from the command well, "Let's hear what you've got Lyon."

Petty Officer Lyon adjusted a few of his controls, "They're sending visual as well, sir."

Lyon flicked a switch and the screen filled with the visage of the alien. The creature was roughly humanoid: two eyes (one on each side of its head), two arms and presumably two legs. The last was difficult to confirm as the creature was seated. It had light purple skin and a low crest rising out of the top of its hairless skull. Deep grooves under the eyes lent the face a menacing appearance. The small slit of a mouth did not improve its features. This one's not winning any beauty contests, Martin thought.

The alien's small mouth began to move. "Yeth shar harth calotia plainr rath barnin pal cort!" The creature said. Martin could hear the sneer in the voice even though he could not see it on its face. The alien's expression did not change at all during its speech.

"Can you make anything out of that Fynch?" Inquired the Captain.

"I'm running translation programs now sir, but this may take some time."

"I have the feeling that these folks are not the patient type" chimed in Commander McMurphy in low tones.

Captain Prescott smiled at his first officer, "I believe I agree with you."

The alien shot another verbal broadside, "Carth planer trespass snee plorcareeth weapons chatygia gol!"

Martin heard the two English words mixed with the alien's native tongue. He was pleased that the translation computer was functioning, but those particular words did not sound promising.

The Captain echoed Martin's thoughts as he said, "That didn't sound good. Lyon send this: We did not intend to trespass, as I said, we are on an exploratory mission in this sector. If you will permit us to stay for a few more moments, our translator will allow us to communicate in a meaningful fashion."

The alien's face visibly darkened after Prescott's address. The bridge speakers filled with the harsh voice of the other vessel's captain, "Snark bleth our territory. Clee baroth gopen cha! Cal leave this space borak borak!"

"I don't like this," muttered McMurphy from the command well.

"I agree," added Prescott. "Ensign Shindessa what are you reading?"

Jaspa concentrated on her board for a moment. "No change sir . . . wait, I'm picking up an energy fluctuation . . ."

Prescott did not need to hear any more. His command instincts for the safety of his ship and crew took over. "Helm, evasive starboard. Weapons: prepare to . . ."

No one heard the rest of his command. At that moment two angry red energy beams leapt from the alien vessel and lanced toward the de Gamma. For an instant the two ships were linked by glowing threads of coherent light. The de Gamma bucked wildly as the beams struck home, but Prescott's order to evade saved her from a direct hit. A cacophony of noise filled the bridge as internal sensors recorded the damage and cried out to be the first one noticed.

"Shut off that damn noise!" Yelled Prescott to be heard over the din. "Weapons: fire at will! Helm, bring all missile tubes to bear on the hostile!"

That was all Martin needed to hear. He remembered his training and took care not to fire a wild shot. "Come on, come on" he muttered as the de Gamma came about. Suddenly the alien vessel was lined up perfectly. It was trying an evasive turn of its own but Martin compensated. He smiled grimly as he pressed the firing mechanism. Two blue streaks pierced the darkness of space and interacted with the alien's defense fields. It was rather beautiful really, with the rainbow effect produced where the FAL's collided with the enemy. Martin did not take the time to notice the interplay of energies. He followed up his laser strike with two anti-matter missiles. The missiles struck home right where the FAL's had weakened the defense fields. Martin saw the alien ship heel over with the force of the blows.

"Nice shooting Lieutenant," said Commander McMurphy in an appreciative tone.

"Don't let up Gammage," interjected the Captain, "Keep pouring that fire on. Helm: 60 degrees to port, 30 degrees inclination. Try to get behind him."

"Aye sir," came the response from the helmsman. His voice sounded a bit shaky, but he executed the maneuver flawlessly.

Then something happened that Martin thought impossible. The huge alien ship seemed to turn inside out. The maneuver was so quick, that is what appeared to happen on the view screen. Suddenly, the alien was in perfect firing position and it wasted no time in taking advantage of it. A sheet of blinding energy engulfed the de Gamma. The ship was tossed like a wooden sailing ship of old on a hurricane sea. As the de Gamma valiantly tried to right herself, a second volley hammered across her hull.

"Damage report!" screamed Prescott from the command well. "Engineering, give me . . ."

At that moment a power conduit exploded beneath the command chair. Prescott was dead before his body hit the deck near Martin's station. The young Lieutenant had never seen death before, and this baptism by fire did not ease him into it. Prescott was scorched over most of his body. His eyes stared out of a blistered and charred face. Gammage was unnerved for a moment, but gathered himself quickly. He turned back to the command well to take his orders from Commander McMurphy. She was lying unconscious next to the well. A vicious cut oozing blood was evident from the center of her forehead all the way to her cheekbone. The fact that it was bleeding gave evidence that she was still alive, but this did not help Martin or the rest of the bridge staff. There were no line officers of Command rank remaining on the bridge!

Something snapped in Martin then, something he always knew he possessed, but it took this situation to bring it to the fore. His natural ability to command leapt through him like an electric charge. He had never been so alive.

"I'm going to end this now," he muttered to himself. He fought the badly vibrating deck to reach his control board. As he looked down to arm the Nova Cannon, a red telltale malfunction light mocked him. The control circuits were fused; the vessel's most powerful weapon was inoperative.

He fired a few shots at the enemy ship. He did not care if they struck home or not; he simply wanted to buy some time.

Martin took a deep breath of the bridge's smoke befouled air and announced, "as senior line officer remaining on the bridge, I hereby assume command of this vessel." Helm, bring us to 270 mark 20. Engineering, get me a damage report, and get someone up here familiar with the weapons systems. Jaspa try and get . . ."

"Belay those orders!" Came a cry from the rear of the bridge. Lt. Commander Fynch was extricating himself from the remains of his language computer. "I am the ranking officer present, therefore, I assume command."

"Sir," said Martin, "You are not a line officer and know nothing about battle situations or the command of a Protectorate vessel."

"Oh, so we should turn the ship over to a green j.g.?" Came the sarcastic reply.

"Sirs," the helm officer broke in, not sure whom to address. "The alien is turning for another pass."

Martin's face took on a determined air as he said "Security, send up a team and have Commander Fynch removed."

"You can't do that!" Screamed Fynch, but Martin was already ignoring him.

"Carry out my orders, helm," Martin continued, "Jaspa can you give me a report on the hostile?"

"We have sensor damage sir, but I think our first volley hurt him. I'm picking up energy interruptions in their defense fields and fusion engines."

"Well they're not indestructible at any rate," responded Martin.

At that moment, the lift doors opened to reveal Ryn and Edward. Ryn immediately moved toward Fynch while Edward gravitated toward Martin.

"If you'll come with me sir," the big Pologian said to Fynch.

The Lt. Commander looked at Martin with fury in his eyes. "I'll see you cashiered for this."

Martin looked back and said in a matter-of-fact voice, "If any of us survive, you're more than welcome to try." With that, Ryn took Fynch off the bridge.

Edward gazed at Martin with an expectant expression. The young lieutenant said, "Eddie get on the Nova Cannon control circuits and see what you can do."

"Aye sir," came the simple reply.

Martin's volley and evasive turn had bought the ship some time, but the respite was rapidly running out.

"Helm transfer fire control to your station and turn to 260 mark 35."

The de Gamma began to turn. The alien ship tried to evade, but Martin could now see that it was definitely hurt. Its turn was ragged and erratic. Martin hoped that his desperate shots at the ship had hit. It was apparent that at least one of its stabilizers was out. He quickly jumped on his advantage.

"Fire!" He cried from his post.

The battered de Gamma poured some of its precious remaining energy into its FAL banks. The beams of light struck the enemy amidships, but not with full power. The alien behemoth staggered but was able to right itself and return fire.

The enemy's revenge was devastating. Two anti-matter devices caught the de Gamma in her aft quarter. The lights went out entirely for a moment before flickering back to life.

Lt. Koor at the engineering monitor spoke out, "Damage report: fusion engines at 62%. Defense fields at 31%. Starboard power coupling has failed, backups in operation. Long range sensors are out as is power on deck nine. FAL's at 70%, and we have a hull breach in the operations center."

This last item struck Martin hard. Marcus was in operations. There was nothing Martin could do but hope that his friend was all right. As for the rest of the report, it sounded bad but not as bad as it could be. Martin still had an effective ship to continue the fight.

The two ships passed one another after their last exchange and prepared to come at each other yet again. The situation reminded Martin of a medieval joust, but he knew that the alien would be able to knock him from his horse before he could do the same. Martin had to change the game.

"Helm, when the alien comes into range again I want full stop as soon as possible. When he slips by, give him as much of the aft weapons array as you can muster."

A sly look crept onto the helmsman's face. "Aye-aye sir!"

The two combatants dove at each other. As the alien grew on the screen, the helmsman "slammed on the brakes." The alien fired, but the lasers and missiles went across the de Gamma's bow, right where they should have been had the ship kept moving forward. The alien shot right by the now stationary heavy cruiser, and the helmsman blasted them. The aft array spit four bolts of blue energy and two missiles at the fast moving target. All found their marks. The alien ship was engulfed in a multicolored pyrotechnic display.

"That got 'em!" Cried the helmsman in celebration.

But the alien wasn't finished just yet. In another rapid maneuver, the de Gamma found herself staring down the weapons barrels of the enemy. Destructive energies poured forth and battered what was left of the de Gamma's defense fields. The ship seemed to try to shake itself apart as several consoles on the bridge exploded in a burst of sparks.

"Damage report!" Yelled Martin.

A bloody Lieutenant Koor answered from her station; " defense fields are down. Port anti-matter missile launchers are inoperative both fore and aft. Port FAL generators are destroyed. Port displacement drive engine has structural damage. Fusion engines are at 50% . . ." She paused for a moment, "and main power is down."

That was it. Without main power they were doomed. They couldn't fight and they couldn't escape on auxiliary power. Martin looked around his first command. The bridge was a shambles. The medical team had removed Commander McMurphy and the body of Captain Prescott, but everyone else on the bridge had wounds from the battle. He suddenly felt very ill himself and realized he was bleeding from a head wound and probably had been for some time. He had no idea how or when it had happened.

The alien vessel wobbled back into an attack posture. She was definitely hurt, but it did not matter. If they could turn and fire, that would be the end of the de Gamma.

Suddenly, Edward poked out from beneath the weapons console. "That's it!" he cried.

"What are you talking about?" Martin inquired. If he was going to die, he did not need Eddie babbling in his ear.

"I fixed it! The Nova Cannon is on line! It won't be as powerful on auxiliary power, but it works!"

A smile crept across Martin's blood and soot streaked face, "Eddie, you're a pain in the ass, but you're the best engineer in the Protectorate."

For once, Eddie took a comment for what it was worth, "That's why they pay me the big money."

"Helm, play dead," Martin shouted forward.

"That shouldn't be too difficult sir" muttered the helmsman.

Martin chose to ignore the comment, "As soon as they're in range fire the cannon."

The motley bridge crew waited a few tense, eternal moments as the alien vessel slowly closed the gap. Martin sat on the edge of his chair as he watched the range number on the helmsman's board decrease. "Wait . . . wait . . . FIRE!"

The de Gamma spent all her remaining strength on one final shot. The Nova Cannon released its energy in a ball of superheated plasma. The alien was surrounded by a halo of destruction for a split second before its entire aft section blew off into space. The remaining hulk trailed a fine mist of atmosphere and debris into the surrounding area.

The bridge lost all power and was plunged into darkness until the emergency batteries kicked in. They were adrift, they were out of power, but they were alive.

Martin stared at the view screen and the wreckage floating across it, "Lt. Koor, Ensign Longly, any chance of restoring auxiliary power?"

The two officers looked at each other, at their boards and back at Martin. "I don't know sir," said Koor. "Main engineering reports that the Chief Engineer and most of her staff are dead or wounded. The starboard engine is intact; we may be able to do something with that."

"Very well," replied Martin. "Do what you can. Petty Officer Lyon, send a message to the Concord informing them of our status and request assistance."

They had survived, but at what cost? The Protectorate was now at war with a race they knew virtually nothing about. Martin sat back and sighed. With the Concord at least six days away, he would have plenty of time to contemplate the repercussions of today's events.

*   *   *

October 26, 2519

Protectorate Command Base 31, inside the "Cooper Acquisition Zone."

"We have all gathered to pay homage to our lost comrade," began Vice Admiral Lucille Jerome, the commander of Base 31, "It is always a tragedy to lose one of our own, but we should take pride in . . ."

Martin began to tune the Admiral out as he recalled the events of the last two weeks. He remembered how the de Gamma hung in space for 18 vulnerable hours with only battery power to sustain her. He remembered sending the message to the Concord to beg for help. He remembered how the sister ship nearly burned out its own displacement drive to get to their position in only four days instead of the six that it should have taken. He remembered the panicked moments when their long range sensors recorded a contact and the subsequent relief when it disappeared from their scopes. He recalled the joy he felt when he found that his best friend Marcus had escaped the vacuum of space. But most of all he remembered the ten day tow back to Command Base 31 and how he brooded over the loss of his Captain and the possible charges he faced from Fynch.

The latter proved baseless. No sooner had Martin disembarked, than he was cleared of any wrongdoing. Fynch, on the other hand, finally got the command he craved; he was assigned as Commanding Officer to a deep listening post in the Playna IX system on the other side of Protectorate space.

As for the de Gamma, it was doubtful she would ever see service again. The old ship reminded Martin of the B-17 bombers of World War II; they would take a beating, but bring their crews home. The Command Base crew would salvage what they could from her and scrap the rest. Martin felt a pang of regret over the old ship's fate.

As Admiral Jerome continued with the service, Martin looked down the line at his friends. All wore the silver insignia of a Lieutenant (j.g.). Marcus sported a silver star as well for closing the emergency bulkheads that saved the entire operations center and everyone in it. Jaspa and Eddie wore Protectorate Crosses for their work on the bridge. Eddie also had an Engineering Excellence Ribbon (1st Class) for repairing the Nova Cannon that had saved them all. Ryn dwarfed the tiny Bronze Star on his uniform. He had pulled a crewman to safety from a burning compartment during the battle. He wore a Unit citation as well.

Jaspa wept openly as the Admiral reviewed the superlative career of their former Captain. Eddie and Marcus stared straight ahead, as if afraid their emotions would get the better of them. Ryn stood silently as a fat tear rolled down his cheek. Captain Prescott was well liked and respected among his crew and it showed at this gathering.

The Admiral stopped speaking. Her voice was replaced by the plaintive wail of the bagpipes playing "Amazing Grace." It was rumored that Fleet Admiral Alexander Kinkaid (the founder of the Protectorate) was fond of this particular melody. It was standard music at Protectorate military funerals even though the last vestiges of organized religion had vanished over 350 years ago. The bittersweet tones of the pipes touched Martin deeply as the song wound to a conclusion.

Vice Admiral Jerome returned to the podium as the last notes died away. "Even as we mourn the loss of one of our finest Captains, we are also here to commend a shining example of courage, fortitude, and valor. Lieutenant junior grade Martin Gammage, front and center!"

Martin stepped out of his rank and walked stiff backed to the podium. The eyes of the surviving crew of the Vasco de Gamma followed his movements. Martin was well aware that 79 individuals were not here to witness this moment. Those men and women had made the ultimate sacrifice for Martin to be here on this day. He marched past his friends to reach the center isle. They all smiled at him as he walked by and he was comforted by their presence. He passed Commander McMurphy in the front row, her head wound nearly healed and her right leg in a regenerative cast. She nodded at him as he approached the Admiral.

"Mr. Gammage it is a privilege to preside at this ceremony. It is rare for a Commander to have such a fine junior officer in his or her fleet. I shall read to all present the orders from Admiral Ooda Calli, Commander 14th Protectorate Fleet: Lieutenant (junior grade) Martin Gammage is hereby promoted to Lieutenant with all the privileges and responsibilities due that rank. He is hereby detached from the 14th Fleet and is assigned to the Protectorate Intelligence Bureau. Finally, by orders of a majority of the Council of Admirals, he is awarded the Protectorate Medal of Honor for his actions of 8 October, 2519."

Martin lowered his head to receive the Protectorate's highest honor. The gold medallion glittered in the light of the chamber as it settled on his chest. A thunderous applause filled the room as Martin executed an about face to look at the crowd. He still felt strangely about recent events. He truly believed that he only did what he had to do to save his ship, crew, and friends. Oddly, as he remembered his history lessons, heroes tended to be men and women who did the right things at the right times.

He peered out into the crowd and wondered who would live and who would die in the years to come. He couldn't help but think that the struggle ahead would be a long one.

Chapter II: Lieutenant
May 17, 2520
Protectorate Command Base 31, inside the
"Cooper Acquisition Zone"

Martin turned in the command chair to face the view screen. The helmsman had lined up the shot perfectly. The alien hung in space spinning without power, waiting for the knockout blow. Martin smiled grimly as he gave the order to fire. The weapons officer pressed the button that would release the destructive energies, but nothing happened. The young man at the tactical station looked at Martin with panicked eyes. The alien ship came alive and fired a devastating volley at Martin's ship. The defense fields collapsed as panels all over the bridge exploded. Jaspa fell dead at her station. Martin watched in horror as Eddie's leg was cleaved neatly at the knee joint by a piece of flying shrapnel. He watched helplessly as a hull breach opened in the center of the bridge. He felt the icy cold of deep space clawing for him as the air and bodies on the bridge were evacuated into the void. He felt his grip on the command chair slipping . . .

Martin awoke sweating in his quarters on Base 31. He had not had that dream in several months and had thought that particular specter was behind him. Unfortunately, the dead of the de Gamma continued to haunt him.

As Martin's breathing slowed, he felt his consciousness slip back into the present. He looked at his bedside chronometer. It read 18:37, only twenty three minutes before he planned to awaken anyway. The P.I.V. Constantinople was due at 19:30 and he had planned to take a nap before meeting her.

His job in intelligence was rewarding. As the first Protectorate officer to engage and defeat a Prescottian ship (the aliens were named for Captain Prescott), his input was valued, but he sometimes wished he had been assigned to a combat vessel.

Eddie and Jaspa had been transferred to the Constantinople shortly after the memorial service for Captain Prescott. The Protectorate had taken action immediately following that first engagement. The 13th, 15th, 19th, and 22nd fleets had all been ordered to the area for the ensuing war. Ryn had been assigned to the Defender and Marcus had been transferred to Fleet Operations onboard the 15th Fleet flagship. Martin knew his work in intelligence was important, but he missed his friends and shipmates.

As he readied himself to meet the arriving ship, he turned on last night's news packet. The announcer droned on about engagements of which Martin was already aware. The war was not going badly for the Protectorate, but they could not seem to gain any ground. Every time the Prescottians seemed to weaken, new ships arrived to plug the gaps in their line. Meanwhile, the Protectorate losses continued to mount. The P.I.V. Diamond Castle had been lost last week with all hands; the first Protectorate battleship to be destroyed in the war had carried over twenty three hundred souls.

Martin left his quarters brooding over such facts. He strolled past a fleet roster board and something caught his eye. As he stopped to read, the word P.I.V. Constantinople jumped out at him. The report indicated that the heavy cruiser had seen some tough action and she was coming in hurt. The casualty list was not yet available, but at least fifty were dead and another seventy five wounded.

Martin sprinted down the corridor and hunted for the dock master. He finally found her near port five.

"Has the Connie docked yet?" He managed to blurt as he caught his breath.

The Lt. Commander snorted at him, "If you mean the Protectorate Interstellar Vessel Constantinople, it is due to arrive at staging area C, docking port nine."

"Thank you," Martin cautiously replied as he puzzled over the dock master's terse response. As he turned to leave, he noticed the speckling on the Commander's neck and determined that she was Calnation. He remembered that the Calnations believe that abbreviating anything is a sign of disrespect. He digested this bit of information as he ran toward staging area C.

He and the battered heavy cruiser arrived at the same time. Martin watched as she hove to, her scorched and pitted hull a testament to the fighting that she had seen. Martin mouthed a silent wish that Jaspa and Eddie were not among the casualties.

It took the crew of the Constantinople about forty-five minutes to finish the docking procedure and start offloading. The huge crew access doors opened to reveal a medical unit transporting several of the ship's more gravely injured personnel. Finally, after what seemed to Martin an interminable wait, he spied Eddie and Jaspa heading toward the station. Jaspa looked all right as far as he could see, but Eddie was wearing a stasis splint on his left arm.

"I'm so glad you could meet us!" Said Jaspa as she hugged Martin, "I was afraid you'd be too busy."

"Nah," continued Eddie, "He's a big muckety-muck in intelligence now. He knew we were coming long before the Captain gave the order."

Martin favored his friends with a smile before asking what happened.

Jaspa was the first to speak up. "We were jumped by two patrol ships in Sector 43J. We managed to destroy one, but the other punched a hole our defense fields and caused a hull breach. Captain Barnett got the other with an anti-matter barrage, but the damage had already been done."

"Yeah," said Eddie lifting his frozen limb, "I took some of that damage when my console exploded; I'm lucky that's all I took."

Jaspa's face took on a faraway expression as she said, "It was terrible. I thought I'd get used to it after our battle, but it just gets harder. I was saved because the kid next to me took the shrapnel that would have killed me. I'll never forget the look in his eyes."

Martin looked at Jaspa intently. "It's over now, brooding about it won't make it any easier." His face took on a softer expression, "I don't know about you, but I'm starving. Let's get some food and discuss something pleasant, okay?"

The three friends headed away from staging area C as they hunted for one of the station's many eating establishments. Martin took a good look at his friends and thought they had aged in the short time they had been separated. He chuckled softly to himself thinking, you probably look even older.

The trio found the Protectorate Pub on the near side of the station and enjoyed each other's company as they dined. Most of the meal was punctuated by half-hearted attempts at small talk. The three friends finally gave up the attempt at forced comradery, and the remainder of the meal passed in a companionable silence.

At the end of dinner, Eddie pronounced that his arm was aching. He excused himself and headed back toward the Constantinople. Jaspa and Martin started a slow walk to the transient officer's quarters where Jaspa had attained a room.

They walked quietly through the nearly deserted corridors of a space station on third shift. For some reason, they reacted awkwardly toward each other. Martin laughed boisterously at an offhand remark Jaspa made. He began to notice, really notice, for the first time what an attractive and remarkable woman she was. Her raven hair cascaded down her back in rolling waves. He was transfixed by the deep purple of her eyes. Eyes that seemed to look at the very heart of him. Martin was befuddled by the range of emotions he felt. He didn't know if it was the effect of wartime or some other cosmic event; but he did know that he was in love with Jaspa Shindessa.

Finally, mercifully, their walk came to an end. Martin stopped at the door to cabin 271 and said, "You know when I read the battle report I kept hoping that you were not among the casualties. It seems silly, we've been through so much . . . I'm not making any sense am I?"

"No," she said as she stepped closer to him, "but I'm used to that" she replied in that teasing tone of voice that absolutely undid Martin's resolve.

Martin's face colored at her retort. Her closeness was nearly intoxicating. "You can come in if you want," Jaspa continued as she opened the door.

His legs seemed to carry him by their own volition. He did not remember giving them orders to move forward, circle the room, or sit him on the couch, but that is where he found himself.

She sat next to him waiting. She seemed to invite him with her eyes, but for the first time in his life, Martin Gammage did not know what to do. Not that he was a novice with women, far from it, but no one had ever affected him like this before.

He reached for her tentatively at first, but when his advances were not spurned, he drew her into a full embrace. His lips probed hers and drank in her softness, her sweetness that seemed to define her. He ran his hands along her form fitting uniform. He possessed the entire universe; right here, right now in this one individual.

"Lieutenant Martin Gammage will report to Captain Johansen immediately! Acknowledge!" Martin sat bolt upright as the summons came over the speaker in Jaspa's room. They had located him by the transponder that all Protectorate military personnel wore in their right shoulder. He exhaled and seemed to deflate as he did so.

"Are you going to get that?" Cooed Jaspa. Apparently she was going to add insult to injury. Her playfulness made Martin want her all the more.

Martin stood and walked over to the comm. unit, "Lieutenant Gammage here. I'm on my way."

"I wonder what the hell he wants" lamented Martin.

"I wouldn't know, you're the intelligence officer."

Martin looked down at her and sighed over what might have been. "I'm sorry about this, but it must be important. The Captain wouldn't have summoned me on a whim." He froze for a moment as if unsure of what to do next. Sadly, Martin turned on his heel left Jaspa's quarters without another word.

Martin stalked down the curved corridor to the lift. His mind kept going on about what his commander could possibly want. He shook his head over how the universe had conspired to rob him of his first chance with Jaspa. As he continued toward the Captain's office, his thoughts turned to the gravity of the situation. Captain Johansen enjoyed his off duty hours, he would not have called for Martin at this time of night for no reason; something was up.

He finally arrived at Johansen's outer office. The Captain's aide told Martin to go right in. The activity in the office was at a fever pitch; further evidence that something big was in the works.

"Lieutenant Martin Gammage reporting as ordered sir."

"Have a seat Marty, we've got something for you."

Martin took the offered chair opposite Johansen's desk. The Captain was a big Swede with a crisp, determined air. He had been an intelligence officer for over 30 years and was nearing retirement. While working under the Captain, Martin had gained valuable experience. The two of them, with the help of several linguists, had successfully translated the Prescottian language with the data Martin had brought back with the de Gamma. They had also broken a series of codes that had been instrumental in an important battle two months ago.

Johansen completed a report he was working on and finally turned his attention to Martin. "Lieutenant, we have what appears to be an unfinished Prescottian base on Endorra V. Our intelligence indicates that the base is only partially manned, however, according to the signals we've been intercepting, both the communications and computer systems are online. I am assigning you a small team to infiltrate the base and acquire whatever information you can from their computer system: fleet movement, technology, ship types, weapons, cultural information, what bedtime snacks they prefer, anything you can get your hands on. This is our first opportunity for a big intelligence break. Your work until now has been exemplary and I'm giving you first crack at this one."

Martin was thrilled at the prospect. He had a chance to make a real difference in the conflict if he could pull this off. "When do I leave sir?"

"We are awaiting the arrival of the final member of your team. I've assigned a friend of yours to work with you. The P.I.V. Defender arrives in six hours. At that time, Lieutenant Ryndock Calplygian will join your squad as head of security."

Martin could not believe his good fortune! Not only was he being assigned to a huge mission, but Ryn would be riding shotgun! Martin couldn't imagine anyone he would prefer to have watch his back than the big Pologian.

"When your squad has been briefed and equipped," continued Johansen, "You will proceed to Endorra V aboard the fast frigate Pelinore. When you arrive on station you will have two hours to penetrate the base, retrieve your information, and return to the rendezvous point. The briefing officer will have all the details. Lieutenant Calplygian is receiving his orders en route. Do you have any questions?"

"I don't believe so sir."

"Very well. Report to conference room 7 in ten minutes to meet your squad and begin the briefing. Good luck to you Lieutenant. I almost envy you. Fifteen years ago and I would have gone myself. You are dismissed."

Martin stood and walked to a secured comm. station. He keyed in the code to Jaspa's quarters. Her angelic face appeared almost immediately.

"I have to leave." Martin said without preamble.

"I understand. It had to be something big to call you at this late hour. I'm sorry things didn't work out."

Martin gazed longingly into her purple eyes. "Not half as sorry as I am" he mumbled.

"What?" Said Jaspa.

"Nothing, never mind. If you're not here when I get back, I'll send a message to the Connie."

A flicker of sadness seemed to cross her face. "You come home in one piece. You hear me?"

"Yes Ma'am." Came Martin's thick reply. His emotions were catching up with him. As he broke the link he silently vowed that he would return to her no matter what it took.

May 26, 2520
P.I.V. Pelinore

"Entering the Endorra System, Captain."

"Very well" replied Commander Clia Colayna, the commanding officer of the Pelinore, "Sensors at maximum; take us in."

The Pelinore was on the final leg of her eight day journey to Endorra V. She had encountered four Prescottian ships along the way, but was able to slip by undetected. The Protectorate had one major advantage in the current conflict: Their sensor technology was much more advanced than their opponent. Thus, Protectorate ships could detect enemy vessels and evade or ambush as needed.

Endorra V swelled on the view screen as the Pelinore entered orbit. Martin thought he had never seen an uglier planet. It was classified as "Earth type" but Martin thought that the cataloguers were stretching the definition. Endorra V did have an oxygen-nitrogen atmosphere, but it was a stormy planet. To add further to its charms, the entire crust was tectonically unstable, and if the earthquakes were not enough, the daytime temperatures seldom rose above freezing. A vacation spot it certainly was not.

"Well Lieutenant, this is where we leave you" said Calayna turning her attention to Martin. "We'll be leaving the system to avoid detection and return for you in two hours. May Shafrah smile on you."

Martin returned the Balnora equivalent of good luck with a grin before heading to the shuttle bay. His squad was already there making last minute preparations. Apart from Ryn, four Protectorate Marines rounded out the group. Master Sergeant William Rawlings was a veteran with 36 years of experience. Next in rank beneath him was Sergeant Christopher Shilling. Privates Ona Cal and Mike Lane completed the roster.

"You boys ready?" Inquired Martin as he entered the bay.

"Sir, yes sir!" Shouted Cal as he patted his FAL rifle.

Master Sergeant Rawlings smiled at the youth. "Save some of that for planet-side son. Y'all don't want to peak too early now."

The young man colored slightly as he boarded the shuttle. The enlisted men clambered into the back of the craft as Martin and Ryn slid into the pilots' seats. The plan was to land the shuttle behind a small rise near the base. The P.I.V. Napoleon had dropped a broad spectrum scrambler into orbit around the planet three days ago. The satellite was effectively jamming the Prescottian's poor sensors. Not only that, but the little device was also sending false images of a clear screen to the base's ground receiver. If all went well, the shuttle would drop in undetected. It would then be a short twenty minute march to the base. This would give the small band about an hour and twenty minutes to complete their mission.

The large shuttle bay doors yawned open to reveal Endorra V. Martin nodded to Ryn and the Pologian began the departure sequence. The small shuttle shot out into the void and began its descent into the turbulent atmosphere.

As the ship hurtled toward the planet, Martin addressed his small contingent, "As you recall from our briefing, the base is mostly sub-terranian, so I am not particularly concerned with their sighting us visually. If there are any outside sentries, I want to try and take one alive for questioning. If we can get one, Sergeant Shilling will be responsible for bringing him back to the shuttle." The sergeant nodded briefly to acknowledge the order. This maneuver would reduce their number by one, but Martin felt it would be worth it to take a prisoner.

"Once we penetrate the base, take no prisoners," Martin continued. "It is imperative that no alarm be sounded if we are to be successful." Martin knew this was painfully obvious but he wanted the squad, especially the inexperienced privates, to be clear.

"Lieutenant," interjected Ryn, "We are closing on target. Looks good so far. I have the rise on my scope and our trajectory is on."

"Okay boys," said Martin, "this is it. Once we land let's move out in formation 'C'." A smattering of "Aye sirs" acknowledged the order.

The shuttle landed without incident. Ryn brought her down smoothly despite the buffeting winds. Martin took note of this for future commendations if any of them returned.

The hatch opened on the desolate landscape. A few gnarled and stunted bushes clung tenuously to the surface, fortunately, the only life to be seen. The cold wind howled and a fine grit blew into the team's faces. They moved out with the officers in the lead. They were flanked by the two privates with Master Sergeant Rawlings acting as rear guard. Sergeant Shilling held out his portable scanner, "Don't read anything else but what you see sir" he drawled. "Not picking up so much as a lizard."

"What about humanoids around the base?" Inquired Ryn.

"Can't tell at this distance, sir."

Martin spoke up; "We were told to expect at least one perimeter guard and one man at the entrance. Hopefully we'll get lucky and manage to avoid the external guard." He had to raise his voice to be heard over the ceaseless wind.

A sudden gust nearly knocked the squad down. As they recovered, Sergeant Shilling noticed a flicker on his sensor. "Don't think we'll be avoiding that guard sir. He should be rounding that small hillock any minute."

Martin wasted no time, "Private Cal, you'll take the shot. Private Lane, cover him."

"Yes sir!" They said at once, delighted that the junior men would be given an opportunity to prove themselves.

The squad found what cover they could in their bleak surroundings. The guard appeared right where Sergeant

Shilling said he would. The young private took aim with his FAL rifle and fired. An angry red beam engulfed the luckless sentry. His death cry did not escape his lips before the killing energies disintegrated him.

"Damn it, private!" hissed Martin through clenched teeth; "I wanted a prisoner. I can't very well interrogate free floating atoms now can I?"

The young man colored visibly, "I'm sorry sir. I could have sworn I changed the setting. I'll do so right now. Sorry sir."

Martin took pity on the boy. "It's all right Cal. We'll get the door guard." Martin could afford to be lenient. After all there was another possibility for a capture, not to mention, the kid had made a good shot.

The squad crept along the base of the hillock until the entrance to the underground complex came into view. As expected, there was one guard. Sergeant Shilling reported no surprises.

"Okay Cal," said Martin, "take him out, but stun this time."

"Yes sir." Cal replied as he took careful aim. He was the best shot in the party and he would have to make a good one. They were at least 250 yards from the target. Cal squinted down his sight and pulled the trigger. This time a stream of blue hit the guard square in the chest. He dropped without a sound.

"Well done Cal. That was a hell of a shot. Sergeant Shilling, you will carry the prisoner back to the shuttle and stand guard until we return."

"Yes sir" replied the Sergeant. He was none too happy at the prospect of carrying the unconscious guard to the ship, but he knew that his part of the mission was important. Who knew what valuable information the guard might possess.

The band scrambled over to the unconscious Prescottian. The sergeant distributed his equipment among the remaining members (except for his FAL pistol) and hoisted the stunned alien into a fireman's carry. "Good luck to all of you" he said before heading back to the shuttle, "I'll be waiting."

"Thank you Sergeant" said Martin. He would give Shilling a special commendation if they returned for his part. It was hard to ask a combat veteran to miss the action, but the prisoner was just as important.

"O.K. Ryn, do your stuff." Martin quipped to the Pologian.

Ryn pulled out a palm sized device from his utility belt. He placed it over the locking mechanism and keyed in a long sequence of numbers. "This should take about 90 seconds Marty. Sorry but the lock is encrypted, we'll have to wait."

The five man squad waited tensely as the lock was picked. Master Sergeant Rawlings' eyes never left the scanner as they stood in that vulnerable position. Finally the device bleeped and the light on it's face went from red to green.

The door slid noiselessly aside to reveal a dimly lit passageway. Martin signaled for Ryn to go in first. The two privates followed with Martin next and the Master Sergeant bringing up the rear. The door slid shut behind them.

The Sergeant indicated that the corridor was clear up to the first turn in the passage. They crept along silently until they reached a T-junction. Martin consulted his map. The small display indicated that they should turn left. The map was a sketchy source of information at best, but it was all they had. Martin signaled that Ryn should make the turn.

After fifty feet they came to what appeared to be a lift. Ryn examined the controls until he figured out their workings. As he did, the door whooshed open to reveal two Prescottians. Both groups were surprised, but the Protectorate men recovered first. Ryn smashed his fist into the face of the first one while Martin and Private Lane dispatched the second with well placed shots. Martin heard a sickening crunch as Ryn connected again with his hapless victim.

"Scratch two bad guys," said Private Cal.

The band disintegrated the bodies to help avoid detection if any more of the enemy came this way. Martin's map indicated they should proceed to level five. It was hoped they would find the main computer complex on that deck. As the lift descended, Martin ordered Rawlings to make a scan. The Sergeant announced that there were no life readings along the first fifty feet of level five. Upon hearing this, Martin ordered Ryn to open the doors.

Level five looked exactly the same as the ground level. The dull gray corridor stretched out before them. They padded slowly down the hall until Sergeant Rawlings hissed behind them. He held up three fingers and pointed at the hallway junction just ahead. All five members took aim and waited. As the first Prescottian appeared at the corner, Private Cal let his excitement get the better of him again. He fired before the third man came into view. He hit his target square in the head, but this gave warning to his compatriots. Ryn downed the second one, but the third hit an alarm panel before Private Lane was able to take him out.

"Well that's it," said Martin, "no need for stealth now. The room at the end of this corridor should be the

Computer Center. We'll head for it. Sergeant, look sharp, we can still fulfill our mission. According to our reports there are only about twenty five men here and we've taken seven already."

They sprinted down the hall to the computer room. Ryn didn't bother with the lock, he simply reduced it to slag. This set off a different alarm, but it did not matter, the damage had already been done.

The door slid back. As it did, an electric blue bolt almost took Ryn's face off. Unfazed he coolly returned fire, reducing the perpetrator to ash. A second technician fired but his aim was poor. A pistol shot from Martin stopped the Prescottian permanently.

As Martin hunted for an access port, the remainder of the squad took cover behind consoles. Master Sergeant Rawlings announced that there were no other life signs in the immediate vicinity. He also said that his scanning range had dropped. Apparently the Prescottians were trying to jam the portable sensor.

Martin finally found what he was looking for. He inserted a modified information module and began downloading the Prescottian database.

"Sir," said Rawlings from his hiding place. "I think we're about to have company. Four at least, maybe more, it's hard to tell now."

"Acknowledged. Stand ready boys. We've got the advantage. Hit them as they come through the door. I'm kind of exposed here so I'm counting on you."

The first of the base guards arrived, firing as they came. Bolts of energy splattered all along the inside of the Computer Center but none found their marks. The defenders returned fire and one Prescottian was dropped immediately, but more came on. A stream of energy just missed Martin but his left arm was caught in the nimbus of the beam. He could not help but cry out as his nerves registered the searing pain. He turned and shot his assailant in the face. Finally after an eternity of waiting, the information cube signaled that it was full. Martin uncoupled it and belly crawled up to Ryn's position.

"What do you think?" Asked Martin.

"Well," rumbled the Pologian "I think we can fight our way out. By the way, have you seen your arm?"

Martin looked to see his forearm red and blistered from the Prescottian laser shot. It hurt like hell but didn't appear too bad. "It'll keep until we get to the shuttle."

Suddenly four more Prescottians took up station behind the blackened door. Martin now counted nine enemy soldiers blocking their escape.

"I think it's time for this little surprise" chuckled Ryn. Martin did not know what the Pologian Lieutenant was talking about until the big man pulled a thermite grenade from his belt. The two men smiled at each other. Ryn threw the bomb as Martin told his troops to duck down.

A wave of intense heat blasted through the hallway and Computer Center. The men of the Protectorate were shielded by their consoles . . . the Prescottians were not so lucky. Screams filled the corridor as the heat did its work. When it was safe, Martin could see no movement beyond the door.

"We're clear!" Shouted Private Lane as he stood up.

"Get down you . . ." started Ryn but it was too late. A badly burned Prescottian got off a final shot. The team watched in horror and despair as Private Lane was engulfed by a disintegration blast. The men of the Protectorate returned fire but it did not matter. The Prescottian died, but so did the young man.

The ragged team collected itself and began to retreat down the charred and smoking corridor. As they left the ruins of the computer room, a lone Prescottian leaned against the scarred bulkhead. He was burned on his hands and face and appeared to have a broken leg. Closer inspection revealed the rank insignia of a Prescottian Colonel on the uniform lapels. Ryn leapt to action immediately by grabbing the officer. The Prescottian male yelped in pain but did not put up a fight.

Martin held his portable translator up to his mouth and said, "You are my prisoner. If you surrender now, you will be afforded medical care. If you resist, you will be shot."

The Colonel looked at the devastated remains of his command scattered on the floor and replied, "I surrender." The words were accompanied by a cold look of pure venom.

"Very well," returned Martin "can you walk?"

"I do not believe so. My leg is broken."

Martin thought out the situation. The Colonel was just too good a prize to pass up. The young Lieutenant gestured with the muzzle of his pistol, "Ryn, if you'd be so kind . . . "

The big man easily slung the outraged Colonel over his beefy shoulder.

"I demand to be treated in a manner befitting my rank!" Raged the Prescottian. "I will not be toted around like a sack of meal!"

"Shut up or I'll break your other leg" replied Ryn. The Colonel, sensing that the encumbered Pologian was not bluffing, wisely bit off another retort.

"Where are your other men Colonel?" asked Martin as he turned his attention back to the Prescottian. The Colonel remained silent.

"All right we'll do it the hard way. Formation "D" gentlemen. Let's get the hell out of here." Martin was already thinking ahead. If they could get out of this mess, he would have accomplished quite a bit. He patted the information module on his belt. What a haul! The info cube and two prisoners, one of whom was the executive officer of the base! All they needed to do now was make their escape with about ten of the base personnel unaccounted for: no problem.

The intrepid group made their way back along the route they had taken. The passageway was eerily quiet. They reached the lift without incident and returned to the ground level, again without resistance.

"I don't like this," said Ryn. Martin was inclined to agree but did not respond. If all went well, they could take their prizes and run.

The squad reached the shuttle. Sergeant Shilling was waiting inside with the first prisoner in stasis bonds. "Quite a collection you're making sir" remarked the Sergeant as he prepared another seat for the Colonel. "Where's Lane?" He continued, although he could guess the answer.

"Didn't make it" responded Rawlings.

"You men tend to the Colonel's wounds. Ryn fire up the engines and get us out of here" Martin said as he found his seat.

Ryn engaged the shuttle's systems and began departure protocols. The small craft lifted off the frostbitten surface and got air beneath her. Martin could still not believe his luck . . . and that's when it ran out.

Ryn looked up from his controls; "I'm reading an inbound craft on an intercept course. They should be on us in about three minutes."

"Well," continued Martin, "that answers the question of where the rest of the base complement is. Intelligence didn't say anything about an attack shuttle."

The Prescottian Colonel chortled from the rear of the craft; "My men will blow you from the sky!"

"And you along with us," said Martin.

"My people are not concerned with hostages. My soldiers will blow you into the vacuum of space. Your blood will freeze in your veins as your breath is sucked from . . ."

Martin turned in his seat and shot the Colonel in the chest with a stun blast.

"Thanks" said Ryn as the rest of the crew shared a chuckle.

The enemy craft closed on the Protectorate shuttle. Martin charged the defense fields and weapons systems. As he worked his control panel he said, "Ryn you're the better pilot so I'm handing control to you. I'll be weapons officer . . . it'll remind me of the 'old days'. The rest of you hang on. If we get out of here I guarantee promotions for the lot of you!"

A ragged cheer went up from the exhausted men as the enemy ship came around. The Prescottians fired a vicious but badly timed volley that Ryn dodged easily. Martin responded with a barrage that flared against the opposing vessel's defense fields.

Master Sergeant Rawlings had manned the sensors when the battle began. "Hit on their port, aft field. Minor loss of stabilizer control."

"Line me up again Ryn, I'm just getting warmed up!" Martin crowed from the copilot's seat.

Ryn brought the box like craft about and started after the Prescottian ship. The shuttle was not like the sleek fighters he flew at the War College, but it would do. The enemy fired a shot from its aft weapons platform that grazed the defense fields of Ryn's craft. The shuttle wobbled slightly, but Ryn held her steady. The cross hairs on Martin's board lined up again as he cut loose on his dodging foe. Angry energies spit from the underside of the shuttle and connected with the enemy ship. The defense field flared, grew painfully bright, and went out completely. The Prescottian ship tumbled out of control as Ryn completed the pass.

"Report!" Yelled Martin from his seat. He was riding the rush he always felt under pressure. "That was some hot flying Ryn," he said as he lightly punched his friend's shoulder.

Rawlings completed his calculations from the sensor board and said, "Their fusion engines are at about 5% power. I don't think they have enough to break free of the planet's gravity . . . check that . . . I'm sure of it now. They're falling back into the gravity well. Their stabilizers are out and I'm reading no power to their offensive system. It looks like they're in for a very short, very uncomfortable return to the planet."

"Outstanding!" Returned Martin, "Ryn take us to the rendezvous point. The rest of you . . . well done!" His tired troops cheered. "And the drinks are on me!"

June 6, 2520

Protectorate Command Base 31 inside the "Cooper Acquisition Zone"

"Captain Johansen will see you now," said Petty Officer Gyn-Lan-Conn, the Captain's aide. Martin was sitting in Johansen's outer office. He now stood and entered his commander's inner sanctum. The trek back to the base was reasonably uneventful. Again the Pelinore had encountered a couple of contacts, but with her superior sensors, was able to evade back to Protectorate space.

"Come in lad" boomed Johansen from behind his desk. "You exceeded my wildest dreams." The information on Martin's module was no less than ship deployment plans for the Prescottian fleet in this sector. In addition, the information cube had contained a list of Prescottian shipyards in the area. Plans were already underway to destroy them. The two prisoners were mere bonuses to a completely successful mission. The Prescottian Colonel was quite correct when he said that his people did not care about captives, so it was likely that he and his underling would be POWs for the duration.

The Captain continued, "I'm putting your entire squad in for the Protectorate Cross. In addition, your recommendation that all enlisted personnel be promoted is approved. The new Sergeant Major, Staff Sergeant, and Corporal shall be notified immediately. Also, I'm recommending expedited promotion for both yourself and Lieutenant Calplygian. Congratulations, Lieutenant. You are dismissed."

Martin stood, nodded to the Captain and walked out. The only thing missing in his homecoming was Jaspa; she had shipped out the day before yesterday. His complete success felt hollow for he had no one to share it with. He had sent a message to his father, but did not expect a reply for at least another ten days. He was in a state of mixed emotions as he hunted for Ryn.

He found the big man drinking it up in one of the base's many taverns. Martin sat down next to Ryn and ordered himself a soft drink. Martin did not drink liquor as a rule.

"Did you attend Lane's memorial?" asked the big Lieutenant.

"Yes," said Martin, "It was very well done. He'll get his Protectorate Cross and promotion posthumously. I said a few words. You know, I don't think I'll ever get used to people dying under my command."

"I don't think you're supposed to." Ryn observed.

Martin went on to tell his friend everything the Captain had said. When he got to the part about the decoration, a wry look passed over Ryn's face, "Great, I'll add it to my collection of costume jewelry."

"I thought you'd be pleased," said Martin.

"Oh I am, I just sometimes think I'm in the wrong line of work. Don't get me wrong, I enjoy my posting, but I think I should go into engineering or command; something more challenging than security."

"Well," said Martin, "After today you can probably get any billet you want. By the way, Johansen is recommending us both for early advancement."

"Hot damn!" said Ryn. "I can probably switch tracks now that I'll be a full lieutenant. This does call for a celebration."

At that the other three members of the squad came in. Martin informed them all of their pending promotions. The newly minted Sergeant Major Rawlings whooped and bought all of them drinks. The war companions drank into the night like old friends. They drank to the Protectorate, Martin, women, Captain Johansen, and their departed companion Corporal Lane. Martin, still cold sober, reflected on how war brought the strangest people together. Surviving unbeatable odds had a tendency to do that he thought. "Ah well," he said to himself "tomorrow I'll send a message to Jaspa and fill her in, maybe she can take her next leave here." With that pleasant thought in his head he turned his attention back to his boisterous comrades.

Chapter III: Lt. Commander
September 29, 2521
Office of Admiral Cyrus Morta,
Commander 15th Fleet

Admiral Cyrus Morta sat at his desk contemplating his life. He caught sight of his rank insignia out of the corner of his eyes (he had two on either side of his head) in the black mirror-like computer screen. His four stars twinkled back at him. The silver metal gleamed. Morta had it all: a seat on the Council of Admirals, the 15th Fleet, over three hundred ships at his disposal, everything that is, except a fifth star.

He had been trying to get that star for over forty years. He had coveted it ever since making Commodore. He had gotten close, so very close, only last year. The Council had given him 62% of the vote and then . . . nothing. That damned fickle group had moved onto another favorite and he had never been able to recapture the lost momentum or nomination. It was in this frame of mind that he greeted his aide.

Captain Calvor Joor entered with the morning report. The green skinned Synestian entered with a steady stride. "Good morning, Admiral. I hope you had a pleasant evening."

As Joor placed a cup of clia before the Admiral (clia was the Loäg version of coffee) the black skinned man gave his full attention to his aide, " 'Morning Joor, what's on tap today?" Morta asked his standard morning question but Joor could tell that something else was on the Admiral's mind. Joor's information would probably not help matters.

The no-nonsense aide began: "First, the P.I.V. Scimitar reports engaging and destroying a Prescottian destroyer. Captain Smith requests a layover at Protectorate base 96 for resupply and R and R."

"Permission granted" said Morta, "My compliments to Captain Smith. He may proceed for resupply at his convenience."

Joor made note of this order before proceeding, "Task Force 47 is still on route to the Xiang System. Admiral Noil believes he will be engaging a fleet of three heavy cruisers, two light cruisers, and six destroyers within three days."

"Noil should be able to handle that. Just in case, prepare an order to assemble Task Force 48 consisting of two cruisers to assist if necessary."

Joor made the appropriate notes. "Third, the P.I.V. Zeus arrived today. She lost eight fighters and suffered some minor damage in a skirmish with a Prescottian frigate and destroyer."

The admiral thought for a moment before responding, "Send her replacement fighters and have her turned around and ready for action in seventy two hours."

"Aye sir" responded the aide. The final item on today's report had him worried. It was with some trepidation he began on this final piece of news. "The computer spit out a name on Project Nova."

This got the admiral's full attention. Project Nova was a codename known only to himself and Joor. The "Project" was a list of officers that Morta felt were a threat to his power base. He did his best to somehow transfer these persons to less desirable posts, give them lateral "promotions," or somehow "remove" them from the promotion ladder.

"Who do you have?" Came the ominous response.

"He's only a Lt. Commander now, but he achieved that rank in only 21 months. He graduated from the Protectorate War College first in his class with a . . . history degree."

"History, eh? Interesting."

Joor continued, "Made first contact with the Prescottians and took command of the P.I.V. Vasco de Gamma when her captain was killed. Awarded the Protectorate Medal of Honor, Protectorate Cross, and a slew of lesser decorations."

"Does this fine, outstanding hero of the Protectorate have a name?" The admiral inquired with impatience.

Captain Joor cleared his throat slightly, "Lt. Commander Martin Gammage."

"I see, and where is this young man now?"

"He just ended a tour in Protectorate Intelligence. He was promoted to his present rank last week and assigned to . . . well, this is interesting . . . the 15th Fleet."

The aged admiral smiled, "How propitious that he be dropped into our laps so easily. What is his recommended assignment?"

The captain looked down at his notes briefly, "destroyer command, sir."

A small, menacing smile slowly crept across Admiral Morta's face. It was not an inspiring sight. That smile chilled the room ten degrees. "Then a destroyer command he shall have."

The admiral engaged his computer. He looked at several maps of the Prescottian/Protectorate border. He then examined ship placement for several minutes. Finally, he found what he was after.

"Joor, assemble a group of six destroyers to be labeled Task force 99. Place it under the command of Commodore Sharma Hammond." I can get rid of that thorn in my side as well thought the admiral. "When that is done give command of one of the ships to our friend Gammage. Assign Task Force 99 to sector 61 immediately."

Joor looked at Admiral Morta with some confusion, "But sir, I thought there was a rumor that a Prescottian Dreadnought was operating in that area. A squadron of destroyers with no back up will be slaughtered."

Admiral Morta speared his aide with a piercing gaze; "You like your posting don't you Joor? Do you know how easily you could find yourself at the front? Do you have any idea how easily I could make sure you never get another promotion?" Morta's four reptilian eyes bored into his aide's green face. "Don't ever question my orders again!"

Joor swallowed hard, "Aye sir" he said as he looked at his feet.

"One other thing Captain. Allow Gammage to pick his own first officer. These precocious officers usually travel in pairs."

"Aye sir" repeated Joor as he went to do the admiral's bidding.

"Excellent" murmured Morta to himself as Joor exited. He could get rid of Hammond, who had been a constant annoyance, and this Gammage fellow with no fuss. Joor was quite right of course; Task Force 99 didn't have a chance in hell.

*   *   *

October 1, 2521
Protectorate Command Base 50

Thirteen officers sat in conference room 4 aboard Protectorate Command Base 50. The most senior of whom was Commodore Sharma Hammond, the extremely attractive and capable flag officer in command of Task Force 99. The other twelve officers consisted of one commander, five lt. commanders and six lieutenants; the commanding officers and first officers of the six destroyers in the squadron. The most junior lt. commander was Martin Gammage. His first officer was his best friend, Marcus Slivnova.

The two of them had grown up on Earth and had been best friends since they had met at the age of three. The two had grown particularly close as both of their fathers had been service men and as such, had been away from home for extended periods. They had formed a brotherly bond of steel from day one.

As they grew, they would take turns pretending to command a Protectorate vessel. The other would be the first officer. As it turned out, Martin would be C.O. first, but they both knew that Marcus' own command was not far off. Their childhood dreams had come to fruition.

Both Martin and Marcus had taken turns at topping their various courses at the War College. Martin had excelled at history and in the sciences. Marcus was a master of operations and the inner workings of a ship. The two had been an unbeatable team. When Martin had learned that he would be able to pick his own first officer, no one else had even crossed his mind.

The two young men now listened to the mission briefing from Commodore Hammond. Their attention was riveted on their commanding officer. There was something about realizing your childhood aspirations that made you feel invincible.

"Task Force 99 welcomes its newest commanding officer. Lt. Commander Gammage will be the new skipper of the Thunder." Martin nodded to the assembled officers as Commodore Hammond introduced him.

"Now to our patrol duties. We have been assigned to Sector 61 Alpha to run between the Kalva and Styana Star Systems. We will use Command Base 50 as our operations point." As the Commodore continued, Martin and Marcus tapped all the information into their computers. They looked at each other, as the picture became clearer. Marcus furrowed his brow and Martin stared at his computer screen in disbelief. "Are there any questions?" asked Hammond.

"I have one" returned Martin.

"Very well."

"Am I correct in assuming that we are the only task force assigned to this sector?"

"That is correct, Commander."

"Ma'am" continued Martin; "I just got off a stint in intelligence. Before I left, I worked on this sector. We believe that a Prescottian dreadnought is operating in the area. I do not believe that six destroyers are sufficient fire power to oppose such a vessel."

Hammond frowned at Martin for a moment before allowing, "This does not leave this room, but I had this discussion with the Fleet Command. They believe that the rumors of a dreadnought in the area are unfounded. If that is the case, then our task force should be enough to secure the area."

Martin chuckled without much humor, "If it's not the case, then we're fried." The other officers in the room shifted nervously.

"That's enough Commander," snapped Hammond, "I am not in the habit of permitting insubordination." Everyone in the room knew that her heart was not in the reprimand, however. The orders stunk and everyone there knew it.

"Now if there is nothing further, I will outline our formation." She took the silence as leave to continue. "Our senior C.O. is Commander Po of the Storm Rider. I will set my flag in that vessel and she will be lead ship. Storm Rider will be flanked by Lt. Commander Layla and Figus. Lt. Commanders Priest and Isleton will draw outside duty and Lt. Commander Gammage will be the stern chaser. If there is nothing else, you are all dismissed to your vessels. We depart in six hours. I look forward to working with all of you." The group broke up on these final words.

Martin and Marcus headed for the P.I.V. Thunder that was currently moored at docking port seven. Marcus broke the silence first, "I'm beginning to regret you making me first officer," he said. He chuckled as he spoke the words, but Martin would not have blamed him if he was at least partially serious. Martin could just not understand these orders! If the reports were not true then sure, their group was more than enough to handle just about anything, but if they were true Martin and Marcus' lives could be cut woefully short.

"What do you think, old friend?" asked Martin.

"I don't know Marty. Fleet must know what they're doing. Maybe they just can't spare any more ships right now, or maybe they do know something we don't. There are a number of possibilities. One Lieutenant and one Lt. Commander just can't know the entire operational picture."

"I know," said Martin, "It's Commodore Hammond's reaction that I don't like."

"There is that" conceded Martin. "By the way, I really am glad you asked for me. My work in operations was fun and rewarding, but I did want to get back in the field."

"Think nothing of it," said Martin "My work in intelligence was getting rather boring. It was all pretty anti-climatic after the Endorra Mission."

"By the way" continued Marcus "Whatever happened to the rest of our group. I admit I've fallen rather out of touch."

"Well" Martin began, "Last I heard, Eddie was promoted and is now 2nd Assistant Chief Engineer aboard the Titanic."

Marcus whistled. The Titanic was a battleship that had quite a reputation. She had a great deal more luck than the original sea going vessel to bear that name.

"Ryn is also a Lieutenant and went into operations. He is on Thor's Hammer as I remember."

Ryn did well for himself apparently, thought Marcus. Thor's Hammer was a battle cruiser in the Hysil sector. Marcus wished either of those ships was around to back up their task force.

"And what of Jaspa?" asked Marcus.

What of Jaspa indeed, thought Martin. He had not seen her in person since before Endorra. They kept up regular correspondence, but Martin longed for her. "Oh, she's part of the Command Staff on Base 13." Martin said this so nonchalantly that Marcus knew there was more behind it, but elected not to press the matter.

The two friends finally arrived at their destination, cutting off any further discussion. Upon arrival it was all business for a while. Marcus saw to the last minute loading and provisioning of the small ship while Martin ordered a meeting of all officers in the Ward room before departure. There was much to do and both lost themselves in their respective tasks.

Martin's stint in intelligence had ended with a whimper rather than a bang. He finished his tenure as an analyst, primarily on the information he had gathered. Johansen's promise of early promotion had come through. Martin finally had a ship of his own. The Storm class Destroyer was a sturdy little vessel. They were extremely fast, and in packs, were a force to be reckoned with. He was understandably worried, however. It was unusual, to say the least, to have a group of destroyers operating in unsecured space. He planned to discuss this matter at the officer's meeting. He also ordered the Communications Petty Officer to send a message to his father. Sometimes his father was privy to information Martin was not.

The hours passed quickly in preparation and anticipation of departure. There were orders to sign, resources to allocate, and drills to schedule. He coordinated with Marcus in everything he did. Martin was a firm believer in having a strong, well informed first officer. Besides, living a childhood dream with your best friend was just plain fun.

Finally the moment was at hand. At precisely 1730 hours, the go-ahead for launch came down. Martin began the launch sequence "Thrusters at station keeping, clear all moorings." Marcus crisply repeated every order. "Maneuvering thrusters: All back one quarter." The Thunder eased away from her berth, the powerful engines thrummed smoothly as the dock slid away. "Helmsman set course for the rally point at system marker 12 gamma. All ahead full."

The Thunder leapt away from the Command base as her fusion engines responded to full power.

"Engineering reports all systems nominal. All decks show green." Said Marcus at Martin's elbow. So far, so good.

The Thunder arrived at the rally point. Commodore Hammond ordered all vessels to proceed to their patrol station at 2400c. Even at that tremendous speed, it would still take ten days to arrive on station. There would be much to prepare for in the intervening time.

*   *   *

October 16, 2521
Sector 61 Alpha

It had been an easy trip so far. The task force had encountered a lone supply ship and jumped it. They subdued it and took its small compliment of fighters easily, took 67 prisoners, and seized a cargo of rare ipsilidium, an important war material. Thus far, the patrol was a complete and unqualified success.

The officers of the Thunder met for their traditional morning meal. It had become standard operating procedure from day one. As usual, Martin arrived first. He still carried his cadet habit of being everywhere at least 20 minutes ahead of time. Ensigns Susan Paul and Karen Feeny arrived next. The two junior engineers were very good at their jobs and were regulars at the breakfast. Truth to tell, only the senior officers were at every meal together; the juniors tended to rotate in and out. Lieutenant Sycarl Ral, the Assistant Chief Engineer pulled up a chair followed by Lt. (j.g.) Kelly, one of the weapons officers. Finally, at exactly 0700, Marcus joined the group.

Command suited Martin. Although his crew consisted of only 175, he treated them all as though they were serving on a battle cruiser. No job was considered too petty or small. He expected 100% from all personnel at all times. He knew that perfection was impossible, but he demanded the next best thing.

Marcus was a superb foil for Martin. As first officer he remained approachable and kept up crew morale. Missions like this could quickly degenerate into monotony and boredom. Bored crews made mistakes. Marcus kept up a constant drill and recreation schedule to keep the crew busy.

The companionable chatter at the table was broken by a signal whistle, "Commander Gammage?"

"Gammage here."

"Sir, we've been ordered to change course to 125 mark 30."

"Very well, inform the helmsman to make the correction. Is there anything that requires my presence on the bridge before change of shift?"

"I don't believe so, sir" came the disembodied voice.

"Very well, Gammage out."

"Guess we're looking for better pickings," said Marcus.

Martin nodded. He wondered if Commodore Hammond was doing what World War II Wolf Pack commanders used to do. If targets were scarce, the subs would hunt in another area. Technology and ships might change, but some things remained the same mused Martin.

The small group of officers felt the course correction as a slight shift in the deckplates. Martin was beginning to ease into his command. He could tell how fast they were traveling by the vibration in the bulkheads. He could sense maneuvers. He thought that if he concentrated hard enough he could be the ship; feel the solar winds on her hull; feel the defense fields kicking space debris out of her way. He actually thought that a ship and her commander could become as one. He also felt the crew becoming an extension of his mind. Each crewmember was a cell carrying out a specific function to benefit the whole. "Ah yes" he thought to himself, "Command is what it's all about."

The group of officers broke up to be about their tasks. Martin and Marcus took the lift up three decks to the bridge. They relieved the night shift and assumed their posts. Martin got the report from the gamma shift watch officer, "We have made the course correction as per Commodore Hammond's order. We are cruising at 1200c. Sensors report a small contact bearing 129 mark 40 distance, .9 light years. We anticipate an order to intercept, but have not received one thus far. End of report."

"Very well" responded Martin to the concise report; "You are relieved. Have a pleasant rest, Steve."

"Good morning Skipper." With that Steven Lemke, the gamma shift watch officer, left the bridge.

"Well, that contact sounds interesting" Marcus said to Martin.

"Yes indeed" responded Martin mentally breathing a sigh of relief. Steve had said a small contact. Martin still half expected a Prescottian dreadnought to jump at them from out of the night.

The order Martin was waiting for came down exactly five minutes later. "P.I.V. Thunder, you are ordered to ascertain the identity of the contact previously recorded. The vessel is small, and we are not reading any major weapons capability. Call for backup if necessary. Hammond, commanding task force, out."

Martin smiled, "The first catch of the day," he said to Marcus. "Helmsman, set an intercept course, flank speed. General Quarters."

The GQ alarm rang out as personnel scrambled for their stations. Martin felt just like a submarine commander of old, stalking an enemy out of the dark, lining him up, and firing torpedoes. He felt the adrenaline surge as he said, "sensor officer, give me a report on contact as soon as you have one."

"I have a positive contact now, skipper," came the immediate reply. "Target is a Prescottian cargo ship. Minimal defense capabilities."

"Very well, let's frag him and return to formation," Martin announced to his crew. The crew let out a cheer. This would be an easy kill.

The Thunder barreled forward. Finally, the destroyer came into action range. "Raise defense fields, arm weapons" came the order from Martin. The ship transformed into an instrument of destruction. The small cargo ship finally saw its pursuer, but far too late. As the target ship gathered itself to flee, Martin gave the all important command. "FIRE." Deadly beams embraced the Prescottian ship. Her defenses were no match for the destroyer. The Thunder would have lived up to her name had sound been able to travel through the vacuum of space. Volley after volley took their toll on the ill fated victim. She eventually broke into free floating particles, glimmering in the fires of her own destruction.

"Well done," said Martin to the bridge crew, "scratch one Prescottian cargo carrier. Lay in a course back to the task force at 2000c. Sensor officer, record the kill. Condition green."

The crew carried out the orders in a euphoric state. The Thunder's first test under fire had left them without a scratch. True, it was a simple test but an important one. Marcus punched up the crew's efficiency rating on his console as if they had performed any other drill. He was pleasantly surprised to see a rating of 97%, the highest on any ship he had ever served. He turned his screen toward Martin and gave him a nudge. Martin looked at the information and smiled. "They're a good crew," was the only comment he made.

The Thunder slipped through the ether on the way back to the rally point. All was well. The ship and crew had functioned as one unit. They were all a captain could hope for.

Suddenly, Marcus looked up from the command pit to see the sensor officer turn an interesting color indeed. Lack of color was more like it. His normally bluish face had turned an ashen gray. "What is it?" asked Marcus.

All eyes turned to the first officer, then toward the sensor officer when it was learned to whom Marcus had addressed the question.

The sensor officer looked down at his scope, turned toward the command pit as if to reply, and back to his scope again, his mouth working the entire time. The situation had Martin's full attention as well.

"What is it? Spit it out man!" he said in a raised voice.

"Sir, I'm reading . . . I don't rightly know what I'm reading, but it's huge!"

"Marcus get up there and find out what he's talking about . . . and ensign, I expect a better report than that." Marcus had vaulted from his seat before Martin could finish the order.

The shaken ensign returned to his scope. "Sorry sir." By this time, he was joined by Marcus. "I'm reading a large body of at least one million metric tonnes moving toward the task force at about 500c."

"One million? Marcus, check that." If the ensign was correct, the contact out massed the Thunder by over a factor of ten; the entire task force by a factor of two.

"Confirmed. Martin I've never seen anything like it."

Martin looked about the bridge before focusing on Marcus again, "get back down here! Condition red! Sound General Quarters. Increase to flank speed. Communications: send a warning massage to Commodore Hammond."

The crew jumped to do his bidding.

"Sir," this from communications, "I get no response from the task force flag ship. I got the message out, but I think something is jamming the return."

"Great" replied the beleaguered commander. "A one million ton contact is bearing down and there is precisely nothing we can do; not even send a warning. Well folks, let's be sure we're ready when we do get there. Open a channel to engineering." The voice of Martin's chief engineer came over the bridge speakers.

"Joaquin here sir."

"Jose, I want all emergency power channeled to the weapons and defense fields. How high can you charge them?"

"Well, I can probably get you 120% on the D.F.'s and about 115% on the FAL's without blowing us across the galaxy."

"Do it. Bridge out."

That was it, that was all he could do. The waiting began. It would be about twenty minutes before they returned to within range of the task force. Martin could only imagine what they'd find. If the readings were correct, and he had no reason to doubt that they were, the task force was sorely outmatched. Martin could only hope that Hammond would do the sensible thing: run like hell and get a message to fleet. Anything else would be folly.

Even at flank speed, Martin felt like they were creeping. He looked at his command console and saw that his engineer was true to his word. His offensive and defensive capabilities were not going to get any higher.

"Keep trying to raise the flagship." It was a futile order, and Martin knew it. It would simply give his crew something to think about for the next few minutes.

"No response." Came the expected reply.

"I want all weapons to bear on target as soon as we drop to sub light." Martin called out to his weapons officer.

"We don't exactly know if the contact is hostile," Marcus dutifully pointed out.

"True, but that's the assumption I'm making. A Prescottian warship was rumored to be operating in this sector, and our communications are jammed." Martin added, "Besides, I trust my gut, and I don't like what its telling me."

Marcus only nodded. Martin's gut had been right as long as he had known him.

The minutes ticked away. "Sensors: Any more information on the contact?"

"Yes sir. The contact is definitely of Prescottian configuration. We should both arrive at the Task Force within minutes of each other. The task force does not seem to be engaging its displacement drive. Sir, they seem to be readying for an attack!"

"DAMN!" Martin yelled. He turned to Marcus, "A lot of good people are going to die for nothing! We can't possibly take that ship."

"Sir!" came the excited peal from communications, "getting something from the flagship."

"Put it on!" Finally they might get some useful information.

"Thunder, you are . . . proceed back to . . . advised . . . Admiral Morta . . . ordered to stand and fight . . . Acknowledge if . . . "

Martin slammed his fist into his palm. So it wasn't Hammond's idea. He started to try and come up with a way to win this fight, but he simply couldn't. He imagined the Prescottian's laughing on their bridge at the pathetic attempt by the Protectorate forces to stop them. They needed heavier ships! Six destroyers could not possibly even slow this monster.

"Sir, I've attempted to respond but cannot."

"Very well, keep trying."

"Aye, sir."

"Helm, time to intercept?"

"Four minutes, seventeen seconds, sir."

It was going to be a long four minutes. The helmsman continued, "The hostile will precede us by about twenty seconds."

Martin digested this, "Very well, put the battle on the main viewer." He did not believe he was going to like what he was about to see.

The two ships raced for the same point in space. The small one about a half minute behind the behemoth. Martin had never felt so useless in his life. He was sure he was about to throw away his ship, his crew, and his life. What the hell was Admiral Morta thinking, anyway?

"The dreadnought has engaged." Came the ominous pronouncement from the helm.

The Prescottian wasted no time. It picked out the flagship and poured fire into her. The sensor officer informed Martin that the enemy vessel was using supercharged FALs and plasma bolts. And use them in good fashion it did. The crew of the Thunder watched in horror as the flagship flared, broke in two, and exploded. The battle had been joined only fifteen seconds thus far.

"We are in range sir!"

"Break to sub light and fire at will!"

The Thunder broke out of F.T.L. and unloaded everything she had at the enemy dreadnought. FALs and anti-matter crashed against the monster's hide . . . and did absolutely nothing.

"No damage." This from the sensor officer, "Its defense fields absorbed everything."

"Maintain fire!" Screamed Martin.

The Thunder lashed out again and again but to no avail, until the dreadnought turned its attention on the irritating gnat buzzing about it. Four plasma bolts leapt from the belly of the beast.

"Evasive starboard! Get more power to . . ." but the order came to late. The bolt crashed through the augmented defense fields to sear the hull below. The bridge exploded around Martin. Consoles blew, the deck buckled, and the overhead crashed down on the bridge, but the hull held. Only the strengthened defense fields had saved them from immediate destruction. The Thunder had been literally drenched in energy, but Martin had survived it.

"Marcus," Martin choked out, "damage report." There was no response. "Marcus?"

Martin turned toward Marcus through the smoke. He saw his best friend lying on the deck, a ceiling strut had neatly impaled Marcus through the chest. Martin's oldest friend had died as a good soldier should, with the look of battle lust on his blackened, blood streaked face.

Martin staggered back into what was left of his command chair. He could not take the time to mourn his friend now. "Anyone still with me; a damage report" he croaked through the smoke.

A voice wafted through the debris to reach Martin's ears "Sir, all systems are red line." A cough broke up the report. "No power to defense fields or weapons. Engines are at bare minimum. Life support is functioning, but just barely. Casualties are reported on all decks."

It seemed that the only thing intact, ironically enough, was the ship's hull. They floated there in space, while the dreadnought nonchalantly picked apart another destroyer. As the ship broke apart on the badly distorted view screen, Martin had a moment of clarity. He knew exactly what needed to be done. With a completely useless ship, he could still win.

"Engineering, anybody home?" Martin almost giggled. The stress, combined with the loss of his friend was getting to him.

"Engineering, Joaquin here" came the sputtering reply.

"Jose, still with us I see, good. Can you get me anything on the displacement drive at all?".

There was silence for a moment, "I can get you maybe 10c for about twenty seconds, but I don't see what . . ."

Martin practically leapt out of his command chair. That was the answer he was hoping for.

"Good." He said. "Here's what we're going to do. I want you to set the FALs to overload. I want you to arm every last anti-matter device. I want you to set the engines to implode after giving a burst of 10c. for . . . let's see," he did some quick calculations, "2.3 seconds. Finally, I want you to set all this up to an activator that will go off when the bridge escape pod is launched. Got all that?"

Jose did not have the slightest idea what Martin was up to, but he was good at his job, "Aye sir. I'll be ready in ten minutes."

"You've got four" Martin responded.

After two minutes, Martin gave the order to abandon ship. Everyone except the remaining bridge personnel and engineering staff found an escape pod and departed the lifeless hulk. On the view screen a fourth destroyer blew apart.

"Hurry up with that switch!" Martin yelled into the bridge speakers.

"Almost got it."

"Helmsman, lay in a course to intersect with the hostile."

"But, sir, won't that . . . ?"

"That's right, we're going to ram him."

"Aye sir."

Engineering responded that moment, "It's set."

Martin grinned wryly "all right, you guys get off this thing. It's going to get awfully hot around here in about thirty seconds."

Martin's face took on a grim expression. All he had to do was make a couple of final adjustments. He was about to lose his first command, but come hell or high water, he was going to take that thing that killed Marcus with it.

He tapped out the final codes on his command pad. "All right, bridge personnel abandon ship. All hell's gonna break loose in about ten seconds!"

He took a last look around. He could not even take Marcus' body as the ceiling strut had gone through the deck. Martin simply did not have time to move it. As he gazed about him, he felt an anger build. He still could not understand the order to stand and fight; Morta was just too experienced a commander to make such a stupid mistake. Perhaps the order had been garbled in transmission. It did not matter. Hundreds had died. Only two destroyers out of six in Task Force 99 remained. Martin slowly walked to the hatch where his bridge crew awaited him. He felt himself grow older with every step he took. It was not easy for a commander to sacrifice his ship, even if it was dead in the water.

He ordered his brave crew to their seats. Several were conspicuously empty; the pod was designed to save the entire bridge crew if necessary. The crew was badly banged up. Mitchell from communications looked as if she might die at any moment. Another crewmember was tending to her as best she could. There was nothing else to do now but press the launch button.

"Helmsman, I want you to orient the pod so that we can see the hostile once we clear the ship."

"Aye sir."

Martin waited. He would only get one shot at this. As the dreadnought came about for another pass on the two remaining ships, Martin uttered a command that may not have been heard for a thousand years.

"Ramming speed!" he yelled as he launched the pod. The lifeboat shot away from the Thunder at 3g's, pushing the crew into their acceleration couches. The ship gathered itself for its last flight. The rainbow effect consumed the vessel as its displacement drive engaged. The Thunder shot through space as if fired from a crossbow. It smashed into the dreadnought at 9.7c, directly amidships. The Prescottian defense fields were good, but not good enough to stop 80,000 metric tonnes of destroyer. The fuel burners exploded in a dazzling display of cherry red. The displacement drive imploded. The FALs emptied their coils in one large explosion, and the thirty six remaining anti-matter missiles unleashed their fury.

Martin was witnessing the finest fireworks display to be seen in galactic space. The huge vessel spilled its atmosphere into the interstellar void. A massive hull breach opened disgorging large bits of detritus and debris. Even with all the firepower the crashing ship had brought, the mammoth vessel remained intact! Now the two remaining destroyers came alive. They took turns firing on the beast. Without its defense fields to protect it, huge chunks of metal were torn from it with every pass. Finally, one of the ships got lucky and scored a hit on the dreadnought's anti-matter pile.

Time stopped for a moment as the huge ship seemed to shrink a bit. Finally, a fiery explosion began to engulf it.

Debris flew everywhere as the destruction continued. A series of explosions ran up the centerline of the ship to the bridge. Another shudder and the superstructure went up in a blaze of orange and yellow. A sheet of flame engulfed it, courtesy of what oxygen remained in the ship. Finally, all grew still. Martin's little pod was just one more piece of flotsam in a field of scattered junk. Martin's plan had worked.

The two remaining destroyers did a victory roll before breaking into a standard search pattern. Martin ordered the locator transponder on his pod activated and before long, one of the remaining ships hove into view. She activated a tractor beam and delivered the little boat to a docking port. The airlock light went from red to green as the door opened.

Martin stood, practically dead from exhaustion as a nurse poked his head in. Martin turned his gaze toward the new arrival, "my communications officer is badly hurt, we also have additional injuries. I need to see your captain."

"Right here," came the response from behind the door. As med techs filed in to help the wounded, Martin exited the pod.

"Permission to come aboard sir?" Martin asked as he gave a very weary salute.

"Permission granted" said Lt. Commander Figus. "You saved our asses" he continued. "Thank you. If it weren't for that call, we'd be dust by now. I can speak for Lt. Commander Isleton when I say that we're recommending you for the Medal of Honor."

Martin waved it off, "I've already got one," he responded. He looked like he was about to drop. "All I want is a place to lie down."

"You can use my cabin," said Figus.

"Thank you. My pod's computer has a list of my casualties. Also, I'd like you to put a recommendation in your log to award the Protectorate Citation for Valor to Lieutenant Marcus Slivnova. Have it read 'He gave his life in the performance of his duty'." The last words caught in his throat and he shook his head "What a waste what a bloody, stupid waste. Figus, do you know what happened?" Martin was starting to babble.

"Just get some rest, Marty. We can talk about that at debriefing."

Martin deflated at that moment. He simply nodded and shuffled to the lift. He hoped the oblivion of sleep would take him quickly. His ship was gone, his best friend was gone. Martin squeezed tears out of the corner of his eyes as the lift carried him away.

*   *   *

Seven hours later
Office of Admiral Cyrus Morta, Commander, 15th fleet.

Once again Admiral Cyrus Morta sat at his desk drinking his clia and once again his stars twinkled back at him. He was in a good mood. He was rid of that troublesome Commodore Hammond. He hadn't liked her from the moment he saw her service record. He had also dispatched that troublesome up start Gammage. What did the humans say? "Killed two birds with one stone." He was thinking about the memorial service he would preside over to mourn the "fallen heroes", when his musings were interrupted by Captain Joor.

Joor's face was a sickly, gray color, not his usual healthy green. His eyes were sunken from lack of sleep, as he had been ordered to follow Task Force 99's progress, and it was he who had relayed the order to stand and fight. Joor was essentially a good man from a military family, but above all, he was trained to follow orders, and they didn't come any higher ranked than Cyrus Morta.

"Morning report sir," he said from ashen lips.

"What's the matter, Joor? Be in good cheer." Morta saw the dispatch pad in Joor's hand and figured it was the report of the destruction of Task Force 99.

"Uhm . . . sir? I have the initial battle report from what's left of Task Force 99."

"What's left?" Said Morta. He didn't like where this was headed. "Someone survived? You must mean reports from escape pods or location transponders."

"No sir. Two vessels survived. The Lightning and the Cyclone."

At least the Thunder wasn't on the list; or the flagship. Morta wrongly assumed that that spelled the end of his problems.

"Shall I read it to you sir?"

"Of course, of course."

"From Lt. Commander Figus, highest ranking surviving officer Task Force 99, to Admiral Cyrus Morta, Commander 15th Fleet: Sir, I am pleased to report the survival of two task force vessels and the complete destruction of the enemy dreadnought. This amazing feat was performed by Lt. Commander Martin Gammage of the Thunder, whom I am recommending for the . . ."

"WHAT?" Screamed Morta. "Is this some kind of joke? How did he survive? More importantly, how did he win?"

Joor took a step back from the thunderclap of Morta's voice, "Sir it appears, and this is only from the first report, that Gammage rammed his ship into the enemy vessel."

"He did what?"

"He rammed his ship into . . ."

Morta glanced up at Joor, "Yes, yes, I heard you."

Joor continued, "Lt. Commanders Figus and Isleton are recommending Gammage for his second Medal of Honor. In addition, the Council of Admirals will likely recommend him for advancement as well. Sir, keep in mind that you also look brilliant in this matter. Defeating a dreadnought with only a loss of four destroyers is amazing."

If looks could kill, then Joor would have left in a basket. "Thank you very much Joor. I have to approve his medal and promotion of course, if I don't I look like an idiot. DAMN!" He smashed his fist on the desktop. Joor left Morta to his ravings.

November 3, 2521
Protectorate Command Base 50.

Martin stood alone at the podium. He faced the seventy four survivors from the Thunder, seventy four out of one hundred and fifty. He still could not believe it. He turned to the crowd with slow, dreamlike movements as the last strains of Amazing Grace died down.

"What can I say about Marcus that Vice Admiral Cheela has not? The Admiral talked of his career and accomplishments. He spoke of his record and achievements.

I could tell you we grew up together. I could tell you what a fine executive officer he was to me. I could tell you of his hobbies and spare time pursuits. Would this help you to know Marcus the way I did? No. What he meant to me can be summed up in these words: He was my best friend and I shall miss him."

Martin returned to his seat on the platform. The stunned crowd stared up at him. Both he and the contingent present knew what came next, and Martin loathed it. He hardly felt that he needed to be rewarded for getting his best friend killed.

Vice Admiral Cheela took the podium once more. "We have a very special ceremony to perform today. I am honored and privileged to be the presenter at this very special and rare gathering. For the first time in 268 years, one man shall receive his second Protectorate Medal of Honor. He is responsible for saving hundreds of Protectorate lives by taking provocative and decisive action. He is responsible for an immense Protectorate victory over its enemies. His tactical genius has won the Protectorate an entire sector. Plans go forth even now to build a Command base in Sector 61 Alpha. I cannot find the words to adequately describe the enormity of this feat. The man I speak of, is, of course, Martin Gammage."

The crowd broke into thunderous applause. Martin stood and slowly walked to the podium. Admiral Cheela smiled and placed the decoration around Martin's neck. He should have been happy. He should have smiled in turn, but could not. He felt as if an albatross was being placed around his neck. The gleaming medal felt as if it were made of lead.

So much death, so much pain, so much destruction. These words bandied about Martin's brain as he accepted his commendation and subsequent promotion to full commander. All Martin could think of was that the decoration and advancement had been bought with his best friend's blood.

Chapter IV: Commander
August 10, 2522
Protectorate Command base 57, Craxella II

Martin stared out his window at the first Craxellian sunrise. There would be two today as there were every day. The first star that Craxella orbited, Shish, poked its head above the horizon. The morning sky exploded in a sheet of green flame above Shish to a deep midnight blue in the western sky. Martin enjoyed this time of day. It was one of the few things he drew pleasure from anymore. He watched as Shish lifted herself clear of the Falton Mountains. As she did so, he prepared the morning report. He did this every day at the same time. Since Craxella II had no axial tilt, the suns rose at a consistent moment every day. He stood and waited for Crax to show her fiery face. The red tinted star was right on time. When it cleared the horizon halfway, Martin left his office to be about his duties.

He was Chief-of-Staff to Vice Admiral Pila Toh, deputy commander, 22nd Fleet. He had been offered several destroyer and frigate commands after his victory at 61 Alpha, but had opted for staff duty instead. He wanted to get away from the fighting and no one was going to refuse the request of a two time Medal of Honor recipient, although his superiors thought it strange. Several had insisted that he be utilized where he had shown unswerving ability, i.e., combat command, but his father had agreed that he take a staff job, if only for a short time. That "short time" was now eight months and showed no signs of coming to an end.

Martin walked the bright corridors of Command Base 57, nodding to several colleagues as he passed. It promised to be another beautiful day as most were on Craxella II. Most passers-by could not help but notice the bank of ribbons on Martin's chest. He did not think of them much anymore. His Medals of Honor were packed away in his quarters collecting dust.

The war was still being fought to a stalemate. The Protectorate had lost 107 vessels to date while inflicting a loss of 201 enemy ships. Even this two to one casualty rate had not deterred the Prescottians. They always seemed to have more ships, more men, right where they needed them. Over 200,000 Protectorate citizens had lost their lives and only the universe knew how many Prescottians. Martin felt himself sinking back into the depression that hovered about him like a shroud. So much destruction, and for what? The war showed no signs of ending. The long days of death and suffering would continue.

He had lost track of his friends after telling them of Marcus' death. They left him transmissions from time to time as their duties allowed. Martin never answered them. He always almost responded, but could never quite bring himself to make the calls. This only added to his ever increasing solitude.

Vice Admiral Pila Toh awaited her aide in her office. The 82-year-old Severnian sat at her desk sipping Earth coffee. She was an excellent commander, but she knew she would never be given a fourth star and she liked it that way. Her skills were primarily administrative; she had no desire to send men and women to their deaths. Toh knew she had a "secret" nickname among her command. She cared so much about every being for whom she was responsible, they simply called her "Mom."

She gazed out her window as she waited for Martin to arrive. Toh could not have asked for a better aide: prompt, competent, brilliant, Martin Gammage was ideal, but she knew he was wasting his skills. She knew his record. She also knew he felt responsible for the death of his best friend and crew. "My poor Marty," she sighed, "perhaps my news today will cheer him."

Martin arrived right at 0730 as he did every day. "Good morning Admiral. Did you sleep well?"

"Good morning Marty. Yes I did. Did you see the sunrises today? They were particularly wonderful."

"I did see them Ma'am. I have the morning report if you would like to hear it."

The old Admiral nodded. Martin began the reading of all the mundane tasks required to run a fleet. He nodded and made notes as the Admiral gave various orders.

Martin was summing up the report, "Finally the P.I.V. Falcon is due to arrive today for reprovisioning."

"Very well, assign them a berth and invite the crew for shore leave."

"Yes Ma'am. If that is all, I will process your orders."

The Admiral smiled slightly and said, "I have one more item for you, Marty."

"Yes Ma'am?"

"We are going to be getting a new assistant for my staff. She should be arriving tomorrow or the next day on the Benjamin Franklin. She is to be promoted to Lt. Commander upon arrival, and I'd like you to conduct the ceremony and, how do you humans say, 'show her the twine'?"

Martin chuckled a bit. He knew full well that the Admiral knew the proper phrase; she just wanted to see him laugh.

"That would be 'ropes' Ma'am."

"Ah yes, show her the ropes."

Martin made note of this on his portacomp. "It shall be as you say."

"Oh and Marty, I think you know her. Her name is Lieutenant Jaspa Shindessa."

Martin was taken aback. This was completely unexpected. His feelings were mixed as he digested the information. Jaspa, after all this time? What would he say? What would he do? She'd be working for him all the time.

"Are you all right Marty?" The Admiral lightly laughed to herself as she made the inquiry.

"Yes Ma'am, quite all right."

"You are dismissed." Marty left as the Admiral smiled. She had put two and two together from reading service reports and listening to Martin ramble on after long days at work. She was gratified to know that she had done the right thing. She only hoped that her efforts would not be wasted.

*   *   *

30 hours later.
Landing bay 19.

Martin paced nervously as he awaited the arrival of Jaspa's shuttle. The Benjamin Franklin had entered orbit 10 minutes ago and Martin's nervousness had been increasing exponentially since then. It was strange, he could command a ship in a fierce, pitched battle, but he could not face this single woman.

He turned to the monitor in the docking lounge. Perhaps the news would take his mind off his roiling emotions. The announcer was discussing the last voting of the Council of Admirals. They still had not elected a Fleet Admiral and it was not likely that they would anytime soon. Admiral Cyrus Morta had received 49% of the vote, a far cry from the 75% that was necessary. Morta was the top vote getter in the badly split election. Martin thought that this was a particularly bad time for such indecision. He felt that the war could only be won under strong, united leadership.

The moments ticked away. Finally, the arrival board announced that the Franklin had launched several shuttles. Some were bound for the orbiting station, but these did not interest Martin. Jaspa's shuttle would arrive in the next five minutes. Martin thought about what he should say, but could come up with nothing. "This is ridiculous" he mumbled under his breath. He and Jaspa were the best of friends; why was he being so foolish?

The shuttle raised a small cloud of dust as it settled on the pad. The gangway arm extended to meet the small docking doors on its flank. Martin stood, took a deep breath and strode to the doors. Several junior officers and crew departed the craft, looking forward to their first leave in some months. Finally he saw her and she took his breath away. She had let her jet hair grow even longer. It cascaded to the middle of her back in long rolling waves. She broke into a radiant smile as she saw him. Her expression warmed his heart, and he felt his face flush. She ran the last few steps and threw herself into his arms.

"Oh Marty, it's so good to see you. I've been worried about you. You never answered any of my communiqués.

Ryn's been concerned too. How are you? Do you like your new post? I'll be working for you, right?"

Martin smiled in spite of his dark mood of the last months. Her bubbly speech was infectious. Energy seemed to flow from her and seep into Martin's tired soul. "Hey slow down. One question at a time. You look fantastic. I hate to press you, but your promotion ceremony is in three hours. Why don't we get some lunch? You can clean up and refresh yourself. After the ceremony, we'll go to the officer's mixer. Afterwards, we can catch up if you want."

A smile played upon her full lips. A mischievous sparkle lit up her eyes. "Have it all planned out do you? All right, lead on."

She linked her arm with his as they started up the concourse back to the base proper. Her face took on a somber cast as she said, "When I heard about Marcus I cried for three days. I tried to get leave to go to the memorial, but I couldn't get away. Most of all I felt for you. It must have been difficult for you being all alone."

"It was all right. After his death I . . . well I just wanted some time away. That's why I took this posting. You'll like Admiral Toh. The station personnel call her Mom."

Jaspa laughed, "'Mom'?"

Martin returned a chuckle, "Yeah. She's a fantastic administrator and takes care of the people under her command. You'll be acting as assistant chief-of-staff. You'll report directly to me."

"Oh, yes sir!"

He was feeling better by the minute. Jaspa's mere presence was like a tonic; her manner contagious. He was so glad she was here. It was like a dark fog over his head was finally dissipating to let in the light of day.

Martin looked into those purple eyes he remembered so fondly, "Come on, I'll give you the 50 cent tour."

A look of confusion crossed her face, "The what?"

He smiled, "It's an old Earth expression, it means I'll show you around."

Her only response was a quizzical look and a nod.

They explored the base for about forty five minutes before stopping for a quick meal. The light of the two stars shined clear and bright through the windows of the galley. As they ate, Martin introduced Jaspa to some of the base personnel. Jaspa's quick wit and charming smile won over a great many people. After lunch Martin showed Jaspa her quarters. They parted so that both could ready themselves for the upcoming ceremony.

*　　*　　*

". . . and by the powers vested in me by the Council of Admirals and Vice Admiral Pila Toh, I hereby promote you to the rank of Lieutenant Commander with all the incumbent privileges and responsibilities."

A smattering of applause wafted up to the podium where Martin had officially promoted Jaspa. The ceremony had lasted only a few minutes, Martin was not the type to be long winded. Both left the stage and joined the officers' mixer.

Martin introduced Jaspa around to several of his staff and other base personnel. He had a drink and then faded into the background. This was Jaspa's moment, and he did not want to intrude. He watched as Jaspa spoke to Lieutenant (j.g.) McPhillips. Jason thought of himself as a "lady's man" and he observed as the young Lieutenant tried his stuff out on the new Lt. Commander. Martin smiled a bit; he rather liked Jason, but knew he wouldn't get anywhere.

The glow of Jaspa's visit was beginning to fade for Martin. He tried to get into the mood of the party, but he simply could not. Every time he tried, he kept imagining Marcus' broken body pinned to the deck of his ship and saw the corpses strewn about the bridge of his command. He could not shake those horrible images and they were beginning to dampen the fiery reaction he had for Jaspa. He felt the dank cloak of depression once again close around him.

*   *   *

January 25, 2523

"I have the morning report for you Ma'am," Martin intoned as he did every day. He had lapsed into a mind numbing routine to kill his pain.

"Marty, I have good news for you," Admiral Toh said without preamble. "They've offered you the P.I.V. Topaz, a new construction heavy frigate."

"Thank you Ma'am," Martin said, "but if it's all the same, I enjoy my posting here and . . ."

Admiral Toh slammed her hand down on the desk. "It's not all the same to me, Marty. You're wasting your talents here. You're an excellent aide, I can't deny that, but you should be in space where you belong. Captains sometimes lose crewmembers. It's a fact of command. You simply cannot torture yourself over their loss. For the love of Necla . . . Marty, you saved hundreds, if not thousands, of lives. You were born for combat command. Please, at least think about this before replying."

"I'll think about it Ma'am," Martin responded listlessly.

Admiral Toh sighed, "All right Marty, you're dismissed. I'll read the morning report myself."

Marty turned to leave, "As you wish, Ma'am."

He walked to his outer office. Jaspa was already there, practically dancing from foot to foot.

"So?" She inquired.

"So what?" Martin said as he adopted a confused air.

Jaspa shot him an irritated glance, "you know what I mean. What did you say about the Topaz?"

"Does everyone around here plan to get involved in my personal life?" Martin said with more than a touch of annoyance.

"Just those of us who care about you." Jaspa shot back.

Martin's tone softened. "I said I'd think about it."

"What's to think about? A new construction heavy frigate. Those usually go to Captains! They're offering it to you Marty because you're the best. You're wasting time here! Marcus would not have wanted it this way."

Martin exploded. "What do you know of what Marcus would want? Did you know him your entire life? Did you request him as first officer? Did you get him killed?"

"Don't think you have a monopoly on grief Marty," Jaspa growled, "I've lost people close to me in this war too."

Martin looked chagrined. Shame crept into his voice as he said, "I'm sorry Jaspa". He managed to continue in a hushed tone, "I don't know what I'm saying" he shook his head, "or what I'm doing. These last months have been awful. I've tried to block out anything that might cause me to be hurt again . . . especially you." Martin looked at Jaspa as if seeing her for the first time. Gods but she was gorgeous. "Buy you dinner?"

A small smile tugged at her mouth. "This is kind of short notice, but I'll try to squeeze you into my busy schedule."

Her smile had its old effect on Martin. "1900 at Section A?"

"I'll be there," she said.

*   *   *

1900 Hours:

Martin and Jaspa concluded their business day and headed for the intra base lift. Martin punched Section A on the control pad and they started off. Base 57 was quite large, and the restaurant they frequented was on the opposite side. It took a ride of almost two minutes to reach it.

They entered the Section-A-Bistro at peak hour but the gold admiral's aide loops on their shoulders got them immediate seating. The Maitre'd showed them to a central table. Martin and Jaspa said hello to many of the patrons as they walked. They were both well liked and regulars at the establishment.

"I hope the table is to your liking," said the Maitre 'd with a pronounced Despoina accent.

"It is indeed," returned Martin in that language. The Maitre 'd never failed to be impressed at Martin's mastery of the Despoina tongue; it was a difficult language.

Jaspa leaned over the table, "I was always jealous of you for that, you know. Languages always came easy to you. I

- 90 -

had to study so hard just to learn Terran, and you know how many, five, six?"

"Actually, nine now. I started learning Darnalian shortly after I was transferred here."

"Well at least your brain hasn't gone completely soft."

Here we go, thought Martin.

Jaspa fired the first volley, "Are you going to tell Admiral Toh that you'll take the Topaz?"

Martin began warily, "my response has not changed from this morning. I said I'll think about it and I will."

"No, you won't" Jaspa's purple eyes blazed as she said it. "I've been working here too you know. This is the third command they've offered you, just since I was transferred in. I know you've had your problems, but you need a field command. I don't care what you think, Marcus would not want to see you build a fortress of self-pity around yourself, and that's what this is Marty, self-pity. Marcus is gone; it's not your fault. The orders you received were horrible, perhaps criminal, and everyone knows it. They don't give Medals of Honor to screw-ups. Everyone else has moved on and . . . "

"All right." Martin's voice was barely audible.

"What was that?"

"I said all right. I'll take the command!"

Jaspa's mood came about like a windstorm in the Greyling Mountains, "Oh Marty, that's wonderful. I knew you'd see reason. Let's finish eating, I have something in my quarters I've been saving for just such an occasion!"

They finished their meal and left for Jaspa's quarters. Once there, Martin seated himself on the couch and could not help but feel a sense of deja vous. His mind was still reeling. This woman had single handedly pulled him from the quicksand his life had become. He owed her so much he did not know how to express how he felt.

Jaspa meanwhile had entered her bedroom to fetch her surprise. She returned in a diaphanous gown that was revealing in all the right places. She was carrying a chunky bottle of liquid that Martin did not recognize. The fluid matched the purple of Jaspa's eyes.

"My parents gave this to me when I graduated from the War College. It's Nari Sharsase."

"Oh yes, I remember it" Martin said as he took in Jaspa's form. "You, me, and Marcus got plowed drinking a bottle of that stuff." Martin's memories carried him back to a time just before their fourth year. They had stayed up all night drinking the Sharsase and talking about their dreams. That was the night Martin had fallen in love with Jaspa.

"Those were good times," she said as if reading his thoughts. She poured two glasses of the electric violet substance. "To Marcus, friend and hero."

"To Marcus" Martin echoed. He drank the potent liquor. He savored its taste and allowed it to trace a warm trail down his throat.

Jaspa turned to him, "you know, I was attracted to you our first year, but you didn't even know I was on campus."

Martin choked on his drink. He sputtered for a moment and burst out, "Like hell! You were the unapproachable one. You always had a crowd of men and women around you." He gathered his courage; "I fell in love with you the moment I saw you. I realized it that night with the Sharsase."

Her eyes misted "I never knew," she said softly.

"To missed opportunities" he said and looked into her eyes.

"To the ones we make ourselves." She put her glass down and kissed him.

The kiss was more intoxicating than the beverage. Her mouth was cool and sweet, just as he remembered. He grabbed the folds of her gown and pulled her to him. She stroked his brown hair and let her fingers lightly brush the skin of his neck.

As he gathered Jaspa up and carried her to the bedroom, Martin sent out a silent thanks to any gods that might be listening

*　　*　　*

March 1, 2523
P.I.V. Topaz, 9th Fleet, Task Force 1

There was just something about a new ship. All the consoles gleamed as Jaspa strolled around the bridge. Eddie had the sparkling engines running at peak performance. Even the crew had an air of anticipation about them. The Topaz had performed above specifications on her trial runs. Jaspa could only hope that the ship and crew lived up to their potential in battle. As executive officer, Jaspa was responsible for the training and performance of the mostly green crew.

"Captain on the bridge," said Ensign Liles from the life support monitor. Liles was one crewmember Jaspa was particularly concerned with.

"Good morning all" said Martin as he strode to the command well. The new vessel seemed to energize him back to top form. He had shaken the guilt he felt over Marcus' death and was now the captain Jaspa knew he could be.

"Morning report, please" he said as he flashed a smile at Jaspa. On duty they were all business, but the crew knew of their romantic life after hours. One could not hope to keep a secret like that on any Protectorate ship, much less a frigate. Their relationship was not quite professional, but it did not hurt their individual performances.

"We are traveling with the P.I.V. Emerald as escort vessels for the Battle cruiser Avenger" began Jaspa, "Our heading is 150 mark 75; our speed: 1800 c. Admiral Bentein has ordered that we, the Emerald, the Sapphire, and the Avenger shall form Task force 1a and scout the perimeter of this sector at 1200 hours today. We are expected to encounter resistance."

A hush fell over the bridge upon hearing the news. It looked like some of the kids in the crew would have to grow up faster than they had anticipated.

Jaspa was not done with the report. "Sector command confirms," she raised her voice so the entire bridge could hear "that the Fleet carriers Lexington and Intrepid have engaged and destroyed a Prescottian Task Force consisting of four destroyers, three frigates, two heavy cruisers, and a battleship. All vessels were obliterated or hopelessly crippled. They report that they will destroy the remaining stragglers by 1000 hours today."

A cheer went up from the bridge crew. There was a major victory in the works today, and they could have a hand in it. The cheer was laced with some trepidation however. Scouting duty was particularly dangerous and one never knew what one would find.

Martin said to Jaspa, "That's excellent. Order a battle drill before we depart on patrol. I'll be below in engineering if I'm needed."

"Very good sir." She gave him a wink that only he could see.

Martin entered the lift and toggled the control for the engineering deck. From there he planned to make a walking tour of his new vessel. He felt fully alive for the first time in a long while and the promise of combat heated his blood.

As he exited the lift, Eddie was waiting for him.

"Jaspa told me you'd be coming down. I'll tell you, these new AX5 displacement drive engines could drive anyone to distraction. The antimatter flow is constantly out of sync and the . . ."

Same old Eddie, Martin thought. He'd find something wrong with any new piece of equipment. Eddie continued on like this for five minutes. It's a good thing he's a top engineer, thought Martin, or no captain would have him. As he left engineering, he moved up one deck to explore the cargo spaces. Everything a ship needed was to be found on this deck. The large containers were still full of supplies. A quiet testament to the mission ahead.

He toured the master weapons room and ammunition magazines. Sleek antimatter missiles lined the walls waiting for action. Fusion Assisted Laser coils lay on the floor like sleeping serpents waiting for an excuse to unleash their energy venom.

He toured operations and the sensor control room. The crew was inexperienced, true, but they all looked ready and eager for the upcoming patrol.

Finally, on deck two he found his chief tactical officer. Ryn looked about the same since their mission on Endorra; if anything, he had gotten bigger, and Martin did not think that was possible.

Ryn smiled warmly as he looked up from his weapons readouts, "I was just on my way up to the bridge when Jaspa told me you were making your walking tour, so I thought

I'd wait for you." The Pologian's voice rumbled like an earthquake.

"I'm glad you did, I wanted to talk to you."

The seriousness of Martin's voice gave Ryn pause. "Oh? What about?"

"When we go into battle, your department will be of greatest import" Martin began in Pologian so that passers by would not understand, "I wanted to know if you were ready."

The big man sat for a moment before responding, "Some of the kids are green, Marty, but they'll dish out more than we take, that I can promise you. The weapons package on this bucket is fantastic. The only thing we lack is a nova cannon, but I understand the Avenger is coming with us so that problem is solved. Oh yes, Marty, we'll be ready for you."

Martin looked his friend in the eye. Even seated, this was difficult as Ryn was a full seven and a half feet while standing, "That's what I wanted to hear. When you're done, come on up."

"You bet Marty," rumbled the big man.

Martin turned to leave when a huge hand grasped his shoulder. "Good to have you back, Commander" rumbled Ryn.

"Good to be back, Lt. Commander" Martin said as he left the compartment.

Martin's tour had taken the better part of three hours as he had hoped. When he arrived on the bridge, the Topaz was preparing to get underway.

He walked down to the command well, "Helmsman, we'll alter course as soon as we hear from the Avenger."

"Aye sir."

"Jaspa, how are we doing?"

"All systems are running despite Eddie's objections to the contrary," they shared a smile at that, " we're as ready as we're going to be."

"Signal from the Avenger, sir," this from communications, "we're ordered to course 200 mark 60 at our earliest convenience."

Martin spoke up, "You heard him helmsman, take us out, set speed at 2000 c."

"Aye sir, 200 mark 60, 2000c."

The frigate came about and joined its two sister ships and the battle cruiser. The four vessels made an imposing sight as they adjusted their courses. They gathered themselves and leapt for the unknown.

*   *   *

March 4, 2523
P.I.V. Topaz, Task Force 1a

It had been three days since Task Force 1a had broken away from the Fleet, and all they had found so far was some dust and free floating hydrogen. It appeared that the "resistance" they had been promised had scurried away.

Martin rather liked that thought. His mighty ships scaring away a weaker foe. Oh well, he thought, a pipe dream from my past isn't going to help now. Even so, he couldn't shake the recollection from when he and Marcus were boys. The two would pretend to command ships so powerful that none could stand before them. If only that were true now.

"Sir, sensor contact."

These three words broke Martin out of his musings. "Give bearing and identify!" he ordered.

"Bearing 260 mark 10, distance: .8 light years. I'm reading five contacts, three small, one medium, one large. I cannot identify ship types at this distance. They show no sign of having seen us sir."

Martin grinned. The Protectorate sensor advantage was still working for them.

He turned to the communications station, "Send to Commodore Wainwright aboard Avenger: Announce our contact and give the coordinates. Tell them we're standing by for further orders."

Martin waited tensely as his message was sent. He was the most junior commander in Task Force 1a and therefore had to await further instructions.

The communications specialist listened at his board for a minute before saying, "Sir, message from Avenger is as follows: Form attack posture Beta. We will engage at once. Proceed on target at 2750c, this will put us in striking distance in approximately two and one half hours. Good work, Topaz, Commodore Sun Chula Wainwright out."

Martin turned toward Jaspa, "Commander, do a thorough check of all systems while we have the time. Helmsman: Alter course to intercept. Sensors: Give me a positive identification of targets as soon as you get one. Communications: Patch me through to engineering."

Crewmembers scurried to carry out their orders. Eddie's voice from engineering came over the speakers, "Engineering responding, Captain."

"Eddie I want emergency power to the defense fields in about two hours and fifteen minutes. Cut all nonessential systems and pour that in too . . ."

"Sir!" cried the sensor specialist, "the targets are altering course toward us. They are closing rapidly."

This was an interesting development. There was no way to tell if the course change was a coincidence, or if the Prescottians had actually seen them. Whatever the case, it appeared that the game was on.

"Condition red, general quarters!" announced Martin.

The vessel came to life as she readied herself for combat. Her sister ships formed a wedge in front of the Avenger forming a spearhead that would hopefully pierce their enemy's defenses. As the vessel that spotted the Prescottians, the Topaz had the honor of lead ship.

"All Task Force ships report ready. All decks are standing by," this from Jaspa who was listening intently to her internal monitors.

Martin looked around the bridge, something did not feel right to him. As his gaze settled on life support, he noticed that a critical circuit had not been closed.

"Ensign Liles! Mind your station. Circuit 6 Alpha is open. If we take a hit in the life support coupling, we'll lose the entire system!" Circuit 6 Alpha was designed to channel auxiliary power to life support if the primary system was damaged.

Ensign Liles turned beet red, "Sorry sir."

"Sorry doesn't cut it on my bridge, mister. Another error like that and you'll be grounded . . . permanently."

Martin was harsh, but he needed to be. A mistake like that could cost him his ship, and nothing was more important than his ship and the lives it housed. His instincts had been proven right again.

"Sir," the sensor specialist spoke up, "positive identification on the hostiles. Three Prescottian destroyers, one cruiser, one battle cruiser. They are now forming to an attack posture. I do not believe they saw us until just now. They had altered course, but their formation had been for cruising until recently."

This was good news. It helped to confirm that the course change on their part had been coincidental. Martin was glad in a way. This meant that the battle would take place much sooner. They were closing at a combined speed of over 5500c.

"Eddie I need that emergency power now."

"You've got it," in confirmation, the power gauge on Martin's panel for defense fields went from 100% to 127%. Eddie was always good for a few extra power points at just the right moment.

Ryn chose this time to announce from his tactical position, "I have the hostiles on my scope now sir. Time to intercept: twenty two minutes. My FALs and antimatter missiles are armed and at full charge."

"Excellent. Let's show those bastards exactly what this ship can do." The bravado went a long way to boosting the confidence of Martin's green crew, especially after Ensign Liles' sloppiness.

The two fleets closed on each other at a space eating pace. Martin felt the familiar rush; he pictured the upcoming battle in his mind. He envisioned moves and countermoves for the upcoming dance of death. He confirmed orders from the command ship and readied his own crew. He smiled at Jaspa and nodded to her knowing full well had it not been for her, he'd still be flying a desk for Admiral Toh. He was ready. His ship was ready. All Martin could do now was wait.

The minutes slowly ticked by. Finally, the enemy ships appeared as small dots on the view screen, this was the moment. "Decelerate to sub light, prepare for action!" Martin ordered his bridge crew.

Task Force 1a shut down their displacement drives. Inertia control systems strained at the sudden loss of momentum. Suddenly a burst of light exploded from the Avenger. She had fired her nova cannon. One of the enemy destroyers flared like a candle flame and was as quickly snuffed out. Its defense fields did not even hinder the blast as the small ship was consumed. The destroyer exploded into sparkling debris as the tremendous energies engulfed it; now the odds were even.

"Let's concentrate on that cruiser. Come to 186 mark 13. Steady, steady, Fire!" Martin's ship did his bidding as the Topaz spat her destructive energies at her foe. The enemy cruiser staggered under the pounding; its defense fields collapsing momentarily under the barrage. Martin saw his chance, "Ryn, target that weak area and fire!"

Two antimatter missiles found their mark. The cruiser wheeled away, heavily damaged and out of the fight temporarily."

"We hit her badly," said Jaspa. "Her port side fusion engine is out as are her port stabilizers. Her defense fields are at 42%."

A good first run for the Topaz. Unfortunately, her combat path had taken her in front of two of the enemy destroyers. They cut loose on Martin's flanks. The Topaz stood up to the beating she was taking as Ryn returned fire. The shots were well timed and coincided with fire from the Emerald. One of the destroyers flared brilliantly with the rippling effect of several FAL hits. The second moved off, jockeying for position.

"Damage report!" cried Martin.

Jaspa consulted her board, "Not too bad, defense fields are at 86%, no other appreciable damage."

"Sir, the battle cruiser is running at us!" screamed the helmsman.

"Evasive, port! Bring us to 90 mark 270." This maneuver probably saved the Topaz. Only a small fraction of destruction found its mark, but it was enough. The frigate shuddered under repeated hits. An antimatter device exploded under her chin. Sparks flew from ruined consoles. Ensign Liles, the luckless life support officer, fell in a bloody mess to the deck. The world seemed to slow as Martin watched a blade of shrapnel sail past Jaspa's head, missing her by inches. Ryn cried out in pain as a piece of flying debris hit his shoulder.

In a moment it was over. The bridge crew caught their breaths as Martin asked for the extent of the damage.

Jaspa choked on some smoke as the ventilators kicked in, "Defense fields are at 55%. We have a hit on the starboard displacement drive engine. Primary power is at 75% due to a ruptured coupling. The infirmary reports six dead. Could be worse sir."

She was right about that. If the battle cruiser had caught them with a full barrage, they'd be floating dust by now.

Martin called out, "Take us to 180 mark 17, let's finish that destroyer."

The Topaz stopped her stagger and got her feet beneath her. The helmsman executed the turn with some difficulty and Ryn lined up the shot. The Pologian was perfect as he released twin bolts of red death at the enemy ship. The small ship bucked and swerved under the hits and then floated lifelessly, its hull breached in several places.

A blinding flash lit up space as the Emerald exploded close aboard. The battle cruiser had caught her with a broadside and the frigate could not stand up to the full wrath of the Prescottian. The players were now down to the Avenger who exchanged shots with the battle cruiser, the untouched Sapphire, and the damaged Topaz. The Prescottians still controlled their battle cruiser, one damaged destroyer, and the badly hit cruiser. The battle was still too close to call.

"Sir, that cruiser is trying to back door us, they're on our tail and closing fast," this from the sensor specialist.

Martin grinned savagely, "Well, I think we can have a little surprise for them. Helmsman, I want full stop on my command. Wait, wait, wait, NOW!"

The Topaz' mighty engines whined as she decelerated from .7c to nothing in a few seconds. The maneuver had the desired effect. The enemy cruiser overshot the frigate by a week and a half. "Fire!" Martin yelled.

Ryn pumped everything through the Topaz' forward weapons array. FALs and antimatter combined in a lethal dose as they impacted the aft sections of the enemy. The already damaged cruiser heaved under the assault. The defense fields collapsed, leaving the engines and underbelly bare for another barrage. Ryn was only too happy to oblige as he cut loose with four missiles; all found their marks. The cruiser's engines overloaded. A fatal chain reaction engulfed the large ship as its antimatter fuel exploded. Sheets of orange, yellow and green flame surrounded the ship as it blew into five pieces, all heading off on their own vectors.

The celebration on the Topaz was short lived, for at that moment, two things happened. The enemy battle cruiser caught the Avenger with a savage blow while the Sapphire was having problems with the remaining destroyer. Martin knew that they could still lose this battle. His quick mind, however, was already formulating a plan.

"Ryn, I want you to put all available power into one burst from the forward FAL array."

The Pologian looked puzzled, "But sir, that will surely overload the coils, we'll lose the array until they can be replaced."

Martin smiled, "If I'm right, we won't be needing them." Ryn did not look convinced. Martin continued, "Sensors: how much power does the battle cruiser have on her defense fields?"

The answer was quick in coming, "32%."

"Ryn, target that blast on the battle cruiser's bridge. As soon as you hit, launch as many antimatter missiles as you can. It will be a tough shot, but I know you can do it. Helmsman: give Commander Calplygian the best shot you can. If we pull this off, the battle cruiser will be like a giant with no brain."

Ryn smiled as the plan came together in his mind, "I'll hit him for you Marty."

The Topaz came about. The enemy battle cruiser and destroyer were busy with their own adversaries and did not immediately notice the maneuver.

Ryn mumbled from his post, "A little more, just a little more, Now!"

He pressed his firing control. The light dimmed as the Topaz put everything she could into one shot. The acrid fumes of overloaded FAL consumed the bridge as an ultra bright light shot from the forward weapons array. The red string lanced through the night to connect with the enemy bridge. As was hoped, the defense fields flared briefly and then died. Ryn followed up his hit with three antimatter devices. They flew through the void and struck home in rapid succession. The front end of the battle cruiser exploded in a beautiful array of colors. The overload indicators lit up all over Ryn's console but it did not matter. The battle cruiser's nose dipped precariously at the loss of mass in its forward section. Without a bridge, the rest of the vessel was just worthless junk.

The Avenger leapt into action. They fired a devastating array of weaponry that spelled the end for the Prescottian giant. The Sapphire too got the upper hand in its duel and blew the destroyer from the sky. It was a clean sweep. For the loss of only one frigate, the Protectorate Task Force had destroyed five enemy vessels, including a battle cruiser. The Protectorate had won the day; it was time to go home.

*   *   *

March 6, 2523
Sector 29G, Task Force 1 rallying point.

The Topaz rejoined a jubilant fleet. Task Force 1 had recorded an impressive tally against Prescottian forces in this sector. Three separate battles had been fought in the last ten days including the scrap the Topaz had been a part of. All were complete Protectorate victories. Martin was in a jaunty mood as he called his senior staff together.

"I'm recommending all of you for commendations, your efforts against the Prescottians were exemplary. Eddie, I understand that our battle damage has been buttoned up. Well done."

Eddie beamed, for once in as good a mood as anyone had ever seen him, "Everything is repaired except the forward

FAL array. Your little shot blew so many circuits it will be another twelve hours before that's up and running."

Martin took the jibe in stride, "Excellent." He turned toward his Pologian tactical officer, "Ryn, that was some of the best shooting I've ever seen. I think you single handedly carried the day."

It was not easy to make a Pologian blush, however, Ryn was becoming a startling red color, "Thank you sir" was all he managed to say.

Martin continued, "I am extremely pleased with all of your performances and will make a favorable report to fleet. In the meantime, let's get our full report from our first officer." Martin could afford to be informal at this meeting, there were only six people in the room, four of whom were the best of friends.

Jaspa stood, "We are being credited with a full kill on the cruiser and an assist on the battle cruiser." Martin let out a low whistle, this was high praise indeed. Jaspa continued, "We lost twelve crew and have an additional twenty one injuries, only one of which is serious." Dr. Tyla Nor Nor Con nodded from her chair at this news. This was her only contribution to the discussion. "As Eddie has indicated, all of our battle damage with the exception of the FAL array is repaired. Total crew efficiency for this engagement was 95%."

Martin nodded as Jaspa took her seat. 95% for a first battle was outstanding.

"You are dismissed; again, thank you for making me look so good." Everyone laughed and turned to leave. "Jaspa, could you stay a moment, please?"

Everyone else filed out leaving the two of them alone. Jaspa looked at Martin expectantly.

He began, "We make an excellent team Jaspa. So good in fact, that it makes what I am about to say very difficult. I was looking at your service record and it appears that you were not entirely truthful with me. It indicates that you are qualified for X.O. duties. It also says that you are qualified for command. You failed to mention that little detail."

"Well, I would have gotten around to it eventually," she teased.

He smiled at her, "I'm putting you in for destroyer command as soon as one is available. I cannot serve on the same bridge with you. There was a moment, if you remember, where you could have been injured or killed. At that moment I was distracted and I cannot have that. If I were to lose you while you were under my command, I . . ."

"I understand" she said as she placed a finger on his lips. "I did what I did for you. You're the best C.O. I've ever seen; just remember me when you're an admiral."

He gave her a brief hug. "I'll always remember what you did for me; now, back to it."

They left the conference room for their stations.

Chapter V: Captain
January 25, 2525
Orbital Space Dock, Baltos VII

It was time for him to have her. He would not be her first. She had been with others, none as deserving as he in his opinion, but she had others nonetheless. It had taken him a shorter time than most, but in the quiet times in his quarters he had dreamed of her. She would be his now, and his alone. No others would take his place; she belonged to him and he would take care of her. And then suddenly, there she was. The sun glinted off her skin in a dazzling display of light and shadow. To his romantic eye, the scene was pure magic. All 600,000 tonnes of her glinted in the star fire of Baltos as Martin's shuttle cleared the limb of the planet. The battleship Indomitable now belonged to him. She was the Fleet's flagship, and Martin was proud to command her.

His command of the Topaz had been perfect. His ship had engaged and destroyed more capital ships than any other frigate in the past one hundred years. He sometimes regretted putting Jaspa off the Topaz, but she was proving her worth commanding a destroyer. Besides, he felt that his record was better without the added distraction, but he sometimes wished he could share his success with her.

Ryn would be coming with him to his new command. The big Pologian sat next to him in the shuttle. He would need Ryn's expertise. The Death Merchant class battleships were the most heavily armed vessels in the Protectorate arsenal. The Indomitable had a third displacement drive engine simply to power her weapons and defense fields. She was a vessel to be reckoned with.

The shuttle was giving the new captain the "Grand Tour." Something all captains got when receiving a new command. The shuttle looped around the bow, showing off the bridge and weapons platforms. Next, the small craft flew over the top of the large vessel, showing everything the Indomitable had to offer its new commanding officer. Martin looked over the three displacement drive housings; saw the huge exhaust vents. He took a cursory glance at the fusion engines and noticed the scars on the hull; this was a ship that was meant for, and had seen, a great deal of action.

Ryn nodded approvingly at the aft weapons array. His eyes grew large over the nova cannon barrel. He could not wait to use it in battle. As Ryn calculated the worthiness of the ship, Martin waxed nostalgic over battleships of the past. Each had been a testament to the might of its maker. Whether it had born archers, sixteen inch guns, or nova cannon, the battleship was the largest weapons platform of its respective place in history, and Indomitable was no different. She was the result of the massive expenditure of treasure and manpower necessary to build such a vehicle. Martin vowed to be worthy of her.

The shuttle completed its flight plan and swung around to the aft portion of the ship. The pilot was ordered to alight in the port side landing bay. The young ensign deftly worked the controls and the shuttle lightly settled to the deck. The gentle hissing of air could be heard as the bay pressurized. As Martin waited, he looked at the rows of sleek fighters that lined the bulkhead. Even though this was not a carrier, she was equipped with several squadrons of interceptors. This served to increase her offensive punch.

The airlock light came on as the bay became habitable. An honor guard strode in, weapons and chins high, to begin the ceremony. A change of command was a welcome break in shipboard routine. Everyone would speculate as to what the new "old man" would be like. Finally, the person Martin would be replacing came in. He walked to a podium set in the middle of the deck and nodded to an enlisted man that raised an antique bosun's whistle to his lips. The shuttle doors opened as Martin was piped aboard.

He and Ryn exited the shuttle. "Permission to come aboard" Martin said to the officer of the deck.

"Permission granted, and welcome, Captain" came the snap reply.

Martin nodded and walked to the podium. Ryn marched to where the other officers were standing and took his place at attention.

The ceremony would be brief and to the point. Martin began, "By order of Vice Admiral Rosh Beela, Deputy Commander 15th Fleet, I hereby assume command of this vessel." He turned to the other captain, "I relieve you sir."

The second man nodded, "I stand relieved." Captain Jason Smith had just been promoted to Commodore and he stood ready to be transferred to his new post.

The two men shook hands, and without another word, Captain Smith turned and walked to the shuttle. Martin and Smith had spoken at length the day before, and this was how Jason had wanted it. No fanfare or speeches, he simply wanted to leave his magnificent ship as he remembered it, and Martin was not about to begrudge him.

The crewmembers present looked on. They gazed at Martin with a mixture of respect, awe and trepidation. All present knew his reputation. The man won victories to be sure, but his casualty count tended to be on the high side. The outgoing captain was well liked but tended to be a bit conservative in his command style; Martin, on the other hand, pulled no punches.

The new captain announced to his senior officers, "I want a staff meeting in one hour. The executive officer and senior weapons officer shall attend me now. Company is dismissed."

Commander Sarah Blaithe, Martin's new exec. shouted, "Attention! . . . Dismissed!"

The X.O. and Ryn both moved toward Martin as the milling crowd left the shuttle bay. They walked to the departure lounge and watched as Captain Smith's shuttle rose silently and shot out into the void. Martin stared at the planet below as he said, "I've heard good things about you Commander Blaithe, but I have a question."

"Yes sir?" she replied inquiringly.

"You are qualified for command, yet you passed it up. Why?"

"They offered me a frigate, but battleships are in my family. Three generations of Blaithes have commanded one. I felt that a tour as an exec. would be of greater benefit to my career, sir."

Martin still watched the planet below, "Fair enough. I demand the best from my crew, and I expect you to make sure I get it. We're both new to this vessel, so we'll have to coordinate with the experienced officers. I plan a rigorous schedule of drills before we get underway. You are to set these up and have a schedule for me by the staff meeting. You are dismissed."

Blaithe did not bat an eye as she said, "Yes sir." The slim commander turned and left.

Martin smiled at Ryn, "Oh, I like her."

Ryn grinned wistfully, "Any woman with battleships in her blood is definitely for me."

Martin chuckled, "Be careful Ryn, she outranks you."

"A temporary situation, I assure you."

Martin laughed outright at this, "Come on, let's take a look around."

The Indomitable was over 30 years old, but she had just been refitted before Martin took command. Ryn and he walked the huge corridors nodding to officers and enlisted men alike. Each being sized up the new captain in his, or her, or its, own way. Martin took it all in. His smile grew broader as his thoughts turned to taking this masterpiece into battle. He would make sure that ship and crew were ready.

As they walked, Ryn turned the conversation to their friends, "I understand that Jaspa has been transferred."

"Yes, she had a destroyer command in the 20th fleet, but she requested the transfer because, and I quote, 'There's no action out here'."

They both shared a chuckle as Martin continued, "She's got the P.I.V. Lance in this fleet now, where I believe she'll get all the action she wants."

Both men sobered at this statement. The 15th fleet was stationed in a hotly contested sector where the war could flare up at any moment.

Martin continued with the conversation, "Eddie is chief engineer on Eagle's Talon in the 19th fleet. I just heard from him a few days ago. I could tell, even through all the complaining, that he enjoys his job. He just received a Bronze Star for pulling their chestnuts out of the fire when his ship took a serious pounding."

Ryn nodded his huge head, "Yeah, I had heard about that. I sent him my congratulations by star gram sometime ago. I don't know if it caught up to him yet."

Martin shook his head, "Eddie is a lot of things, but he keeps up his correspondence. If you haven't heard from him, he didn't get it yet."

The two friends passed the time in companionable silence, both men absorbing the power around them. Battleships brought out the best in both of them. The Pologian practically drooled with anticipation as they inspected the master weapons room and ammunition magazines. Martin was already plotting in his head the best way to maneuver this monster against smaller, faster ships. The time moved quickly as they both occupied themselves with their own thoughts.

Finally the hour passed and both headed for the Captain's conference room. "Attention!" said Commander Blaithe as Martin walked in.

"As you were folks, and we can dispense with that from now on. I want my senior officers to feel just that . . . senior. In most cases, I'm only one or two steps in rank above everyone in this room, so let's keep it friendly."

This seemed to break the ice. Martin knew that military tradition was important, but this was one he could do without; besides it was a pain having to say "as you were" every time he entered a room.

The other officers sat and Ryn walked around to the opposite end of the conference table. Martin took a moment to study his officers. Commander Blaithe sat at his right with Lt. Commander Tila Rogger, the operations and 2nd officer, next to her. Continuing around the table would take an observer to Commander Arram Goldbloom, the vessel's squadron commander. Next came Ryn. Commander James Crane, the chief medical officer was next. To his right was Lt. Commander Manix Sarchul, the chief engineer. Lt. Commander Laura Peel, the sensor specialist and science officer was next with Lieutenant Lyah Noor, representing security, completing the group.

To Martin's practiced eye, it looked like a good bunch. He began the meeting, "I am not going to take up your time with any welcome speech. You all came highly recommended. Some of you served with my predecessor, some are new. We don't have time to spend on the normal pleasantries for an incoming commander. We need to be turned around and underway in a week's time. We will have a crew mixer at 1700 hours this evening. I expect all of you to attend. I run my ship in a democratic fashion in private, that is to say, I am always willing to listen to my officers, but outside of this room, my word is law. You may not agree with me, but I expect this group to show a united front at all times. You will be permitted to run your departments in any way that suits you as long as I get maximum performance. I am not into micro managing. Our job is to inflict as many casualties on the Prescottians as we can while keeping ours to a minimum, it's as simple as that. If we can all remain focused on our jobs, we certainly have the vessel to obtain that goal. I will be running an inspection of each of your departments before we get underway, so be ready for me. As I have said throughout my career, I don't expect perfection, but I do expect the next best thing. Are there any questions?"

Commander Goldbloom's hand shot up immediately. Martin took that as a good sign. He wanted his crew to serve him out of respect and, truth be known, a little fear, but he did not want them to think him unapproachable.

"Yes Commander."

"Sir, will we be getting the new Hades System I requested for my fighters before departure?"

Martin nodded, "Last I heard, it was all set, but I will ask the base commander again. You need to light a fire under these people sometimes. Excuse me."

He turned to his private comm line in the center of his workstation and toggled a switch.

"Yes sir" came the immediate response.

"Yeoman McGregor, send a message to the ordinance section of this command base and make sure the new Hades System is ready to incorporate into our fighters. And tell them I want it set up in the next 72 hours."

Commander Goldbloom smiled ever so slightly, "Thank you sir." The Commander could tell that Martin was a captain that did not suffer desk jockeys gladly.

"Is there anything else?"

There was not, and Martin dismissed the gathering.

"Good group" Ryn said as the last person filed out.

"I got that impression as well. Do me a favor, tell Commander Blaithe to meet us in my quarters about a half hour before the mixer. I want to review our orders."

It was not entirely necessary that Ryn be there for that particular meeting, but Martin had picked up on the fact that Ryn rather liked the fiery X.O.

Ryn smiled, knowing full well what his friend was up to, "I'll do it" he said, "Oh, and by the way, thanks."

Martin just smiled as Ryn left the conference room.

He took a moment to collect his thoughts. Martin was not one to be sentimental, but he wished Marcus could be here to share this moment. This was what they had dreamed about as kids. He also wished Jaspa could be with him. He knew full well that it was because of her he had been able to achieve command of this vessel. Had it not been for her support, he would probably still be languishing behind a desk. He decided then and there to send a message to her.

He pressed the control for communication with the bridge.

"Bridge, Lieutenant Capole here."

"Lieutenant, this is the captain, patch me through to communications please."

There was a brief pause, "O'hara, Communications."

"O'hara, I want to send a personal message, please."

"Very well sir, but I must tell you that personals are taking seven to ten days to arrive."

"There's not much to be done about that, I'll send it anyway."

"Yes, sir. One moment please."

Another brief pause, "You're on Captain."

O'hara's face disappeared from the comm. screen to be replaced by the Protectorate seal. Martin began: "From Captain Martin Gammage, C.O. P.I.V. Indomitable, to Lt. Commander Jaspa Shindessa, C.O. P.I.V. Lance.

My dear Jaspa, I was thinking about you and thought I'd send you a message before we got underway. As you know, they gave me the Indomitable and I just took command today. I know you have your hands full with your ship as well. I just wanted to tell you good luck and good hunting." He paused a moment, "and to tell you I love you. Message ends."

He leaned back in his chair to await confirmation. "Message away sir" O'hara informed him.

"Very well" Martin said as he clicked off the screen. He felt better already for sending it.

*   *   *

- 116 -

"Our mission is a simple one," began Commander Blaithe. It was precisely 1630 and Ryn, Martin and the X.O. were gathered in Martin's quarters.

"We are to seek out and destroy the Prescottian dreadnought operating in sector 116G. In addition, we are to eliminate any other Prescottian vessels we encounter."

Ryn favored Commander Blaithe with a wry grin, "Sure, simple. No problem."

She tried to ignore him, but a smile played across her face nonetheless. "Our Task Force shall consist of this vessel and four destroyers."

Martin thought back to the last time destroyers were sent out without heavy ships. It seemed as if Admiral Morta had learned his lesson. Martin felt the anger over the loss of Marcus start to rise, but he forced it back under control.

"The Task Force will be commanded by you since a commodore is not available."

Now this was a surprise to Martin. It would be a quick way to move up in rank, if he was successful.

Commander Blaithe continued, "You will be meeting with the C.O.s of the other four vessels in two days. We will be traveling with the P.I.V.s Dark Hunter, Lion Heart, Lance, and San Diego."

The Lance! Martin kept his face impassive, but his mind swam. He would be seeing Jaspa in two days, but there would be no way to keep her safe on this mission. He remembered what happened the last time he went toe to toe with a dreadnought. True, he was in a much larger vessel, but the destroyers were fragile compared to those million ton monsters.

"We will be designated Task Force 7."

"Well that's lucky at least" said Martin.

Ryn looked confused, "Care to enlighten him Commander?" said Martin.

"In Earth numerology, 7 is considered a lucky number, it is also a winning combination in the ancient Earth game called 'craps'."

Both male officers looked impressed. Ryn shot Martin a look that said, "Oh, I want this one!"

Martin gazed briefly at his chronometer, "Shall we?" He was referring to the impending crew mixer.

"May I?" inquired Ryn as he offered his huge arm to Commander Blaithe.

She didn't seem to react at all, but said, "I'd be delighted."

Martin walked behind them down the corridor. The crew looked baffled as they passed. Martin couldn't blame them, the two made an awkward pair. The big Pologian at seven and a half feet dwarfed the five feet, three inch Commander. "Oh well," Martin thought, "Love is where you find it!"

They were headed for the rec deck for the mixer. This gathering was an opportunity for old and new crew to get to know each other. Martin thought the tradition was an important one, and even though there was much to do before departure, he would not let this opportunity slip by.

The mixer was already in full swing as the trio strode into the rec. hall. The huge room could accommodate roughly a third of the 2500 being crew, and it looked close to capacity. Ryn immediately asked Commander Blaithe to dance. She accepted and they walked to the center of the chamber, leaving Martin to his own devices.

The young Captain looked over his crew. He felt slightly overwhelmed at the diversity in the room. He could easily make out over a dozen races with a quick scan of the area. What made the sight even more impressive was the fact that he was responsible for the well being of all of them. It was an awesome prospect, and he felt a mixture of pride and nervousness at the thought.

He caught the eye of his new Science Officer, Lt. Commander Laura Peel, at the refreshment table. He nodded to her, and she excused herself from the young Lieutenant she had been talking to.

"Good evening, sir," she said in a decidedly English accent.

"Good evening Ms. Peel. Are you enjoying the party?"

She looked rather put out as she said, "I never really liked these things, sir. For some reason they've always made me feel . . . well, odd."

Martin smiled at her, "If you can keep a secret, I can tell you that I feel the same way."

Laura grinned, "Then why did you order all of us to attend?"

Martin replied in all seriousness, "Because I think it's important that the crew see that their senior officers were once like them. I think that a good officer leads by example, instead of being some isolated icon."

As Peel thought this over Martin added, "In that spirit Ms. Peel, may I have the honor of the next dance?"

Laura did not hesitate to give her assent. He took her arm and led her to the dance floor. The two officers shared a moment of enjoyment as the other crew looked on. As Martin danced, he could not help but wish that it was Jaspa in his arms, but it was important, that his crew see him at ease before a major engagement.

The party continued under its own power for several more hours. Many crewmembers left to relieve their shipmates so that they too had the opportunity to attend. Martin mingled with the crew of all ranks and he thought that he made a good impression. He needed them as much as they needed him; only in this traditional symbiosis of captain and crew could they hope to survive the upcoming battle.

*   *   *

Two days later.
Captain's Briefing Room, P.I.V. Indomitable

Martin strode into his conference room, "Remain seated, please." His eyes caught Jaspa's for a moment before he took his seat. He turned to Commander Blaithe and favored her with a brief smile, "Good morning, Sarah."

"Good morning sir. I have the honor this morning of introducing your Task Force Commanders."

"Proceed." Again, he looked at Jaspa briefly, evoking a smile from her.

Commander Blaithe began, "To my left is Lt. Commander Falnoth K'nar, skipper of the San Diego."

Martin nodded to the young Talnite.

"Next is Lt. Commander Jaspa Shindessa of the Lance."

Martin couldn't stop the smile that broke over his face, "The Commander and I are . . . acquainted."

Jaspa couldn't resist the chance to goad him on a bit, "A pleasure to see you again, Captain," she stressed his new rank as she said it.

Blaithe next introduced Lt. Commander Cyndi Blackmoor of Lion Heart.

"Last, but not least," she continued, "We have Commander Charlotte Simmons, senior destroyer Captain and C.O. of Dark Hunter."

"A pleasure" Martin said as he acknowledged the senior commander. She nodded back pleasantly.

"If you would continue with the briefing, commander" Martin said.

"Yes sir. Our orders have changed slightly since you received your Fleet bulletins. Intelligence reports that our quarry has moved on to Sector 117B, it is still our job to seek out the dreadnought and destroy it. She is responsible for large Protectorate losses in this area, and Fleet wants her dispatched as soon as possible. I will send your formation assignments to you in 72 hours. Are there any questions?"

Commander Simmons took this opportunity to speak up, "Do we have any backup?"

Commander Blaithe nodded, "Task Force 19 will be within 18 hours at all times. The group consists of," she consulted her pad, "three cruisers, five destroyers, and five frigates, so our backs should be well looked after."

The destroyer captain nodded, "Thank you."

"Is there anything else?" No one offered, so Martin dismissed the group.

Jaspa waited for her fellow commanders to depart. When they were gone, she stood and said, "Those eagles look good on you." She was referring to his rank insignia.

He broke into a radiant grin, "It's good to see you." He stood and embraced her. "How have you been? It appears that command agrees with you too."

"Oh, I love it" she said. "I'm glad you kicked me upstairs."

His grin took on a wistful character, "The eagles are because of you. I truly wish I could have you here, but I can't. I do, however, have a surprise for you."

"Indeed" she said as she raised an eyebrow.

"Hold on one second." Martin went to the communications panel, "Lt. Commander Calplygian please report to the Captain's Conference Room."

Jaspa smiled as the page went out, "I didn't know Ryn was here!"

"He's been looking forward to seeing you."

Jaspa's smile grew broader, "It's been such a long time, how is he?"

"You'll be able to ask him yourself. By the way, I think he and Commander Blaithe are becoming close."

"Really? But she's so tiny."

Martin chuckled, "I know, they look a little funny walking the corridors together, but they really seem taken with one another."

The two of them looked into each other's eyes for a while; simply enjoying the sight of the other's face. Martin sincerely hoped that the war would end soon so that Jaspa could be with him permanently.

Ryn lumbered into the room, "Jaspa!" he boomed.

"Hello Ryn, I . . . oof!" He had scooped her into a crushing bear hug. Martin grinned as he looked on. Finally, Ryn released the bedraggled Jaspa.

"Playna, it's good to see you," he said referring to the ancient Pologian god of war.

Jaspa caught her breath, "It's fantastic to see you too, Ryn. You haven't changed."

"I wish I had more time, he rumbled, "but I have to get back. Can the three of us have dinner tonight?"

Martin nodded, "I'm free, what's your schedule look like Jaspa?"

"I can have my X.O. look after things and stay aboard tonight." A twinkle caught her eye, "That is… if it's all right with you, sir."

"Permission granted," Martin dead panned.

Ryn said, "Then it's all settled. Is 1900 okay?"

"Sure," returned Martin.

"I'll be going then. Until this evening . . . Oh Marty, is it all right if Sarah comes along?"

Martin knew this was coming, "Of course."

The huge man smiled, winked at Jaspa and returned to his duties.

"Come on," said Martin, "Let me give you the tour."

"There's really only one area of the ship I'm interested in right now," Jaspa said.

"Oh?" inquired Martin.

"Yes. I'd very much like to see the Captain's quarters."

Martin grinned, "That can be arranged."

The both smiled in anticipation as they left the room.

*   *   *

Five days later.

Martin gripped the arms of his command chair. The moment had finally arrived. He was about to embark on an important mission in a wonderful ship, it didn't get any better than this.

"You may clear all moorings Commander Blaithe."

"Aye sir, clear all moorings."

"Helmsman, maneuvering jets at station keeping."

"Station keeping, Aye" the helmsman said as he repeated the order.

"We are floating free," said the exec. as she checked her board.

"Very well. Helmsman, maneuvering jets ahead one quarter."

"Maneuvering jets one quarter, Aye."

The huge ship slipped majestically from the shackle that bound her to the repair station. Martin watched the view screen as scaffolding and lights coasted by. Space opened up before them.

The helmsman turned to Martin, "We have cleared the station and are free to navigate."

"Very well. Fusion engines ahead full. Set course for the rally point."

"Aye sir, fusion engines ahead full. ETA at rendezvous," the young man consulted his board, "four hours, twenty minutes."

Martin was feeling grand, "Lieutenant Jacobs," he said referring to the helmsman, "give us the 'grand tour'."

The young man smiled, "Aye sir." He entered the new course. "ETA now six hours, fifty four minutes."

The Indomitable visited several of Baltos' planets as she toured the system. A beautiful green-gold gas giant slid by as the helmsman just brushed Indomitable by its gravity well. It was clear he was enjoying himself.

After a spectacular view of the system, the Indomitable finally arrived at the rendezvous. The other four destroyers were already awaiting Indomitable's presence.

"All vessels signal readiness to depart" said the comm officer.

"Very well" responded Martin, "Send to all ships: Set course 17 mark 119. Dark Hunter shall take the point. Speed: 2700c."

The comm. officer repeated the orders and Task Force 7 got underway.

The days slipped by quickly for Martin as he settled into his command routine. The crew grew to respect him all the more with each passing day. Martin worked them hard and they responded well. On the fourth day, Task Force 7 happened upon a small Prescottian convoy. The Indomitable made quick work of the guard destroyers as Martin's Task Force obliterated the three cargo ships. The mission was off to a fine start. Vice Admiral Hiro Isagamma, deputy commander 15th Fleet, congratulated them for their engagement and ordered them to continue to hunt for the dreadnought.

Finally, after two weeks of cruising, Task Force 7 arrived at their patrol station. Two Prescottian cruisers greeted them.

"General quarters, condition red" said Martin. This would be their first real test.

"Weapons armed, defense fields energized" said Ryn.

"All ships, attack at will! Ryn, arm the nova cannon."

Ryn took great pleasure in carrying out this particular order. The nova cannon was a powerful weapon, but it took an extremely long time to recharge. In addition, as it drew power directly from the displacement drive, it made escape nearly impossible if it was used. The firing ship simply could not outrun anything after firing the cannon. These drawbacks were easily offset, however, by the destructive capability of the weapon. Martin was about to demonstrate this fact.

"As soon as you have a target, fire."

No sooner were the words out of his mouth before a bolt of angry energy flew through space to splatter against one of the cruiser's shields. The enemy vessel wobbled precariously as its stabilizers failed. One of its fusion engines exploded in a rainbow of colors. A hull breach was evident in its flank.

In a perfectly coordinated attack, the destroyers of Task Force 7 concentrated their firepower on the crippled vessel, taking it out of the fight for good.

Unfortunately, the remaining cruiser got off a devastating volley on the San Diego. The small ship shuddered under the beating she took. The little craft bravely held together as its crew frantically abandoned ship.

Ryn fired a series of FAL blasts into the remaining cruiser as the San Diego finally broke apart.

The cruiser's defense fields flared as Ryn's shots struck home.

"Sir, they're trying to use their displacement drive!" This came from Lt. Commander Peel, the science officer.

"Oh no you don't" Martin said through clenched teeth, "You're going to pay for the San Diego. Ryn, target their engines, antimatter missiles, full spread."

Ryn worked his controls like a piano virtuoso. Six streams of death shot from the Indomitable. The first three annihilated the defense fields around the cruiser's engines and the final three found bare hull. The enemy vessel's port side F.T.L. engine collapsed in a silent explosion as the support struts sheared off into space.

Ryn did not let up. He fired fusion assisted lasers with the precision of a surgeon, leaving nothing left of the enemy cruiser but debris of varying sizes.

"Well done everyone" said Martin. His ship had not even sustained a hit. "We'll pick up the San Diego survivors. Communications: send news of our victory to 15th Fleet. Tell them we lost the San Diego, but all other vessels are in perfect shape. I'll take two cruisers to one destroyer any day."

The crew settled down as the adrenaline, or alien equivalent, left their systems. The casualties aboard San Diego were light, only sixteen persons were unaccounted for. Martin made plans to continue the patrol. His ship and crew had performed perfectly. He could not wait to face his adversary again.

*   *   *

Three days later.

"Flight 3 reporting in sir. No contact."

Martin met Commander Blaithe's report with a despondent sigh. He had been sending out his fighters in the hope of picking up some trace of his quarry; so far with no success.

"Very well" he finally responded, "let me know when Goldbloom reports in and we'll call it a day." Commander Blaithe acknowledged the order and returned to her duties. This was the 23rd sortie with no results.

"Sir, I'm receiving a report from Flight 1," said the communications specialist.

"Put it on audio, crewman" Martin responded. It was probably a routine check-in from Commander Goldbloom.

"This is Flight 1 to Indomitable. I've picked up an ion trail from the engines of something very large. By the looks of things, it's an old trail, but very distinct. I'm logging the location and direction and heading for home."

Martin immediately snapped into command mode. "Acknowledge the message crewman. Helmsman: set a course to intercept our flight. Communications: when you've completed the acknowledgment, inform all other commands that we will begin pursuit immediately. Then send the following message to our command base in this sector: P.I.V. Indomitable has detected a trace of what we believe to be our intended target. As soon as we have recovered our scouts, we will begin pursuit. Telemetry from our scout fighter indicates that the dreadnought is traveling without escort. If this is the case, my vessel and my three escort destroyers should have her outgunned. Captain Martin Gammage commanding P.I.V. Indomitable and T. F. 7 out. Get all that crewman?"

"Yes sir. Message away. All other commands have acknowledged and await your orders."

"Helmsman, bring us to 147 mark 100. Best speed to recover our fighters."

The orders were acknowledged and Task Force 7 was on its way. Finally, Martin thought, we could do what we were sent here for. The upcoming battle did not concern Martin much. They had the opposition outgunned. In addition, Martin's destroyers were far more maneuverable than their prey. The smaller ships could distract the dreadnought, while the Indomitable did its work. The battle would not be a cakewalk, but Martin had every confidence in his ship and crew.

Commander Goldbloom and his wingman were picked up without incident nearly ninety minutes later. The commander immediately reported to the bridge.

"What have you got?" asked Martin as soon as Goldbloom set foot on the deck.

"We encountered the ion trail of a large contact. There is no way to be certain if it is the dreadnought, but whatever left it is big. It would be worth going after anyway. The trail is definitely of Prescottian signature, no doubt about that. We picked up only the one trail. We orbited the sight four times to be certain, but picked up no traces of any other vessels."

"Excellent work, Commander," said Martin, and he meant it. "You are dismissed. Please give your information cube to the helmsman." Martin smiled at his senior pilot. "You found him, now we'll go crush him."

Commander Goldbloom returned the grin, "I'll hold you to that, Sir."

He gave the cube with all the pertinent information to the helmsman before retiring. The young man at the helm fed the coordinates into the computer. An extrapolated course appeared on the view screen, like an arrow pointing to a buried treasure.

"Follow that course helmsman, flank speed."

"Flank speed, Aye."

The whole bridge was charged with excitement and anticipation as Indomitable shot forward, her three escorts in close proximity.

"Message from P.I.V. Lance sir" said the comm. specialist.

"Martin nodded, "On screen please."

Jaspa's beautiful face lit up the bridge. She began without preamble. "Our science specialist has made a positive

I.D. on the trace we are following. The trace matches the exhaust of the Prescottian Dreadnought Redeemer that badly mauled one of our supply convoys five weeks ago."

"Well done, Commander" replied Martin. He made a mental note to get the name of her science specialist so that he could write up a commendation. Identifying a specific vessel in such a manner was no easy task.

Jaspa gave Martin a smile just for him, although no one on Indomitable's bridge missed it. "Thank you sir, Lance out."

The screen faded to black as the transmission was cut. Martin's own science officer confirmed Lance's findings. At least Martin now knew what he was up against. Redeemer was a giant, but it was a ship that could be beaten.

Another three hours passed in regular routine. The trail was becoming stronger as the ships flew along it, but no sensor contact had yet been made.

The comm specialist broke the relative silence of the bridge, "Captain, we're receiving a response to our last message to base."

Martin thought this strange. Normally, they would just send an acknowledgment.

"Let's hear what they have to say."

The comm officer punched a few buttons and the message came over the bridge speakers.

"From Admiral Cyrus Morta, Commander 15th Fleet to Captain Martin Gammage, P.I.V. Indomitable. You are hereby ordered to suspend your pursuit of your target. You are to return to base at once for reassignment. Admiral Morta out.

This was insane! After all this hunting and their excellent battle record so far, command wanted them to turn back? Martin thought about this for a while in stunned silence. He came to a decision that could very well end his career, but he felt it was the right thing to do. He was about to disobey a direct order from an Admiral.

"Stay your course helmsman."

Those four words were perhaps even more shocking than the first message.

Commander Blaithe immediately spoke up, "But sir, the message said to return to base."

"That's what you think it said Commander, I think it was garbled in transmission. Comm: request confirmation of previous message. That should take another three hours or so." Martin decided to test his crew. "Could you make anything of that message, Commander?"

Blaithe thought for what appeared to be a long time. She would be sticking her neck out too, but she had learned to trust Martin. He won victories. "Couldn't make heads or tails of it sir," she finally responded.

"Anyone else?" asked Martin.

"Couldn't hear a damn thing with all that static" said Ryn, but Martin knew he could count on him.

"Message? What message?" said the comm. officer as he absently fiddled with his controls.

Martin smiled, his crew would back him. He just hoped he wasn't making a catastrophic mistake.

"The transmission could have been a trick" offered Blaithe, "I think it's wise that we get confirmation." Never mind that all the command ciphers and codes were correct.

Martin smiled. Now all they had to do was find the enemy ship and destroy it. No problem. Martin was really at a loss to explain Admiral Morta's order, but this was not the first time that had happened.

"Stay your course," Martin repeated to the helmsman, "We'll ride this out until we find her, or our message is confirmed."

A reassuring chorus of "Aye sirs" echoed around the bridge.

No sooner had Martin made his pronouncement than the science officer turned her head, "Sir, I have a positive contact. Two vessels bearing 164 mark 17. One small," she checked her controls, "one very large. It's the Redeemer, sir, no question about it."

Martin sat ramrod straight in his command chair, "Comm send to all ships: This is Captain Gammage. We will alter course to intercept this contact immediately. This is what we came all this way for folks, let's go get 'em."

The appearance of a second ship altered Martin's plan slightly, but not significantly. The smaller vessel was at best a cargo ship, at worst a destroyer. His Task Force should be able to take them.

Martin felt the charge of battle surge through him. He thought back to one of his personal heroes, General George Patton of 20th Century America. He thought about what one German officer had said about him, perhaps anachronistically, but accurate nonetheless. It was at the end of World War II when the American army was smashing through Germany. The young officer was burning papers when he said, "Patton will be destroyed too; the absence of war will kill him." Martin felt a thrill of fear when he remembered the remark. He hoped that he was not becoming that type of officer. His past experiences had honed him to a razor's edge, sharpened and shaped him; made him an instrument of war. But deep in the recesses of his mind, he hoped that when this war ended, his usefulness would continue.

His reverie was broken by a report from the helm, "Sir, we have fifteen minutes to intercept. The smaller vessel appears to be moving off."

"Confirmed," said the science officer. "There is a great deal of communications traffic between the Redeemer and the small vessel which I have now identified as a Class II courier."

This was an interesting bit of news. That type of vessel was used for the transportation of top brass. Had the Indomitable caught a Prescottian Admiral with his pants down? Only one way to find out.

Martin swiveled around in his chair. "The plan remains the same: We will engage and destroy the Redeemer. Once that is accomplished, we will return to capture the courier if we are able."

The minutes wound down. The two large vessels sized each other up as they drew closer. Weapons ports were heated, missiles armed, defense fields raised. Anticipation crackled through the air. For once, Martin had the superior force, and he was going to use it to score a victory, orders or no orders.

"Two minutes to intercept," said the helmsman with a quaver in his voice. He felt the responsibility fall about his shoulders. Dreadnoughts had massive firepower but they handled like bricks. His ship handling could be the difference between victory and defeat.

Commander Peel readied herself at the science station. Her quick identification of the enemy's strengths and weaknesses could give the Indomitable the upper hand.

Commander Blaithe sat quietly at her post beside her captain. She had chosen to support him and, that decision made, she waited with outward calm as the ships prepared to unleash destruction.

Commander Sarchul watched his engines thrum with barely contained power. His patching of a conduit, or repair to a critical system could save everyone aboard.

Dr. Crane readied the sick bay. The waiting was perhaps the most difficult task for the doctor. He knew that he would soon have "customers" and he dreaded the fact, but until they arrived, there was precious little he could to.

Martin sat at the eye of the storm. His ship and crew relied on him to make the right decisions at the perfect moment. Any mistake could spell disaster. He was already out on a limb by disregarding his orders. A failure here could end his career or even his life and the lives of his fellow officers and crew.

The only being on the entire ship not feeling trepidation was Ryn. He lived for this. His meaty hands clenched and unclenched over his weapons board; his children. All was in readiness and he waited in ill-concealed impatience for the order to fire.

Martin waited one more minute before crying "All vessels: Break formation and attack at will!"

This time, however, the Prescottian was faster. As soon as T.F. 7 went to fusion power, a bolt of violet destruction shot from the enemy ship. The purple of Jaspa's eyes connected with her vessel. Martin could only watch helplessly as the Lance spun out of control and off the main viewer.

A sensor specialist called out, "Direct hit on P.I.V. Lance. Defense fields out, stabilizer out, main power out. I'm detecting a hull breach. Estimating 22 seconds until hull collapse."

Martin breathed a silent goodbye to Jaspa and then tried to put the incident out of his mind, he had to, the safety of his ship and crew was at stake. He could barely force the words past his lips as he ordered the two destroyers to harry the monster's flanks while he brought the Indomitable into firing range. The smaller ships herded the larger vessel into position, their weapons doing little damage, but the tactic worked.

Ryn watched as the huge ship crept onto his screen. Suddenly he opened up with everything he could. Missiles and beams of energy impacted on the enemy's defense fields. She shuddered away under the onslaught, but gave as good as she got. The Indomitable groaned under repeated hits. The bridge lights flickered as the two ships passed each other like knights on a jousting field. They both started the turn that would send them after each other once again.

"Damage report," yelled Martin. As he said this, an explosion ripped across the screen. A yellow blossom erupted and as quickly died as oxygen was consumed.

"The Lance just exploded, sir" said the sensor specialist.

Meanwhile, a report came up from engineering. The Indomitable had weathered the first attack well and was still fully operational, although her defense fields were down to 70%.

The Redeemer reached out and swatted another destroyer. This time the Lion Heart swerved precariously on her prearranged course.

The Indomitable came around and unleashed another volley. Martin watched as all of Ryn's shots connected. The Redeemer's defense fields had begun to flicker in some places.

"Target those weak areas and fire!" Martin screamed over the din.

Ryn reset his controls. An FAL found a chink in the armor of the beast and tore a gash in her side. The Redeemer swung away, trying to keep her wounded flank away from her tormentor.

The angered vessel let loose with a volley of her own. Some of the fearsome energies found their way through the Indomitable's defenses. An overhead conduit on the bridge exploded in an arc of energy as the big ship righted herself. Smoke poured from the opening as the large ventilators kicked in.

"We got her that time!" Came a victory cry from the sensor station. I'm reading a hull breach and power fluctuations from her main power couplings."

A grim smile appeared on Martin's soot blackened face, "The question is: How badly are we hurt?"

The answer was quick in coming, "Hull integrity stable. Defense fields are at 42%. We have power leakage in energizer 3. Engineering is buttoning it down. Main power is still on line."

It was time. Martin told Ryn to ready the nova cannon. All hopes of pursuing the courier faded as Martin heard the damage report. His ship was taking a pounding, and he wanted it to end. The nova cannon would temporarily negate the displacement drive, but he was going to end this here and now.

"Nova cannon ready," crowed Ryn as he brought the appropriate system on line.

"I'm going to bring you into point blank range Ryn, so be ready," Martin called over his shoulder.

The two ships came at each other. Each a bit more uncertainly this time. Martin's final destroyer peppered the big ship with irritating, but negligible shots. The Redeemer unleashed its last attempt at victory at the Indomitable. Martin's ship bucked and heaved as hammer blows fell on the hull. Defense fields flickered and died. Stabilizers failed, conduits erupted, but still the Indomitable flew on without returning fire.

The barrel of the nova cannon glowed with pent up energy. Ryn waited as long as he could, and with the press of one button, let that energy loose.

A bolt of green-gold fire shot from the belly of Indomitable. The ball of energy punched through what was left of Redeemer's defenses and expended most of its wrath on her hull. As the Indomitable slipped by, a series of explosions tore through the fatally wounded monster. She got off a last shot at her conqueror. The Indomitable swayed but got her feet under her as the death throes shook the Redeemer. A few escape pods sailed away with much larger pieces of debris. Finally, a rainbow of light erupted from the aft quarter of the ship as her displacement drive went up. The Redeemer would fight no more. This thought saddened Martin just the smallest bit as Redeemer exploded in a cacophony of light and flame.

"Boom!" Bellowed Ryn from the tactical console. He followed this up by giving an authentic Pologian war cry.

Martin grinned briefly before his thoughts brought him crashing back to reality. "Commence a search pattern for survivors from our lost ships" he ordered. Now that the battle was over, Martin's grief over Jaspa took full root in his mind. "Get me a complete damage report as well," he ordered of his exec.

Officers scurried to do his bidding. The communications officer turned to Martin and said, "Communication from our command base: you are reminded that you are not to engage the Redeemer."

Martin's reply was immediate and sarcastic, "Ask them if they want me to rebuild it."

This seemed to break the tension on the bridge. Martin received his damage report. All in all, the Indomitable came through with only moderate damage. After a half hour of cruising however, Martin got the report he was waiting for. A young ensign reported from shuttle bay 2 that the commander of the Lance had been picked up with only minor injuries. Martin relaxed for a moment and breathed a silent thanks to the Universe before going down to meet Jaspa.

*   *   *

13 days later.
Office of Admiral Cyrus Morta

Martin sat in the antechamber outside of Admiral Morta's office. A rare sensation washed over him; for one of the very few times in his life, Martin did not know what to expect. True, he had violated orders, but he had also won a major victory. He remembered what his father once told him: You can't argue with success.

The trip back to base had been virtually uneventful. The Indomitable had encountered a lone Prescottian scout on the return journey and had eliminated it easily. Martin and Jaspa had enjoyed a joyous 10 days together. Martin's ship and crew had performed admirably. The only thing that worried him was the silence of his command base concerning his victory. He had duly sent several communiqués telling of the battle but had received no reply except to return to base. So here he waited, unsure of what was to come next. He had never personally met Admiral Morta and so was doubly in the dark.

"Captain, the Admiral will see you now," said the pretty aide behind her receiving desk.

"Thank you," Martin returned as he stood.

Admiral Morta's office was austere. The only decorations were battle paintings along one wall. The Admiral himself did not rise but gestured to the chair across from him. In utter silence, Martin lowered himself into the offered seat.

The Admiral began, "Congratulations on your victory." His tone was so icy that the temperature in the room seemed to drop twenty degrees.

"Thank you sir," Martin replied hesitantly.

"I believe you will find that particular victory a costly one . . . very costly." The Admiral said.

"I don't follow you sir." Martin replied.

"Ah, then let me enlighten you. You proceeded against an enemy vessel despite my direct order, and don't give me any nonsense that it was 'garbled in transmission'." A dark shadow passed over the Admiral's face. He pounded the desk as he said, "No one defies me! No one!"

Martin was taken aback by this tantrum of a career officer.

The Admiral got himself under control and continued, "I've been ordered by the Council of Admirals to promote you, so here . . ." He tossed a pair of metal studs on the desk. Martin stared at, not the star of a Commodore, but the wreathed eagles of a Fleet Captain. Admiral Morta smiled as the truth sunk in. Fleet Captain was an honorary rank bestowed on Captains nearing retirement. They held the same rank as a Commodore but with no corresponding seat on the Council of Admirals. In addition, due to the very nature of the rank, promotion out of it was nearly impossible. Martin stared at the end of his career represented by the two small metal pins.

But the Admiral was not finished yet. "I'm reassigning you to the 1st Fleet where you'll be out of my way for good. You should have been a good lad and died a hero's death when I set you up the first time, but no, you had to win that little fight. You then compound the problem by winning a major victory, again. Well no more. If I can't kill you, I can kill your career. Good day!"

Martin was absolutely shocked. A myriad of images tumbled through his troubled mind. The smell of burnt insulation, Marcus' broken body on the deck, the screams of the dying. All to further the ambition of this madman. Something snapped in Martin then. He had been used in the worst possible manner. His dream of a career in the Protectorate Fleet faded. His accomplishments vanished like a whiff of smoke. His anger and revulsion came to the fore.

"You bastard," Martin whispered.

"Excuse me?" Came the smug reply from Morta.

"You bastard!" yelled Martin.

"I suggest that you watch your tone Captain. I can still add a court martial to your list."

Martin's eyes blazed as he framed his reply, "You can, but you won't. You've got what you wanted." Martin shook his head as if trying to ward off a blow. "At the cost of hundreds of lives . . . What a contemptible creature you are.

It will be, from this day forward, my mission to make you pay for what you've done."

Morta stared back with an unrepentant gaze in his four eyes. "You may indeed make me pay, Captain . . . but not today. Now get out of here before I have you removed."

Martin's hatred blazed in his eyes as he rose from his chair. This bastard would pay. Nothing else mattered.

Martin promised himself, as he walked back to the Indomitable for the last time, that a day of reckoning would come. He didn't want Morta's death, that would be too easy. If it was the last thing he ever did, Martin would see Morta humiliated, broken in disgrace. Marcus, and all those that died with him would be avenged. This thought was Martin's driving force as he entered the airlock of what used to be his ship.

Chapter VI: Fleet Captain
April 14, 2525
Sol System

Martin gazed out the viewport in the observation lounge of the P.I.V. Hermes. His eyes were just able to discern a fuzzy cloud of matter that drew closer with every passing second. Martin grinned briefly out at the Oort cloud that surrounded the system of his birth.

The gentle whisper of the displacement drive gave way to the more palpable thrum of the fusion engines. It would be a six hour trip into Earth orbit.

The trip back to Earth had been a two month affair even by ultra fast courier. The service aboard had been exemplary, but strained. Everyone wanted to know how such a young man found his way into a fleet captaincy, but were far too polite to pry. The awkward silences at the Captain's table, the double takes in the corridors, the shy glances of junior officers all served to compound Martin's feelings of anger and loathing toward Admiral Morta.

The electric blue disk of Neptune slid by as Martin looked out upon its wonder. Perhaps the only good thing to come out of this mess was that Martin would be coming home. Many humans were born out of the Sol System in Martin's century and millions would never even see the planet that gave rise to their race. No matter where Martin's travels had taken him, he always felt an attachment to this place. He was fighting for a little rocky ball orbiting an average yellow sun.

The king of the planets loomed through the void as the Hermes continued sunward. A rainbow of reds, pinks, yellows, and browns swirled in the turbulent atmosphere. One of Martin and Marcus' first leaves from service had been spent on a cruise of the Jovian System. Jupiter still did not fail to impress Martin as the giant drew near and finally fell astern.

The Hermes put on a show as the asteroid belt appeared. The captain had ordered some target practice and the gunners picked out some of the smaller rocks to fire on. Fusion Assisted Lasers split the night to explode the chunks of nickel and iron.

Still the Hermes flew on. The orbit of Mars came and went until finally Earth and her companion appeared. They would be coming in near the night side of the Moon. Martin could just pick out the lights of the twin cities Armstrong and Aldrin as the Hermes requested orbital parking instructions. The vessel glided around the Moon's limb to reveal the Earth. The shining blue sphere that was Martin's home grew in size until it filled half the view port. City lights winked back at Martin as the Hermes settled into her programmed parking orbit. The weather control net was breaking up a hurricane over the Atlantic as Martin's sight seeing was interrupted by a page. "Fleet Captain Gammage please report to the docking lounge," came the neutral voice. The sound of the title still rankled Martin but nevertheless, he rose and walked to the shuttle deck.

A young pilot and the Commander of the Hermes were there to meet him. Lt. Commander Loita Rote shook Martin's hand, "It was a pleasure to have you aboard, sir. I wish you the best of luck on Earth."

Martin returned the warm Lingallian's handshake. "Thank you for having me, Commander. My compliments to your crew and yourself." With that, Martin entered the small shuttle that would take him on the last leg of his journey.

The young pilot introduced herself as Ensign Cali Parker. She deftly operated the controls and soon the small shuttle cleared the mother ship and was on her way. A crimson glow surrounded the small craft as it entered Earth's atmosphere. Martin broke the silence by asking, "So Ensign, how long have you served on the Hermes?"

"This is my first cruise sir. However, I just learned of my transfer to the 4th Fleet. I'll be serving as a junior tactical officer," her face beamed with pride.

Martin smiled at her youthful exuberance. "My very good friend was tactical officer aboard my last command. I wish you the best of luck; tactical positions can be very rewarding. You should be proud."

The ensign puffed up even more at the praise of a Senior Captain. The shuttle was zipping toward the North American Continent. Details were becoming visible. The pilot was flying them over the Mojave Desert on their way to the capital of the entire Protectorate.

Suddenly, there it was, the city that controlled everything. Phoenix had changed a great deal over its six hundred year history. The desert had given way to lush parkland surrounding the capital. Several hundred square miles had been preserved in its natural state, however, to be used by the native wildlife. Martin had never been to Phoenix, he had gone to school at the Protectorate War College in St. Louis, and for some reason, he had never gotten around to seeing the sights of the capital. Even though Phoenix was the heart of the Protectorate, there were many more interesting cities on Earth. As a history major at the college, Martin had visited many of Earth's more ancient metropolises.

The shuttle swung low over the outlying housing areas and made its way to the spaceport. The ensign manipulated her controls and brought the shuttle down without even the slightest bump to betray its arrival. Martin had planned to head straight for the senior officer's quarters and secure lodgings before leaving for the Protectorate Building, but these plans evaporated as soon as Martin saw who was waiting for him.

A Lt. Commander bearing the loops of an Admiral's aide stood at the entrance to the shuttle, "Fleet Captain Gammage?" the man inquired while holding out a hand, "I am Lt. Commander Joseph McKraken, one of Admiral Higgins' assistants. The Admiral sent me out to meet you. He would like to see you immediately."

Martin shook the proffered hand and replied despite his surprise, "Very well, let's retrieve my belongings and be on our way."

"That won't be necessary, sir. My orders are to have your luggage sent to Admiral Higgins' home where you will be his guest. We are to proceed to his office immediately."

This was certainly a pleasant surprise. Martin truly loved the old Admiral and was happy to see that he had taken such an interest in him. The Lt. Commander led Martin to a ground car and they were soon on their way. Martin killed some time by inquiring after the health of the Admiral and asking how Earth was holding up during wartime. Martin took in the sights of the city as McKraken drove on. They passed the Admiral's Hall where the Council had its meetings. The Kinkaid Building loomed majestically over the city as the car drove past. Finally, they arrived at 1st Fleet Headquarters.

The Lt. Commander dropped Martin off at the front edifice and asked him to wait while he returned the ground vehicle.

Martin was impressed by the vastness and grandeur of the headquarters building. No expense had been spared in the construction of the grand old complex. Only the ancient Pentagon in Washington D.C. had more office space than the Protectorate Building.

Martin was soon reunited with McKraken who led him to the offices of Admiral Donald Higgins, Commander 1st Protectorate Fleet. It had been a long time since Martin had sat in Admiral Higgins' history classes. The Admiral enjoyed teaching so much that he insisted he be allowed to continue even after assuming the rank of Commodore. In all, the admiral had over seventy years experience in molding the minds of young Protectorate officers. Martin had spent a great deal of time doing research for Higgins' and had learned invaluable lessons. Martin felt that a great deal of what he had accomplished in his career was due to this one man. Now, Martin had to ask his help one more time. If for no other reason that to see that Marcus had not died in vain. If it ruined him, Martin would see that glory hungry son-of-a-bitch Morta broken.

Martin was ushered into the admiral's outer office. McKraken said, "If you'll wait here sir, I'll inform the admiral of your presence."

Martin sat and admired the portraits of Caesar, Napoleon, Patton and Kinkaid that adorned the walls. He remembered Admiral Higgins' speeches on each of them and recalled daydreaming of the day that he would have a command of his own.

A booming voice interrupted his thoughts, "Come in, come in my boy." The admiral was a moderately tall man with snow white hair and a neatly trimmed beard. His face had craggy features and his nose remained smashed from a training accident of no one knew how many years ago.

Martin entered the office, "You're looking well, Admiral."

"Everyone always tells me that. I'm 104 years old Marty, I look like shit."

Martin couldn't help but laugh at the profanity. The admiral had always spoken that way for as long as he could remember.

Admiral Higgins sized Marty up for a moment, "Fleet Captain, eh? Morta's got you in a real fix, but I think we can do something about that."

Martin's hope soared, "What can we do sir?"

Higgins waved his arms. "All in good time. All in good time, my boy." You know, I saw your father a few days ago. A fine officer, until that accursed disease laid into him."

Martin smiled a little wistfully, "He was one of the best, sir. I plan on seeing him the first chance I get."

"Good, good. I was sorry to hear about Marcus. Next to you, he was one of my best students. Never could convince him to major in history, though." The Admiral's old eyes narrowed to slits, "We're going to make that bastard Morta pay for what he's done. When I read your communiqués I almost went through the roof."

Higgins stood and began to pace his office, "Morta has always been ambitious as hell, but to sacrifice fine ships and officers to further his own agenda is inexcusable," he pounded his desk with a fervor that belied his age, "inexcusable!"

The old Admiral's features softened as he said, "I'm going to let you in on a secret. I've seen officers come and go. I must have lectured to half the fleet at one time or another, and you're the finest officer I have ever seen. In my opinion, you could very well be the next Fleet Admiral, and that's what Morta is afraid of."

Higgins sat down again, "I'm an old man Marty, but if it's the last thing I do, I'm going to see things set to rights. There is a reception tonight. I want you to go back to my house and prepare for it. Dress uniforms. I have a big announcement to make that should clear this mess up. Now go on." Higgins shooed Marty toward the door to his office. "My home is your home. McKraken will take you."

Marty left to find McKraken in something of a daze. He could not imagine how a simple announcement could eliminate his problems. All he could do was wait and see what the old man had up his sleeve.

*   *   *

5 hours later
Protectorate Hall Banquet Room

Martin entered the banquet hall resplendent in his dress uniform. Banks of ribbons decorated the facings of his tunic while his two Protectorate Medals of Honor hung around his neck. He gazed up at the portraits of former Fleet Admirals that lined the room. He wondered, for what seemed the millionth time, what Admiral Higgins was thinking and what his ultimate destiny would be.

Martin remembered going over his appearance at the admiral's house before leaving for the banquet. The only thing marring an otherwise perfect picture were the two wreathed eagles on his rank tabs where single stars should have been. The eagles mocked him from their perch on his shoulders, bringing back memories of Marcus and Martin's ruined ship.

His train of thought was broken as Admiral Higgins, complete with entourage, entered the hall. The stately gentleman looked even more dignified in his dress uniform. Martin always wondered why the admiral never tried for the top spot in the Protectorate. Whenever Martin asked, Higgins would simply reply, "Don't want the job." Martin guessed that this simple answer was the true one.

A young aide found Martin in the crowd and invited him to the admiral's table. Martin strode through the throng of guests and was greeted by the same response he had aboard the Hermes. Polite and not so polite stares followed the young fleet captain wherever he went; everyone wondering how such a young man had fallen afoul of the powers that be, and yet seem to be an honored guest of the commander of the 1st Fleet. It was an interesting puzzle and a topic of conversation at many tables.

Martin sat and ate in near silence, only pausing to exchange a random pleasantry with a neighbor. Let these idiots think what they want, Martin mused. He still could not figure out what Higgins had planned, but it looked like he was about to find out.

The old admiral was signaling for everyone's attention. When he had it, he rose from his seat and began speaking, "I have gathered you all here today for two reasons. I'm not sure which will shock you more."

Uneasy glances passed through the crowd. Martin just sat back and prepared to enjoy the ride. He had heard many similar pronouncements as a cadet.

"The first reason is to conduct a promotion ceremony."

Oh no! Thought Martin. What is he thinking of? Suddenly, like a light being cast into the darkness, Martin knew exactly what was about to happen.

The admiral continued, "By the powers vested in me by using Admiral's Prerogative, I hereby promote Martin Gammage to the rank of Commodore with all the incumbent duties and privileges intact."

A collective gasp went up from the crowd as an aide came down to change out Martin's rank insignia. Admiral's Prerogative was almost never used as it had the effect of destroying, at least politically, the admiral who employed it. The Council did not look favorably upon admirals who usurped power in such a fashion. Martin knew, however, that it did not make much of a difference in this case as he had guessed the second part of the admiral's announcement.

As the crowd settled down, Admiral Higgins dropped his second bomb, "I would also like to take this opportunity to thank my staff and all those who have worked for me in years past. It has been a true honor to have served with such fine people for so long. All good things, however, must come to an end, and after eighty six years of service, my time is at a close. I hereby announce my retirement, effective immediately."

Pandemonium broke throughout the hall. This created a massive power vacuum in Protectorate politics. The command of 1st Fleet was a prize that many would be striving for in the coming weeks. It appeared that Vice Admiral Capstair would take over temporarily.

Martin sat dazed in his chair. His stars heavy on his shoulders. He still could not believe the events that had transpired here today. An aide came up to him and said, "The admiral would like to see you in his home when things calm down here. He says that 'he's not through with the young fella yet'. It is my understanding that a mission goes with your new rank. By the way, congratulations, Commodore." Martin could only nod.

*　　*　　*

Martin sat in Admiral Higgins' opulent living room when the admiral himself arrived, "Well Commodore, what do you think?"

Martin didn't know if he meant this evening, his surroundings, or both. He responded with a neutral, "I'm very impressed sir."

"Those flint locks over there are from the American Civil War as are the sabres in the far corner."

Martin nodded. "I also recognize that old Navy Colt." Martin's face turned somber. "I'll never forget what you did for me this evening admiral."

Higgins turned toward Martin, "Why, whatever do you mean?"

"You sacrificed your career for me."

The laugh from the old man startled Martin, "I did no such thing, Marty. It was time for me to retire. The timing of this entire incident was merely . . . fortunate. My, what an ego you've developed. I wouldn't wreck my entire life just for you, no matter how fond I am of you."

Martin blushed at the mostly good natured ribbing he was taking at the hand of his old teacher. Martin realized that the admiral was absolutely right, "Nonetheless," Martin recovered, "I owe you a great debt. I don't know how I can repay you."

The admiral smiled, "Fortunately, I do. You can fulfill what I am convinced is your destiny. You can defeat Morta once and for all and become Fleet Admiral. Do it for me, your father, the Protectorate, and do it for Marcus' memory. You can honor him by adding some meaning to his death. As a means to that end, I have one more mission to assign to you before I finish my last tour."

Martin listened in rapt attention as the admiral outlined this extremely difficult mission. Fortunately, Martin would have an old friend to assist him. The admiral continued, "I've detached Ryn to help you out on this one. You're going to need him. I'm giving you my flagship, P.I.V. Dauntless. You will proceed at maximum speed to sector 154J where you will take on a compliment of marines and Commander Calplygian. Your mission is to subdue a Prescottian capital ship intact. You will then board said vessel and capture the remaining crew. In this way the Protectorate will have an unprecedented and necessary look at Prescottian technology. If you can pull this off, you'll be able to write your own ticket Marty."

Martin nodded, "If it can be done, Ryn and I will do it."

The admiral clapped a hand on Martin's shoulder. "I know I can count on you my boy. I'll keep your seat on the Council warm for you. I'm going to turn in. You're on leave for five days while the Dauntless is prepared. I look forward to talking with you some more before you leave. We'll invite your father over for dinner."

"That sounds just fine admiral. Have a pleasant rest."

The admiral winked at Martin, turned around, and left Martin to think about his new mission; both short and long term. Martin's thoughts turned away from Earth and toward deep space where Jaspa still had a command. He couldn't wait to tell her of this new turn in his life. He also thought about going into battle with Ryn one more time. He smiled and shook his head at the audacity of his old teacher and went to bed.

Chapter VII: Commodore
June 20, 2525
Sector 154 J, P.I.V. Dauntless

The Dauntless slipped through the interstellar void. Martin's command had picked up Ryn, his tactical staff, and three companies of marines at Nalkar four days ago. The ship was now on patrol, searching for a prime target to disable and capture. Martin paced the bridge uneasily, for although the mission was his, the ship was not. The Dauntless was commanded by Captain Polnar Jens. The Pologian was an able leader and every inch as big as Ryn. Martin did not like being out of direct charge of the vessel and this was disquieting to him. That being the case, he tried to stay out of Jens' way.

The Dauntless was a light carrier. She had five squadrons of fighters in her flight decks. Three fighter groups, one heavy fighter group, and one missile group. The heavy fighters were just that, craft that were more heavily armed and shielded than their counterparts. This tended to make them a bit slower and less maneuverable than their contemporaries. The missile squadron was designed to carry several antimatter devices with which to disable a capital ship. All in all, the Dauntless packed quite a punch. In addition to her complement of fighters, she had sixteen FAL emplacements, six missile launchers (4 forward, 2 aft), and a light nova cannon. Ryn had mentioned that the Dauntless was a ship to be reckoned with, and if Ryn said it, it must be true.

After another ten days of cruising, Martin picked out a likely patrol area. They were in the space lanes of an oft used Prescottian military artery. Martin ordered Captain Jens to send out several patrol sorties. All Martin had to do now was wait. He played numerous games of chess against the Captain, Ryn and the computer. He also read up on ancient battles. He still loved reading history even though he was now a flag officer. Martin felt this helped to keep his skills sharp. Why repeat mistakes that had already been made?

The patrol stretched out another week with no sightings. Martin ordered a shift in position. The Dauntless shot off into the void heading for the Deruda Cluster. There were several stars there that supposedly supported planetary systems. Martin was playing a hunch based on probe information that was several years old.

To keep everyone alert, Martin ordered several drills. Ryn started treating them as games and often wagered on the outcome or offered prizes to the junior officers for highest efficiency ratings or best marksmanship. Even Martin took a turn at the weapons console to keep his hand in. According to the computer, the Dauntless had been able to capture five capital ships; she had also been destroyed twice, or her boarding party had been listed as "annihilated." The crew laughed this up and simply said, "What does a computer know?" Martin also did not take the results too seriously, but he kept the drill schedule at a fever pitch to hone the ship and crew to a razor edge.

Finally, a patrol fighter listed an anomalous reading orbiting the sixth planet of the Koner System. Martin immediately shook off what threatened to evolve into major boredom and sprang into action. He ordered a stealth approach course, trying to take advantage of the Prescottian's inferior sensors. It was Martin's plan to coast through the Oort cloud surrounding the system, all the while keeping the planet between the Dauntless and the unidentified vessel. This would require an extremely long and arduous corkscrew approach, but if the Dauntless could achieve surprise, it would be well worth it. Besides, Martin did not yet know what they were dealing with.

As the fusion engines kicked in, the navigator announced that it would take seventeen hours to complete the approach. Martin was undaunted by the time estimate although he did hear a groan from Ryn's post. The big Pologian always wanted to get into a scrap as soon as possible. Martin imagined back to the days of submarine warfare. This would be like chasing down a target at night and then crawling beneath the surface to avoid detection once the sun came up.

Martin announced to the crew, "Captain Jens, I want a briefing of all senior officers in sixteen hours. We will outline our attack plan at that time. Remember, this is not simply a search and destroy mission. It will be our job to disable the target and bring it home intact. This will be perhaps our most difficult assignment in our respective careers."

The Captain smiled, "Very good, sir. I'll order Major Harris in on the briefing as he will be leading the Marines in the assault phase. Have you given any thought as to who will be in overall command of the assault?"

Ryn cracked his knuckles in anticipation of Martin's response. Unfortunately for him, Martin was about to disappoint him. "Yes Captain, I have." Martin responded. "Commander Calplygian will assist Major Harris and I will lead the assault."

A slight gasp went up from the bridge staff. It was almost unheard of for a flag officer to lead such a dangerous mission. Martin felt a slight explanation was in order, "I led a mission against a Prescottian surface emplacement several years ago. I feel that my experience will be necessary."

Ryn flashed Martin a "Let's talk" look while Captain Jens merely said once more, "Very good, sir."

"What are you, nuts?" said Ryn in an exasperated tone. Martin smiled at the human slang. Ryn continued, "You're a Flag Officer now. You can't just lead a dangerous assault mission because you feel like it!"

"I'm not doing this on a whim," Martin responded. "I have more experience than Harris does on this kind of mission."

"I know all that," Ryn continued, "I was there, remember? If you don't want Harris leading this, then let me do it."

Martin thought for a few moments, "No, my mind is made up. I'm going."

Ryn threw his muscular arms up in frustration, "When you get a thought in your head, I know better than to argue. Just do me a favor."

"What's that," Martin smiled at the big man.

"Go in behind me, and try not to get killed."

"That's a deal." The two men shook hands.

The briefing room was full of senior officers as Martin prepared his strategy. He began addressing the complement present, "Our mission, as you well know, is to capture a Prescottian capital ship. We will have to do this with our fighters as they are far more accurate than ship's guns. The Dauntless will stay nearby in case things get out of hand. I don't want to sacrifice fighters unnecessarily. Once the vessel is disabled, we will dock and the assault phase will begin. Something we have to watch out for is whether or not Prescottian ships have a self destruct device. Our intelligence says no, but I'm not going to take any unnecessary risks. The assault team will dock via assault shuttle."

There was some murmuring around the table as Martin continued. "The fighters are going to have to screen for the missile ships whose targets will be weapons and engines only. The Dauntless will only be able to assist in a superficial fashion as I am giving orders not to fire unless our gunners have a perfect shot on those key systems. As our target appears to be a cruiser or similar craft, you will not have to concern yourselves with enemy fighters. Anti-aircraft guns will be your chief problem. I want this ship, gentlemen. Capturing it intact will be a tremendous boon for our intelligence sections and hopefully bring a successful conclusion to this war that much closer. Pilots are dismissed. Stand by your ships, and good luck."

Several men and women stood and filed out of the briefing room. When they were gone Martin continued. "Major Harris and Marine Company D will conduct the assault under my supervision. Until the vessel is secured, we will take no prisoners. The ship is the important thing here gentlemen. If possible, we will take captives when the vessel is under our control, but not before. This raid will be difficult enough without any added distractions. I want to get in, take the ship, and get out with a minimum of casualties. Dismissed."

The remaining complement stood to a man and departed. Martin and Ryn left for the armory to draw weapons and supplies. Martin ordered Captain Jens to close on the enemy vessel. Ideally, the fighters would engage in thirty minutes.

Martin and Ryn appeared on the bridge twenty minutes later in full battle regalia. Martin was the picture of competence and courage in his black battle carapace. Ryn was a hulking figure in his battle armor. They both only lacked a helmet to complete their costumes.

"Range to target?" Martin inquired of the man in the center seat.

"Seven minutes and closing" replied Captain Jens.

"Order the crews to their fighters and prepare to launch."

Lt. (j.g.) Daniels at communications announced, "All pilots to stations, launch in seven minutes."

"General Quarters" barked Captain Jens.

An ant's nest of activity ensued as the Dauntless prepared for battle. Fighter crews finished arming and fueling their ships. Blunt nosed antimatter missiles were attached to the fighters. FAL' s were charged.

Martin stepped down into the command well and took the microphone from Captain Jens' seat. "This is Commodore Gammage to all weapons emplacements. Your targets are weapons and engines only. You are to shoot only if you have a lock on target. The fighters are going to have to do the bulk of the damage today. That is all."

The moments ticked by. Ryn busied himself by preparing the Dauntless' defenses. Captain Jens sat confidently in his command chair. Finally, Martin gave the order they were waiting for, "Launch fighters!"

The massive bay doors opened to disgorge its cargo of ships. Seventy two fighters shot into the night, ready to engage the enemy.

Captain Jens ordered, "Squadron leaders, call out when ready."

The response was swift, "Eagle leader standing by. Falcon leader standing by. Viper leader standing by. Cobra leader standing by. Fox leader standing by. Bear leader standing by."

"Keep a channel open, Captain. I want to hear every phase of the battle." Martin ordered.

The fighters set up a phalanx in front of the Dauntless. The missile ships hung back waiting for an opening. The Prescottian vessel took up a defensive posture, when suddenly something went wrong.

"Captain! I'm picking up another vessel closing with us. 173 mark 14."

"Have the fighters stay on target. Recall Cobra group to assist us here. What do you make of the target?"

The sensor officer examined her readings. "Target appears to be a light cruiser. It was hiding from our sensors behind the system's primary."

Martin thought about this. It would be close, but he still felt he could accomplish his mission. "Captain, you may fire at will. Have Cobra group engage at point blank range."

Ryn opened up with a devastating volley at the new target. Its defense fields lit up with radiation as Ryn's FAL shots struck home. The cruiser returned fire. Structural supports groaned as the Dauntless' helmsman took evasive action.

"This is Cobra leader. Break formation and fire at will." Cobra squadron opened up on the cruiser's weakened defense fields. The fighters peppered the enemy hull. Metal was shredded and exploded off into space as the nimble fighters showed the enemy ship no mercy. Martin watched as one of the fighters was hit by an anti-aircraft bolt. The flaming ship exploded against the cruiser's hull.

The Dauntless was rocked as an anti-matter weapon found its mark. The ship rolled and returned fire. Ryn's weapons found a weak point in the Prescottian's armor. The hull buckled and collapsed where Ryn's energy bolts impacted. Cobra Squadron, minus three, kicked in the afterburners as the light cruiser exploded in a noiseless ball of fire.

Martin examined the smoking bridge. The Dauntless had taken several hits, but appeared to be intact. He turned his attention toward the other battle. He ordered Captain Jens to bring the ship around and back into the battle zone.

*   *   *

The Dauntless made an awkward turn and proceeded away from the debris that was once a Prescottian light cruiser. Captain Jens knew the feel of his ship was wrong. "Damage report," he ordered.

"Our starboard stabilizer is gone. Some structural damage as well. I recommend minimum maneuvering until the stabilizer can be replaced." The captain was not terribly pleased by this report, but there was little he could do about it. "Very well. Have all engineering damage control parties work on that stabilizer. Recall Cobra Squadron to attack primary target."

The Dauntless completed her turn, and swung around to face the other battle. It was still very much undecided. Martin could make out the shells and pieces of several fighters that had been destroyed. Still, the small ships had done damage. One displacement drive engine was blackened and spewing plasma from its side. The pilots had shown pinpoint accuracy. Martin could also make out several weapons pods that would fire no more.

As the Dauntless came into range, the enemy fired two anti-matter devices at her. The helmsman hit his console in frustration as he tried to make evasive maneuvers. Because of the ship's damaged stabilizer, he was only partially successful. One missile found its mark near main engineering. The entire ship moaned in protest as she tried valiantly to right herself.

Captain Jens punched his command console, "Engineering, report." He heard a great deal of coughing and other background noise before his chief engineer answered him.

"We have six dead in this compartment, sir. Our defense fields are down to 42%. No power to the starboard FAL pod. Starboard structural supports are also badly damaged."

Jens flinched a bit at the report. "Button up what you can, and hold her together. We'll get a med team to you as soon as possible."

Martin shouted over the din, "Ryn, get a lock on that ship and fire at will. Stay with pre-chosen targets if you can. If you cannot, then destroy it. We'll try again if we have to."

Ryn's face was a mask of concentration as he tried to salvage the mission. He took careful aim and fired. Two of his shots went wide, but the rest found bare hull where the enemy's defense fields had already collapsed. A massive explosion tore through the Prescottians underbelly as the weapons exploded. Another explosion engulfed the crippled ship's fusion engine.

Ryn bellowed a victory shout as he reported, "Their main energizer is destroyed. I am reading that no defense fields remain. Their fusion engines are also destroyed."

Martin slammed his hand down on the armrest of his chair. "Excellent! Have the fighters destroy their remaining weapons emplacements just in case. Then recall those ships. Captain, move us in. Order the strike team to the shuttle. Ryn and I will join them presently."

The big man and Martin made their way through the damaged bridge. Martin clapped his hand on his friend's broad back, "This is where the fun starts." Ryn's only reply was a huge grin on his sweat soaked face.

The two men stopped to don helmets to complete their uniforms. Both resembled strange black beetles in their protective armor. They arrived in the shuttle bay without incident and watched as the large assault shuttle was readied for action.

Martin was introduced to Sergeant Major Kelly Marsh, the senior enlisted marine present. The Sergeant replied with a simple, "Good afternoon, Admiral." The team was waiting for the all clear to depart. The Dauntless was still recovering her fighters. After about fifteen minutes, Captain Jens announced that the enemy vessel was completely incapacitated and that the shuttle team should ready themselves. As the marine company boarded the box like craft, the Sergeant Major walked up beside Martin, "Ready to go, Admiral?"

Martin smiled stiffly at the older man, "Sergeant Major, my correct rank is commodore, not admiral."

The weather beaten face smiled at him, "Sir, with all due respect, anyone that would head a mission like this when he bloody well doesn't have to, deserves a promotion."

Everyone present got a good laugh at this and Martin was only too glad to join in. Tension breakers like that were an absolute necessity on a mission of this type.

As the marine company continued to file on board, Martin checked his gear. He was outfitted in a Mark VII battle carapace that protected his head, torso, arms, legs, and groin. For offense, he packed a Type 16 FAL rifle and Mark 7 FAL pistol. He was also equipped with a FINDER sensor device that could detect almost anything; life forms, booby-traps, etc. Ryn had all the same equipment. In addition, Ryn carried several grenades of different types. A menacing looking dirk completed his regalia. The Pologian cut an imposing figure as he trotted aboard.

Presently, all was made ready. The pilots closed the hatch and Captain Jens ordered the bay depressurized. The ninety or so passengers bolted themselves in and prepared for departure. The plan was for half the company to board the ship in the engineering sections and work forward while the other half entered near the bridge area and worked aft. Martin believed they could accomplish this as the Prescottians had already taken many casualties. He still expected stiff and spirited resistance, however.

The large craft lifted smoothly from the deck and coasted out into space. Four fighters took up position around the shuttle for its short trip to the enemy cruiser. Martin ordered a sensor scan of the Prescottian ship. The Sergeant Major made the report, "Sir, I'm picking up sporadic energy readings throughout the ship. All propulsion systems appear to be out along with weapons and defense fields. There are major hull breaches, one near engineering and one amidships. Our second team will need to board near the first breach, but this shouldn't be a problem. It is difficult to say with any accuracy how many men we will face. The ship is throwing off a good deal of radiation that is making life form readings difficult. Their hanger bay is also trashed, so we cannot enter there if our other access areas are blocked." This last piece of information could cause a problem as Martin had planned to enter through their flight deck if they could not get in any other way.

The shuttle made its way along the hull of the battered ship. A gaping hole yawned out into space near the engineering section. Ice crystals and other flotsam floated near the breach. A few feeble lights flickered here and there, but apart from this, there were no signs of life. The assault vehicle flew past some markings in the Prescottian language. Martin ordered Ryn to put them through the translator. The characters turned out to reveal the vessel's name. The translation program gave several possible alternatives: Tempest, Cyclone, and Hurricane, to name a few. Martin hoped that this particular ship already had the wind knocked out of it.

The pilots began to search for a likely area to board the hulk. After several minutes, they found what appeared to be a maintenance air lock. It was large enough for three men to walk abreast. This was ideal in Martin's estimation. The shuttle nosed up along side. Martin motioned Ryn to take his position in an attempt to open the lock doors. A small clang could be heard in conjunction with the slight rattle as the large shuttle made contact with the air lock. Ryn opened their side of the lock and attempted several electronic methods to open the door. Nothing worked. One of the junior officers piped up, "This whole party will be for nothing if we can't get in."

Martin felt they had no choice, "Bring up the laser cutters. We'll try to blast the lock. If that doesn't work, we'll cut through the door. This will of course mean that everyone will have to don respirators." There was a collective groan throughout the cabin. The respirators would add to the bulky equipment everyone was already wearing.

"Wait!" shouted Ryn. "I've got the lock." He had tried a different code sequence while Martin was giving his last set of orders and had gotten lucky. Martin patted the big man's shoulder, "Can you get a reading of life forms beyond the door?"

The Pologian shrugged, "Not really, but since their sensors are down, they might not even know we're here. I'll set my scanner on maximum and give it a shot though." As Ryn fiddled with his controls, Martin gave everyone the sign to get ready and standby, things were about to get messy.

The door slid open noiselessly. Immediately FAL bolts filled the air. Ryn and Martin owed a lot to the designers of the shuttle. The assault craft was built with an empty corridor running the width of the vehicle from the airlock door. Because of this feature, the Prescottian fire landed harmlessly against the far bulkhead leaving only some carbon scoring as a testament to their fury.

Ryn and another marine lobbed two grenades down the passageway into the enemy vessel. The explosion rocked ship and shuttle alike as their energies were expended. Instantly, the enemy fire died away. Martin ordered half the company forward. Forty seven marines, Ryn, and Martin flowed into the blackened, smoky corridor. The air lock doors closed behind them and the shuttle departed for the engineering sections. Martin and his team were alone. Ryn had felt it best that Major Harris lead the second half of the assault. This left Ryn in charge of this group of marines with Martin in overall command of the mission.

A couple of Prescottians moved slightly on the deck. The rest had been pulped by the titanic explosion. Martin brought out his scanner and began to take stock of their situation. There were several Prescottian crewmembers about, but they were not moving in any kind of organized pattern. Martin thought that internal communications must be out. If that were the case, it would make his job much easier. Martin ordered his people to fan out. They would make for the computer section to ascertain if the system was still intact.

As Martin started forward, a blinding flash took him by surprise. The corridor spun crazily and suddenly, for no apparent reason, he was staring at the ceiling. He heard a brief commotion and then silence. The sound of footfalls approached his position and then Ryn's face filled Martin's vision.

"Are you all right?" queried Ryn in a concerned tone.

Martin did a quick internal check. Everything seemed to be in working order. "I'm okay, I think. What happened?"

"One of the wounded on the deck had an FAL pistol concealed beneath her. She shot you in the shoulder." Sure enough, Martin saw a burnt patch in his armor where the beam had struck home.

As Ryn helped Martin to his feet, the Commodore gave this order, "All Prescottians, wounded or not, are to be considered live targets. Sergeant, forward this order to Major Harris."

The sergeant complied as Martin dusted himself off. "I think we can move out now" he said as he breathed a silent word of thanks to the man who invented the anti-energy armor.

The team moved out, following the path the sensor recommended to the squad leader. This was of course only guesswork, but it was the only information Martin had to go on.

As the team glided stealthily down the passage, their radioman picked up a signal from the other group, "This is Major Harris. We have penetrated the engineering section and control two compartments --crackle-- heavy resistance. We have two dead and five injuries --crackle-- minor. We are moving forward, but --crackle-- pace. Please respond."

Martin turned to the com-tech. "Send an acknowledgment and tell them good luck."

A sandy haired kid looked up from his equipment, "Aye sir."

The team was snaking up the corridor in a five by five cover formation when they ran into the first real pocket of resistance. One man fell immediately, a smoking hole blossomed in his armor where his chest used to be. Ryn yelled over the noise, "Take cover. Anything that moves is a target. Fire at will!" With that he took careful aim and dropped a Prescottian with a perfect shot to the head.

Martin dove behind a wall of debris next to two privates. He drew his FAL pistol and squeezed off a shot. His bolt hit a Prescottian officer in the groin. One of the marines next to Martin smiled and said, "Ooh! That's gonna leave a mark." Martin chuckled and continued to fire. He was beginning to like the chemistry of this particular group and hoped, not for the first or last time, that casualties would be light.

A small explosion went off in front of Martin's cover followed by a human female flying through the air. She hit the deck hard, but was still moving. Ryn ordered a medic to assist her.

The firefight went on for some minutes. The Prescottians were reinforced at several points, but their numbers never exceeded fifteen at any one time. Another of Ryn's well placed grenades significantly lowered that total. A scream to Martin's right drew his attention to a corporal who seemed to have misplaced his left arm. The unfortunate man's armor sealed the wound in a tourniquet as Martin helped him to the deck.

The fight ended abruptly as Ryn lobbed four grenades down the corridor. The blast blew three of Martin's own team backward, but no one was seriously hurt.

Martin looked up at the big man, "A little bit of overkill, don't you think?"

The Pologian smiled, "The only thing I regret is that I'm out of grenades."

Martin ordered two privates to stand guard over the wounded. One man was dead and three more had been injured. The female marine had a severe concussion and could not be moved. The injured included the one armed corporal and another private who had multiple blast wounds in the chest and abdomen. Overall, a good engagement, Martin thought as he counted twenty seven Prescottian dead. Again, the enemy wounded were dispatched promptly and dispassionately. Martin did not have the time or manpower for such encumbrances.

At this point, the com-tech reported that Major Harris' team had secured engineering. In his report, the Major had mentioned that even though the displacement drive housings were completely destroyed, most of the control circuits and other equipment was intact. This meant that Protectorate scientists could study the Prescottian displacement drive in exacting detail.

Martin's team followed up this good news with a renewed drive for the computer center. Martin's sensor device indicated that the area contained several life forms. The rest of the journey to the compartment would not be an easy one. To make matters worse, the corridors were becoming more narrow. Martin ordered the team split to take advantage of two separate routes to their goal. It was his hope that the two groups could catch the defenders in a pincer. Marine Captain Bridgit van Horst led the other team down the second corridor.

Martin's group made good progress along their passageway. Ryn picked off a Prescottian rounding a turn in their path. He then laid down cover fire allowing members of the team to advance down the wreckage strewn route. When they arrived at their destination, Martin saw that attaining their goal would be a problem. Fully thirty Prescottian crew were dug in behind hastily built fortifications of cargo containers and other junk. Presently the fight for the computer center began.

A young corporal fired an explosive charge into the Prescottian position. Two cried out in pain as shrapnel tore into their bodies. A third never got the chance to scream. The crafty Sergeant Major threw a flash pod into the melee temporarily blinding several of the defenders. Ryn took this opportunity to drop another of the defenders with a well placed shot in the man's side.

A private next to Martin bellowed a challenge as he lobbed a grenade at the defenders. It blew a nice size hole in their defensive wall and caused a woman near the front to double over in pain. A Prescottian at the far end of the line took aim and felled one of the attackers. Another of Martin's men fell as a bolt caught him in the belly.

The Prescottians began to find targets and the battle began to take a bad turn. Just as Martin was about to order a retreat, the second part of his team appeared at the far end of the corridor. Now the defenders were themselves trapped. Martin toggled his FAL rifle to full power and loosed a shot. A defender's head exploded with the force of the blow. Martin was hit again as an FAL shot grazed his wrist, but the energy was dispersed by his armor and the hit was not a solid one.

Martin looked around the battlefield. Ryn was bleeding freely from a cut over his right eye. A piece of shrapnel from an exploding bulkhead had skittered past the big man's head, Captain van Horst was dead on the deck, her abdomen reduced to a smoking hole.

The attackers began to advance from both sides. There were fewer than ten Prescottians left. Two grenades from the advancing group landed squarely among the defenders. Bodies flew in all directions as the grenades' fury was spent. Martin's team had won its way through to the computer center.

The area looked intact. Martin could not take the time to examine the equipment as thoroughly as he might like. He motioned to a technician who took a small box like device from his pack and attached it to the nearest terminal. This device downloaded key information from the computers. Martin ordered the emergency data dump in case the Prescottians were able to sabotage their systems later on. Martin hoped he could salvage most of the information in the memory banks. Protectorate scientists were going to have a field day with the captured machines.

So far the mission was an unparalleled success. Of the forty seven that started with Martin, he had lost only nine. This specially trained marine shock force was an excellent fighting instrument. He planned to place every crewmember of both teams in for promotion and the highest commendations.

It was now Martin's intention to move down several decks, eliminating pockets of resistance as they went. He ordered Major Harris to begin moving up. The idea was to link up on deck 8.

Martin's team started for the through deck ladder. They ran up against three more Prescottian guards and took care of them easily. Martin ordered some members of his team to field strip the Prescottians of any equipment they were carrying. This would provide further trinkets for Protectorate scientists to examine even if the capturing of the ship was a failure.

Major Harris chose this time to make a progress report. He was pleased to say that engineering had been completely secured and his team was on deck six. He had lost ten people, but had inflicted over sixty casualties. Martin ordered his team to pick up the pace. With any luck the two groups could link up in less than ten minutes.

Major Harris had taken it upon himself to close off several internal bulkheads when he captured engineering. Many of the Prescottian defenders were now trapped and, as the good major had control of all the ship's lifts, they were immobilized as well. The major also reported that the vessel did have self destruct capabilities. He went on to say that the battle had fried the activation circuits. To make doubly sure that the mission would not come to a fiery end,

Harris destroyed the computer subsystem that governed the destruct mechanism.

At this point, Martin's luck seemed to desert him. Ryn's readings indicated that the Prescottians had managed to place about eighty soldiers on deck 8. In order to capture the vessel, those troops would have to be eliminated. They were the final obstacle to the taking of the vessel. All other enemies were accounted for; either killed in the ship battle, killed in the shipboard action, or trapped. This would not be easy as Martin's forces were down to some sixty five operatives.

Martin would have the advantage of attacking from the flanks however. He ordered the major to come up from behind while he took his marines in front.

The battle was joined shortly thereafter. Ryn lobbed in a flash pot that blinded and stunned the defenders. This advantage was short lived however. The Prescottians in the defensive phalanx had had plenty of time to prepare. They wore polarized visors and battle armor. They also had jury rigged a defensive wall around themselves. The situation was deteriorating quickly.

Martin watched as three of his team were hit and vaporized. The Protectorate forces were inflicting casualties, but the battle was degenerating into one of attrition, and Martin was not sure he could win it. Even if he emerged victorious, his casualties would be extremely high. If the young commodore was anything, he was extremely conscious of the people under his command.

Martin started thinking frantically for a plan. Major Harris reported that his troops were not faring much better. Time was running out. A young private next to Martin screamed in pain as his arm was blown off at the elbow. Martin decided then and there that this was enough.

"Sergeant!" he screamed over the cacophony. "Bring up the comm gear."

The older man did as he was told. Martin took the set and activated it. "Major, I want your team to pull back to deck 4."

"But sir," came the reply, "We must secure this area to capture the ship."

This statement of the painfully obvious did not improve Martin's mood, "That is an order Major, clear out."

"Aye sir."

Martin changed frequencies, "Gammage to Dauntless, respond please."

"Dauntless, Captain Jens."

Martin took a deep breath, "Captain, I want you to fire on these coordinates in thirty seconds."

"But, sir. You will be perilously close to the blast zone."

"I'm aware of that, but I have no intention of dying today. You have your orders."

"Aye sir. Thirty seconds . . . mark."

Martin turned to Ryn, "Get everyone but ten men out of here and back up to deck 5. The rest of us will hold those people down until the Dauntless fires."

Ryn immediately carried out the orders. Martin told his men to fire in a constant barrage. He told them not to concern themselves with ammunition. The idea was to cover the other's escape.

With fifteen seconds to go, Martin and Ryn gave the order to throw all remaining grenades at the defenders. They also laid down a furious FAL barrage. Through the blinding explosions, Martin gave the order to retreat. The defenders were surprised by the sudden ferocity of the attack and were confused for a few precious seconds, seconds that would cost them their lives.

Martin's team sprinted down the corridor. When they got halfway to the ladder well, Martin halted. The rest of the team scurried up the stairs, all of them that is, except Ryn.

"What are you doing?" screamed the big Pologian.

Martin could not take the time to respond. He was punching a code into a wall terminal. Ryn looked up to see the blast doors closing on either side of the Prescottian defenders. Ryn shook his head in wonder and admiration.

The two men hit the deck as a massive explosion rocked the ship. The Dauntless was right on time. The emergency bulkheads bent, groaned, and buckled. A large crack opened in one of them. Immediately, air began to hiss.

"Let's get off this deck!" screamed Ryn.

The two men bolted for the ladder. They followed their team just as another emergency bulkhead clanged shut three inches below Martin's boot, leaving the Prescottians to their doom.

The plan had the desired effect. The back up weapons officer of the Dauntless had made an extremely difficult shot with wonderful precision. The FAL had opened the Prescottian ship like an old fashioned sardine can. The defenders, jury rigged fortifications and all, were blown out into the night. The emergency bulkheads had bought Martin and Ryn just enough time to make their escape. The ship was now theirs.

Martin ordered both teams to link up on deck five in an empty cargo bay. Within six minutes the two teams were reunited. Martin, Ryn, and the major quickly congratulated each other on a job well done. Ryn sent a message to the shuttle to re-dock at the cargo bay's airlock. He then sent a team to recover the wounded parties the individual groups had left behind. A scan of both areas using internal sensors showed a clear path to both groups.

As these mundane tasks were being taken care of, Martin ordered his communications specialist to try and patch in a device that would allow intra ship dialogue. The internal comm. system had been badly damaged in the initial fight.

After about twenty minutes, the wounded began to arrive. The medic had stabilized his patients and they were laid neatly on the deck. The sergeant in charge of the comm unit announced that he had been able to reactivate the intercom. Martin stepped up to the grill and activated the unit. He ordered a linguistics specialist to translate. "Attention Prescottians. Your vessel is now in the hands of a Protectorate strike team. Your engineering section has been secured. We have used your internal emergency bulkheads to cut you off from one another, therefore, you are broken up into small groups. If you wish to surrender, please select a representative from your party and report back via the ship's intercom. If you surrender, you will be well treated. You have five minutes. After that time, my strike team will hunt each small group down and destroy you one at a time." Martin closed communications with a small click.

The Dauntless had by now run an extensive sensor sweep of the Prescottian ship. They had found that no group of survivors exceeded fourteen, and many of these were wounded. The Dauntless had also destroyed the bridge to completely negate any chance of a Prescottian counterattack.

This was unfortunate but necessary in Martin's estimation. Protectorate scientists and engineers would still have their hands full with the computers and their buried treasure of information, engines, sensors, defense field generators, weapons suites, and a host of other technological goodies.

Martin detached forty marines into a group to round up the surrendering prisoners. According to sensor sweeps, there were only seventy three survivors aboard. Martin also ordered that another shuttle be launched with an additional fifty security troopers to relieve some of the more battered and fatigued soldiers.

All went well at this point. The wounded were flown back to the Dauntless. A makeshift force field was erected with a portable generator to secure the growing population of prisoners. Only one group of seven refused to give up. Those brave but foolhardy individuals were dispatched with only one casualty being inflicted. The wounded man suffered only a burnt hand as a Prescottian FAL bolt found his palm.

When the prisoners had been removed to the Dauntless, an engineering team arrived to prepare the prize for towing. They set to work shoring up the more heavily damaged structural supports. They also buttoned up the hull breaches with portable force fields. A complete inventory of the ship was also made. In addition to the vessel itself, including the invaluable computer core, two shuttles had been captured intact. Martin and Ryn could hardly contain their excitement and glee as they read the salvage reports. For the first time, the Protectorate had captured a Prescottian vessel.

*   *   *

Two months later
Protectorate Base at Nalkar

Captain Ryndock Calplygian sat at a small corner table in the officer's club on Nalkar. His newly minted eagles were perched on his broad shoulders. The bright silver metal a reward for a job well done. He had earned a promotion and the Protectorate Unit Citation for his work in capturing the Prescottian cruiser, but he was, at least temporarily, unemployed. He had yet to be reassigned and was becoming bored.

A familiar figure entered the club. Ryn waved the new arrival over to his table. Martin shook his friend's hand and took a seat. He was practically oozing good cheer as he sat.

"Notice anything different?" Martin inquired as he called for the waiter.

"Yeah," his large friend replied, "Some moron put an extra star on your uniform. The cleaners must have made a mistake." Ryn left all kidding aside as he congratulated the new admiral.

Martin ordered a round of drinks and grinned at his friend. Martin's promotion had come through this morning. Rear Admiral Gammage pondered Ryn for a moment before saying, "If you have nothing better to do, I'm going to need a Chief of Staff. Interested?"

Ryn thanked Martin for the offer. Staff duty was an important step on the career ladder, but it would mean sacrificing a command of his own. Ryn's quandary did not last long, however. He would follow his friend to the last. Besides, Martin was an up and coming flag officer, guaranteed to be in the thick of the fighting until the war ended. Ryn accepted his new post by saying, "It has been, and will continue to be an honor to serve with you. Any service I can give you, I will be happy to provide."

Martin smiled at his friend, a smile that went all the way into his eyes. "I will undoubtedly be offered a task force of some kind. Your first duty will be to cut orders for one Captain Jaspa Shindessa to report to me for the center seat of one of the new vessels under my command."

Ryn nodded. He was unaware of Jaspa's promotion to Captain, but he was looking forward to seeing her again. Ryn would bet everything he owned that Martin was even more pleased to be in a position to see her again.

Martin continued to rattle off surprises. "I'll need a senior engineer on my staff as well. See if one Commander Edward Longly is available."

Eddie! Thought Ryn. They had not seen him since they were junior officers together. The fortunes of war had driven the friends apart. Edward had proven himself an excellent engineer. Now Martin was going to give him a shot in the command structure.

"Ryn, I'll want you to serve double duty as my tactical adviser as well. I looked through the available officers, and you're still the best choice. We'll talk about rounding out my staff later. As of now we're on three days liberty."

The two men lifted their glasses and toasted each other. The capture of a Prescottian ship had opened new doors to the compatriots. Ryn could barely contain his excitement as he pondered his new office and the battles to come with his friends by his side.

Chapter VIII: REAR ADMIRAL
September 14, 2525
New Freemantle Shipyard

Rear Admiral Martin Gammage sat in the well appointed waiting room of his new commanding officer. His transfer to the 11th Fleet had gone through without a hitch. Ryn had accompanied him on the short trip to the New Freemantle Shipyards. Edward had arrived a couple of days earlier and the three friends had shared a cheerful and alcoholic reunion. The person that Martin had wanted to see most however, was not due to arrive for three more days. Jaspa was being cut loose from her present command to take up the reins of a ship in Martin's new task force. Exactly what those ships would be was the reason for Martin's visit to the commander of the 11th Fleet.

Martin turned his head to get a good view of the active shipyard. A destroyer was getting her finishing touches awaiting her shakedown cruise. Beyond the sleek ship, Martin could see a mammoth battle cruiser, her hull pitted and blackened from a recent encounter. Martin stood and walked to the window. At the limit of his vision, he could make out several fleet carriers being readied for yet another mission against the Prescottians. He could not help but wonder which of those ships, if any, he would be taking into battle.

The war was dragging on interminably. Neither side seemed capable of breaking the stalemate. Martin was reminded of his home planet's World War I. The Allies stared at German troops from their trenches, neither side able to move more than a couple hundred yards at any given time. Thousands had died on both sides to gain a few precious feet. Martin could see the Prescottian war stretching on, and on, and on, without end. Something had to be done to break the deadlock.

His thoughts were interrupted by a pretty young lieutenant who had strolled up beside him while he was ruminating. "Admiral Beedle will see you now sir."

Martin simply nodded and allowed the young lady to lead him to the commander's inner offices. A large portrait of Alexander Kinkaid, the Protectorate's first Fleet Admiral, dominated Beedle's office. The older admiral smiled and indicated that Martin should have a seat.

"I am pleased to meet you at last Admiral Gammage," Beedle began, "your reputation precedes you."

Martin smiled at the compliment. "Thank you sir. I am anxious to get back into the fighting."

"I'll bet you are. The capturing of that Prescottian cruiser was a master stroke. It has suitably impressed me to entrust to you a major task force. T.F. 92 will consist of four vessels: a command ship and three fleet carriers. Commodore Randolph Scott will command your screening ships. You will place your flag on board the P.I.V. Europa."

Martin was ecstatic over this news. The Europa was a Titan class command ship. These vessels were among the best all around ships the Protectorate had. As the news sunk in, Admiral Beedle continued, "Your three carriers will be the Yorktown, Hornet, and Enterprise. I understand you are bringing in a new commanding officer for the Hornet." The Admiral consulted his desk, "One Jaspa Shindessa if I am not mistaken.

"Martin could only nod. His mind was spinning over an extremely strange coincidence. The Hornet, Enterprise, and Yorktown had been the names of the carriers that the United States had used at the battle of Midway over 500 years ago. That battle had been the turning point of World War II. Martin sincerely hoped that this bizarre happenstance would have similar results for the Protectorate. When Martin explained this historical fact to Admiral Beedle, the old man echoed Martin's sentiments; "I hadn't realized that myself. Perhaps this is a good omen for you Admiral." The elder man raised a glass in Martin's direction; "May those ships bring you a similar victory."

Martin smiled. "Thank you sir. I understand there is a briefing of all officers at 1600?"

"That's correct, Admiral. We will be discussing our next move in this sector. You are dismissed until that time."

Martin stood. "Thank you again sir."

Admiral Beedle nodded as Martin withdrew.

*   *   *

The meeting room was already quite crowded as Martin entered. He did a quick scan of the space, trying to identify anyone he knew. As his eyes surveyed the individuals present, he noticed Commodore Scott beckoning him. Scott was the commander of Martin's screening vessels. Martin smiled and made his way toward the Commodore.

The two shook hands as Martin took a seat. The burly Commodore was the first to speak. "It will be a pleasure serving with you sir. I am happy to finally meet you.

"Thank you Randolph. I want to waste no time today. Let's have a staff meeting of all ship commanders and first officers immediately following the briefing."

"Aye sir."

Martin continued, "I just received my assignment today. What does your task force look like?"

The commodore thought briefly before responding, "I've got two fast battleships, four cruisers, and six destroyers. I'm trying to wrangle another cruiser before our mission; whatever that turns out to be. The Lynx is in dry dock, but the dock master assures me she'll be ready in fifty hours."

"Very good," replied Martin, "I'll try to get her attached to our task force before . . . "

"Attention on deck!"

Admiral Beedle had just entered the room. "As you were," he said, and with that all the senior officers took their seats.

The Admiral walked to the podium and made eye contact with all the officers present before he began. "Our purpose here this evening is to try and determine the next move our friends will make. With this in mind, I give you Vice Admiral Fliathal."

The middle-aged Lanthanian took the podium. A small lift built into the stand raised the admiral's 2 foot 11 inch height to a more comfortable level. Fliathal worked some controls and a large map of the sector appeared behind him.

"As you can see here," began the admiral as he gestured to the map, "we believe that the Prescottians will make an attempt to take the Kaly System. It has been observed by our scouts that the Prescottian Fleet has been massing here . . . at a point 13.5 light years distant from said system. Kaly is important for several reasons, not the least of which is the fact that it can be used as the perfect jumping off point into three Protectorate sectors. If you'll examine your . . ."

Martin was gazing at the map while analyzing what the admiral had said. He knew that the Prescottians were indeed massing at Kaly. He knew that Kaly was strategically important. He also knew that the admiral was dead wrong. The Prescottians would not attack that system. Martin was certain the Prescottians were after something else.

"Excuse me sir." Martin interjected. "I have a different interpretation of this data."

The diminutive admiral did not take kindly to being interrupted. "We can discuss that later admiral. In the meantime . . ."

"I'd like to hear this," said Beedle from his seat.

"Very well sir" grumbled Fliathal.

Martin looked around the room before beginning, "As most of you know, I've been involved in many campaigns against the Prescottians. In that time I've come to learn a great deal about their strategy." He walked up to the map and pointed dramatically, "They will attack here . . . In the Dryad System."

Pandemonium broke loose in the hall. Several admirals were trying to question Martin at once. After a short time, Admiral Beedle brought the gathering under control. The senior officer appraised Martin for a few seconds before beginning, "Admiral Gammage, I am at a loss to explain your interpretation. There is nothing of significance in the Dryad System. Further, it would appear that Kaly is of greater strategic import."

Admiral Fliathal seemed mollified by this until Martin responded, "It does seem that way at first Admiral. If you'll look closely you can see that the Dryad System rests on our flank. The Prescottians are hoping that we'll see their build up at Kaly so that they can swing around and surprise us from the rear."

Admiral Beedle appeared to consider this before saying, "I think we should follow Admiral Fliathal's recommendation. You are dismissed to your commands to coordinate the attack. Admiral Gammage, I want to see you before you leave."

The meeting broke up. Many of the older admirals were shaking their heads at Martin's audacity as they filed out of the hall. Martin for his part was ignoring the others as he made his way to Admiral Beedle.

The four star looked at Martin, the large map behind them, and back at Martin again. "Son, I think you have a point, and since you raised it, you will be responsible for holding that area."

Martin was surprised to say the least, "But sir, my small task force will be no match for a Prescottian Fleet should they attack at Dryad."

"True, my boy, but your job will not be to face the enemy head on. What I want you to do is to hold them until the rest of the fleet can arrive to relieve you."

Martin still did not like where this was going, "Even so, my forces stand to take tremendous losses."

"Also true, lad, but if we can pull this off, we'll be attacking their flank. Also, if you're wrong, I'll have three carriers and assorted support vessels ready to surprise the enemy at Kaly."

Martin had to admit that this was a good plan, but he also knew that his troops were in for a hard time. He was bound to lose at least 50% of his ships before he could be relieved. It would be worth it if, if the fleet arrived and was able to decimate the enemy's flank. Martin was thinking he should have kept his mouth shut. He also knew there was no way he could have; he knew he was right and Admiral Beedle was taking advantage of his young underling's insight.

The old man looked at Martin with sympathy, "Sometimes a fleet commander has to take chances to win battles. If you have to bait our trap then that's the way it has to be. I also know your record and have every confidence you'll be able to hold until we arrive."

Martin felt the weight of his two stars now more than ever. He was at high enough rank to command many ships, but still too low to make large policy decisions. Deep down he knew Beedle was right, and if the roles had been reversed, Martin would have done the exact same thing. He nodded to Beedle and strode out of the hall to break the news to his staff.

*   *   *

Before telling his people of their "good fortune," Martin needed to take care of something. He walked slowly through the large base nodding to junior officers as they passed him by. New Freemantle was bustling with the activities of war. The habitat area was swollen with beings from every part of the Protectorate. Martin thought briefly about the wonder of it all as he finally reached his quarters.

Martin entered the spartan living room and sat down before the computer terminal. He entered his security code and said, "Request access to voting procedure for Fleet Admiral. Vote of the year 2525." The computer whirred almost silently for a moment. It then took a retinal scan, fingerprint, and voice identification for Rear Admiral Martin Gammage before allowing him to proceed. A brief message lit up the screen that Martin merely scanned before a copy of the ballot took center stage.

Martin began reading the list of names. Admiral Cyrus Morta was the very first. Martin frowned; he definitely was not going to vote for that bastard. Vice Admiral Colya Giapar, a Rosnosiclanian was next on the list. Martin pondered her career briefly. She had served well in several theaters, but her career was not a spectacular one. Martin bypassed her name to the third on the list, one Vice Admiral Paul Phillips. The human admiral had a mediocre battle record at best. He was said to be a superlative administrator, however. Martin shook his head slowly. No, the Protectorate would need a being of action, not a paper pusher. Martin was beginning to fret. None of the names on the ballot were appealing to him. That is until he saw the final name on the screen . . . his.

Martin stared at his name for a long time. He had certainly not nominated himself. This, however meant little as any officer of command rank could submit an admiral for consideration. Who had nominated him? Martin had not paid much attention to the news of late, so it was possible that he had remained uninformed. He smirked at the screen knowing full well that he did not stand a chance. Still, a sense of excitement began to well up in him. He touched the key next to his name and ordered his ballot sent to Earth for counting. He then rescheduled his staff meeting for forty eight hours later. Martin wanted time to think, not only about this new twist in his life, but to try and figure out a way to reduce his casualties to a minimum. In the face of this thorny problem, the slim prospect of becoming the next Fleet Admiral faded to insignificance. Trying to save thousands of lives in the here and now pushed to the fore of his thoughts.

* * *

September 16, 2525

Martin finally emerged from his quarters a mere thirty minutes before his staff meeting. He had remained secluded, taking his meals in his rooms and refusing to reply to messages from junior officers. Jaspa had called twice, and twice he had told her that he would see her after the staff meeting. Martin had been unable to see a way around his current predicament. If the Prescottians attacked his force at Dryad, as he was sure they would, Martin was certain to take appalling casualties before help arrived. The prospect of being nominated for Fleet Admiral was small consolation as it was possible that Martin would not live to enjoy it.

As the young admiral rounded a turn in one of the uncountable passageways of the station, a junior aide on his staff caught up with him. The woman was slightly out of breath and seemed excited. She began, "Oh sir! I've been looking all over for you."

Martin smiled at her, "I have been incommunicado for a while Lieutenant. What's on your mind?"

"I waited in the communications office all day for the news from Earth. It was very close you see. When he heard the news he must have gone out of his mind. To be denied the promotion by a young upstart, begging the admiral's pardon, must have just driven him crazy. I didn't even know you were running. I don't know whether to congratulate you or not. I mean you usually don't congratulate someone for losing, well you didn't exactly lose, but well you know . . . "

Martin stared at the lieutenant completely nonplused. "What are you talking about?" he asked with a sense of desperation.

"Oh, I'm so sorry sir, it's just that I'm so excited and happy for you sir. Well not happy that you didn't win. When I heard the story it was just so . . . "

Martin stopped her before her comments could devolve into babble once again. "Lieutenant Kensington, tell me in plain English what has happened." The edge in his voice finally got through to his aide.

"Yes sir. About an hour ago I received the results of the Fleet Admiral election. Admiral Morta received 60% of the vote. You got 31% and the others split the rest. Everyone's talking about it sir. They say that if you had not split the vote, Admiral Morta would have won for sure. They are reporting that the admiral was apoplectic! I'm sorry you lost sir, but I'm glad he didn't win. 31% for a first time is really quite good especially since you are so junior. I mean . . . "

Martin did not hear the rest. His head was swimming. A small smile began to creep across his face. He did not know who had nominated him, but he was going to find that being and give him or her a medal. Martin had achieved a small measure of revenge against his hated enemy. He had blocked the advancement to the prize Morta wanted most. A change started in Martin at that moment and began to grow. If he survived the upcoming battle, if he could bring his troops home, if all the "ifs" worked in his favor, Martin was going to do his best to be Fleet Admiral. He wanted it now. He wanted it badly.

"Admiral? Admiral?" The voice of his aide shook him from his reverie.

"Sorry Lieutenant. I was lost in thought. Thank you for the message, it is good news indeed. Shall we?" He gestured down the passageway toward the conference center. They continued their walk to room 365 where Martin had assembled his entire staff.

Some thirty beings came to their feet as Martin entered. Lieutenant Kensington left his side and found a seat. Martin's full staff was present along with the commanding officers of his task force. He surveyed the room slowly making eye contact with everyone present before asking the assembly to take their seats.

"Good evening everyone. I have our battle assignment which I will impart to you. We are to be assigned to the Dryad System."

A murmur whispered through the crowd. Martin could hear snatches of conversation . . . "I can't believe they listened to him." "I hope he's right, if the fleet is off at Dryad and they attack at . . ." "He must have some serious weight with the three and four stars . . ."

A woman at the back raised her hand. Martin smiled when he recognized the individual, "Yes Captain Shindessa?"

Jaspa rose from her seat. All eyes turned to her as she said, "Are we to take it Admiral, that your suggestion has been followed and the fleet will be stationed at the Dryad System?"

"Not exactly Captain." Jaspa looked confused as she took her seat. "I said we will be stationed at Dryad. The remainder of the fleet will take up positions at Kaly."

Martin watched as this information sank in. Eddie immediately bolted up and said, "If you are correct Admiral, and the Prescottians attack at Dryad, we'll be decimated."

Martin chose to ignore the comment and continued, "Our orders are as follows: if the Prescottians attack at Dryad, we are to hold our position until the fleet can arrive. If they attack at Kaly, we will be a reserve force. If they attack anywhere else . . . may the universe have mercy on us."

The assembly erupted. Everyone was talking at once. Martin allowed his captains and staff to blow off steam. He tried to conduct his briefings rather informally. The only person not speaking was Jaspa. She caught the Admiral's eye. They looked at each other for what seemed a long time. Jaspa broke the encounter by giving Martin a jaunty wink.

Martin let the gabble continue for a full minute. He then straightened at the podium and said one word in a forceful commanding voice, "Silence!"

Immediately, the noise stopped. Martin put his hands behind his back and stepped out from behind the podium. He paced the length of the stage and back before he addressed the gathering. "I know how you feel. If I'm right and Dryad is attacked, well, we're in for a bad time to say the least. If I'm wrong and Kaly is attacked, we are subjugated to the unenviable role of "reserves." We must watch as our comrades die without being able to do anything about it. Both possibilities are unpleasant. I feel you have the right to know what we are up against. For the last two days I have been running battle simulations in my quarters. The results are not encouraging. In our best case scenario we will suffer 40% casualties before we can be relieved. In the worst case . . . our task force will be totally destroyed before help arrives. You all know me. I have beaten the odds before and have every intention of doing so now. We have a chance for a major victory. If we can hold the enemy and inflict good damage, the rest of the fleet can obliterate the Prescottians. This is our duty, and we will be victorious."

The crowd stared up at Martin with pride and adoration. Martin was certain that he would get the best out of each and every crewmember on every ship. Martin took in glances of respect before continuing, "Commodore Scott, I have procured another three ships for our task force. Under the circumstances, the fleet commander could not refuse me. We have two more cruisers and a front line battleship; the P.I.V. Kraken. From there you will command the screening vessels."

Commodore Randolph Scott simply nodded before adding, "Aye sir."

Martin stepped back behind the podium. "I have only one more item of business before we adjourn. As you all must be aware by now, my name was on the Fleet Admiral voting ballot this time around. As I did not submit my candidacy, I can only assume that someone in this room did. Would that person please identify his or herself?"

At first no one moved. Then a hand went up at the back of the room. It was Jaspa's. Martin had a feeling that this would be the case, but as soon as he was about to say something, another hand went up. Ryn smiled at him. Eddie's hand soon followed, and soon another hand went up. Within fifteen seconds, every hand in the room was raised.

"I see," said Martin softly. Jaspa looked around the room and continued, "We all signed the application Admiral. All officers of command rank and above submitted it, but every crew member on this station signed it." She grinned, "I believe it is a record, Admiral. I don't think that any application ever submitted had 54,000 signatures attached."

Martin was truly touched. He took a moment to gather himself. "I appreciate the confidence this gesture shows. I will see to it that it is warranted. I promise that I will keep our casualties to a minimum. Loyalty such as this is precious and deserves to be protected." For one of the few occasions in his life, Martin was at a loss for words. He finished lamely, "You are dismissed."

*   *   *

September 26, 2525
36 light years from the Dryad System

Martin sat in his tall backed chair on the bridge of the Europa. In the command well, Captain Jilayah Soord had the con. Martin was still uncomfortable not having command of a ship of his own, but he was getting used to it. His task force was on course and on schedule. They were an impressive sight. The three carriers were in the center of the formation with the Europa in position just behind them. In the front, the Kraken flew majestically along with two slightly smaller battleships. A perimeter of cruisers and destroyers completed the force.

Martin had time to think of inconsequential things as his ships cut through the inky black of space. He thought back to the rendezvous he and Jaspa had shared before departing New Freemantle. Their lovemaking had been poignant and sweet. Martin smiled slightly at the memory. His body still ached from the crashball match he had reluctantly played with Ryn. Martin had taken two of the five games from his large companion, but Ryn's sheer strength and size had decided the outcome. Martin had also had time to debate some of the finer points of temporal mechanics with Eddie. The young admiral had tried to enjoy himself in the days before their departure. Martin felt he had done everything possible in insuring the safety of those under his command and he did not want to get burned out, so he had spent time with his friends as his ships were readied for battle.

Now the fleet had launched. Most of the ships were headed for Kaly. Martin's lonely group rocketed for Dryad. Martin had outlined his strategy to his staff. The carrier had been the most important vessel in naval warfare since it's inception. This idea had been proven true in Earth's World War II, Bringolad V's War of Succession, and Plinto's Catsystan Wars. The importance of the carrier had left the seas and gone into space. Martin wanted all of his fighters and war vessels to concentrate on the enemy carriers. If he could inflict heavy damage on the Prescottian's carrier force, the rest of the fleet would have a huge advantage when they arrived. The plan had been debated and finally approved of by his staff. No matter how one sliced it, Martin's group was in for a bad time; they might as well aim for the enemy's most important ships.

The hours slipped by. Soon the orange dwarf star that was called Dryad could be seen on the view screen. Dryad was a desolate system. Two ponderous gas giants made their way around their unremarkable star. A small rocky world tumbled in its orbit some 85 million miles from the orange globe. The planet was habitable but unoccupied. Martin believed that the Prescottians would try to take this world. With it they could set up an advance base on the Protectorate's flank. He was sure of it. In addition, Dryad's thick girdle of asteroids were rich in minerals. No one could argue that Dryad was as attractive a catch as the heavily populated Kaly System, but

Martin believed that this was exactly why the Prescottians would go for the overlooked planets. The Prescottians could grab an advance base with no indigenous population to control. They could simply walk in, set up shop, and still have the asteroids and the small planet's crust from which to extract much needed materials. The Prescottians predilection for taking the path of least resistance was exactly what Martin was counting on.

The orange ball was shining brightly now as Martin's task force flew closer. He was planning to set his ships up just inside the cloud of cometary bodies, ice, gas, and dust that comprised Dryad's Oort cloud. He wanted to use the cloud as camouflage from the Prescottian's already inferior sensors. In addition, Martin quickly ordered his vessels to use their tractor beams to make "windows" in the cloud so that his fleet would have a clear picture of events outside the system.

A few hours after their arrival Martin turned to the communications officer, "Lieutenant, send a coded transmission to Admiral Beedle's flag ship in the Kaly System. Tell him we are on station and awaiting further developments. All vessels arrived without incident. At present, we have no enemy contact and are detecting nothing within sensor range. Admiral Martin Gammage commanding Task Force 92 etc. etc. . . . " The dark lieutenant acknowledged the order and sent the message.

Now the waiting would begin. Martin had no idea how long it would take the Prescottians to attack, if indeed they attacked at all. The latest intelligence reports indicated that a force of at least 35 ships had massed near Kaly. Martin was still convinced that this was a feint. Intelligence also reported that the Dryad System was completely clear up to fifty light years out. The reports did not bother Martin. He still believed that he was in the right place. The waiting and watching would be the hardest part of course. Martin remembered a quote that had followed him throughout the conflict; "War was stretches of absolute boredom punctuated by moments of sheer terror." This phrase was to describe the next few days.

*   *   *

September 29, 2525
Dryad System

Admiral Gammage rested in his quarters, waiting. Before him was a very old paperback novel. The book was a gift from Jaspa who knew how much Martin enjoyed reading. He handled the book with extreme care, and though this was about the tenth time he had read the thing, it was still able to bring him great pleasure. It was amazing to Martin that Isaac Asimov could still spellbind readers many centuries after his death. This fact was even more impressive for much of the book was now science fact as opposed to fiction.

Martin leafed through the pages at a good clip, gobbling the words they contained when a small beep interrupted him. "Admiral Gammage here."

"Admiral," came the voice from nowhere, "we are receiving a message from the 11th fleet, priority one."

"On my way." Martin stood and tugged on his uniform jacket. The ship was not on alert as yet so Martin was not terribly concerned. Still, he strode briskly through the passageways until he arrived on the bridge.

His arrival was duly noted by the bridge contingent. He ignored the standard "Admiral on the bridge" and made his way to the communications station. The head of the department, one Lieutenant Commander Zachary Armistad, greeted him, "Admiral, this message just arrived."

"Very well commander, let's hear it."

The officer punched a few buttons and the communiqué began: From Admiral Beedle, 11th fleet to Rear Admiral Martin Gammage, Commander Task Force 92. The fleet has picked up many enemy vessels moving into this system. We detect at least ninety ships. You will stand by to receive orders to depart for the Kaly System.

Martin listened to the message with a growing sense of disbelief. Had he been wrong? He was convinced that the Prescottians would attack here, but ninety ships? That certainly sounded like a battle force to him.

Martin shook off his confusion to issue orders, "Commander, inform the c.o.'s of all vessels to prepare to depart." He turned to the command well, "Captain, in the meantime we will hold this position, but have the navigator plot a speed course for the Kaly System."

His orders were acknowledged. Martin slumped down into his command chair. How could he have been so wrong? Something about this was still not right, but he had no evidence. Ninety ships were on their way to Kaly and Martin's task force would undoubtedly be recalled. He just could not understand it. Ryn looked at him from the tactical post with a confused expression on his face. He had been as convinced as Martin that the enemy would come after this system. Be that as it may, both men made preparation to leave this area of space. Task Force 92 hovered in the darkness and made ready for departure. All was going well until the situation took a turn.

The sensor officer looked up from his board with a nervous expression, "Admiral, I am detecting numerous targets at extreme range. They are moving at hyper-light velocity and closing on our position rapidly."

Martin frowned. "Type and number?"

"Unknown at this range sir."

Martin waited only a fraction of a second, "Battle alert: General quarters. All pilots to their fighters. Ensign Smig, identify those vessels as soon as possible."

Could the Prescottians be launching a two pronged attack? Beedle had said that he was engaged with over ninety enemy ships. If the incoming group was small, perhaps a double victory could be achieved.

Departments from every ship in T.F. 92 reported ready. The pilots were standing by. Martin rose from his chair and walked slowly over to the sensor position. Before he could arrive, however, Ensign Smig lost all color and turned to the admiral, "Sir, my scans are picking up individual targets. They are definitely Prescottian. Sir, there are one hundred and four of them."

A hundred and four! This could not be possible. The Prescottians simply did not have that kind of strength in this area. Over a hundred vessels here and nearly one hundred at Kaly was a total that Martin simply could not account for.

Martin took a deep, calming breath, "Ensign DeWit send to Admiral Beedle on a secure channel and scramble: T.F. 92 is under attack by one hundred and four, repeat one hundred and four, enemy vessels, please advise."

Ensign Smig delivered additional information to an already grim scene, "Admiral, I can now identify ship types: thirty of the vessels are troop transports apparently for the occupation of this system, another twenty are support ships. Of the combat vessels, twenty are destroyers, fifteen are cruisers, five are battleships," the young man swallowed nervously and ran a hand across his brow," the remaining ships are carriers, fourteen of them."

This was devastating news. There was no way that Martin's ships could stand up to firepower of that magnitude. He could only bring three carriers, four battleships, six cruisers, and nine destroyers to bear. The enemy carriers were the problem. Fourteen on three were not good odds. Thoughts whipped through Martin's mind. He could still escape, as his force had not yet been detected. Staying here with no chance of relief was suicide. He opened his mouth to issue the order to withdraw when his communications officer turned to him, "Sir, we are receiving a transmission from Admiral Beedle."

The speaker crackled to life with the voice of the elder admiral, "Martin, you will hold your ground at all costs! We've been tricked. As our fleet closed on the enemy we noticed something strange about their configuration. When we entered visual range, there was noting out there! The Prescottians had sent ninety or so sensor drones. The robots broadcast large ship silhouettes to confuse our scanners. Their plan apparently was to hold our fleet while they attacked Dryad. You were right. We are breaking off now and will proceed to your position at maximum displacement. Hold your ground! Thanks to you we can flank their fleet and crush them. Our surprise will be complete! Beedle out."

Being proven right was of little consolation to Martin now. He was hopelessly outnumbered, but a firm resolve welled up inside. He would not give up his position.

He turned to the sensor officer, "How long until the enemy is in weapons range?"

"One hour, seven minutes sir."

"How long until reinforcements can arrive?"

"If Admiral Beedle departs in the next five minutes at maximum displacement," the ensign performed some calculations, "two hours, nineteen minutes."

A plan coalesced in Martin's mind. It was their only chance. He moved to Ensign DeWit, "Order all ships to activate their sensor countermeasures. Ryn, Captain Soord, come with me."

The order went out and instantly a field of sensor scattering particles enveloped the task force. Martin hoped that this, combined with the shield of the Oort cloud would keep his ships masked until the last possible moment.

Martin led his two officers off the bridge to a small conference room. Without preamble he began, "This, in my estimation, is our only chance. We will remain hidden here until the enemy closes to short range. We will launch our fighters about five minutes before that time. The fighters will hug their carriers in order to remain inside our jamming field. When the enemy closes we will spring from hiding and hit them with everything we've got. I want to concentrate on their carriers. It is my hope that we will achieve complete surprise and hit them before they have the opportunity to launch their fighters. The Prescottians will then find it very difficult to launch in the middle of a battle. Do you have any suggestions or refinements?"

Captain Soord, who had been a carrier captain before accepting command of the Europa spoke out, "I have only one problem, sir. Five minutes will not be anywhere near enough time to launch our fighters. You must remember sir that we will be virtually pushing the fighters out. They will not be able to use their fusion engines if you wish to avoid detection. They will have to fly on maneuvering thrusters only and then take up an extremely close position to their mother ships. I don't like it, but I do have to recommend at least thirty minutes for the maneuver, and even that will be cutting it fine."

Martin nodded, "Your suggestion is noted and approved. Ryn, you will send the appropriate orders to all vessels. Arrange the task force however you see fit; I trust your judgment. Remember, the carriers have unconditional priority as targets. I want to take as many of them out as we can before the main fleet arrives."

Martin dismissed Captain Soord. He was about to leave himself when a large hand closed on his shoulder. Ryn looked down at him, "It's a good plan," he said simply.

Martin smiled thinly, "It's the only one we've got."

*　　*　　*

31 Minutes To Weapons Contact

Martin paced nervously on the bridge as the Prescottian vessels closed the range. He waited in near silence; the bridge crew was concentrating intensely on the their tasks. As the chronometer ticked down to the appointed moment, Martin uttered two words, "Launch fighters!"

He watched as the first fighter off the Yorktown nosed its way out of its launch tube. Tiny flickers of light pushed the small craft away from the mouth of the tube and up along the body of the sleek carrier. This maneuver was being duplicated throughout the fleet. The carriers would be fielding one hundred and forty four fighters each. Martin's own Europa another seventy two. The battleships each had four squadrons, the cruisers, two. Soon the space around the large ships swarmed with tiny shapes. Martin knew however that the strength this suggested was a mere illusion. Prescottians carriers, while not as large as their Protectorate counterparts, still held ten squadrons apiece . . . and there were fourteen of them.

Martin felt a sense of pride as the tricky dance of fighters and capital ships continued flawlessly. The feeling was short lived, however, as he realized how many of the tiny flickers would not be coming back. Each point of light represented one or two beings. These men, women, and others were being sent on an impossible mission, and Martin was sending them. He felt the weight of responsibility heave itself onto his shoulders. He had never been responsible for so many lives. He kept reminding himself of the big picture. If they could only hold the Prescottians long enough; if they could make the Prescottians pay dearly for every inch of space they gained, the fleet would come and win a huge victory. Martin continued to watch the spectacle unfold. He muttered a line from one of his favorite works of literature, "Theirs is not to question why, theirs is but to do or die."

"Thirteen minutes and closing," announced the helmsman. This was the signal to the destroyers to take position. Maneuvering thrusters fired and the small ships took their places. The fighters continued to launch. The cruisers and battleships had completed their part. The Europa still had some twenty fighters left, and the carriers were about half done. Everything was proceeding on schedule.

"Seven minutes and closing." The Europa had completed her launch. The carriers were nearly done. The view screen could now, at maximum magnification, just make out the pinpricks that were the enemy. The stalwart task force with the designation 92 had still not been detected.

Ryn was making final preparations. He was warning the tactical officers on the other ships to charge weapons and raise defense fields at the last possible second. He worked his own board placing the mighty weapons of Europa on standby. Energy was being fed to the nova cannon as Ryn began the pre-warm sequence. Missiles came off their racks and, still unarmed, made their way to their launch tubes.

"Four minutes and closing," came the monotone from their helmsman. The young man began working on the maneuver that would spring the Europa on her unsuspecting enemy. Complete communications silence was now ordered as the Prescottians entered the task force's control sphere.

"Three minutes and closing." The last fighter from the Hornet edged out into space. Hundreds of little fireflies dotted the void around the capital ships. The Prescottians began their breaking procedure in preparation to enter the system. Velocity bled away as their displacement drives fell into reverse. The ships were closer now. Some detail could be seen as the enemy slipped closer, still unaware of the Protectorate ships crouched behind lumps of ice.

"One minute and closing." The Prescottians dropped into normal space, their massive fusion engines taking over the burden. Not one enemy fighter could be seen. The fleet sailed on, blissfully unaware of their peril. Martin watched the sleek destroyers, blunt nosed battleships, and huge carriers loom ever larger and closer. He could make out fleet insignia on fuselages and engine nacelles.

"Thirty seconds and closing." The black circles of weapons ports could now be seen. They lacked the dull red glow that would betray their activity. Weapons offline, defense fields down, the enemy flew on secure in their superiority; not expecting a fight. Martin's fighters fired their maneuvering thrusters for a final push forward. This would clear them from their mother ships and give them room to maneuver.

"Ten seconds and closing." Martin gripped his command chair as the first Prescottian destroyer slipped by. He was waiting for the vanguard to clear so his ships would have an open strike on the carriers. Ryn barked an order to all vessels, "Arm weapons, raise defense fields."

"In range now, sir," came the announcement from the sensor officer. Martin nodded and said, "Ensign DeWit, send this on an open channel, I want the Prescottians to hear me, the transmission will be only one word."

The confused comm officer turned to his board to comply. A large battle cruiser flew by on the screen, the last vessel before the carriers. "Now, Ensign DeWit." The young man touched a button. Martin drew a breath and then yelled, "Surprise!"

As one, the task force shot forward. The fighters had already jumped on the nearest carrier. The unshielded ship was blasted all over her port flank. Metal blistered and buckled before a fighter found a sensitive spot. The great vessel heaved and rolled, finally exploding in a gush of plasma and fire. Martin's crew cheered as bits of debris hit their defense fields and flew harmlessly away.

Ryn grinned viciously as he targeted another victim. He plied his controls and let loose with a shot from the nova cannon. The ball of fire tore through space and blew the nose off a second carrier. Numerous secondary explosions followed as the ship began its death throes. Its front end gone, the vessel tipped precariously downward as it was struck by an anti-matter missile from another ship. The once proud carrier erupted gouts of flame; her sides were pitted and blackened. At last she exploded noiselessly in the dark of space.

The Kraken joined the hunt soon after. She swooped in from above a hapless Prescottian. Missile tubes launched their deadly cargo. An FAL blast sheared the enemy's bridge right off its foundation. The missiles found their marks seconds later. The unshielded carrier was buffeted by six successive impacts. She slewed one way then another as the warheads did their work. Another FAL blast ended it as the lifeless hulk began to drift.

The Kraken was not yet done. It followed up its scrapping of the third carrier with a shot of its nova cannon on the fourth. This vessel was not quite as unaware as her doomed sisters were. Her defense fields were partially raised by this point, but it mattered little. The nova cannon, at point blank range, went through the field like a flimsy curtain. Raw energy splattered over the hull. A breach opened up amidships. A blizzard of frozen atmosphere clouded the view screen as equipment and men were blasted into space.

Martin could not believe his luck. The confusion his tactic had caused was more than he could have hoped. The troop transports and support craft bringing up the rear began to back away in panic. Their retreat was uncoordinated and soon became a rout. Martin watched with unsuppressed glee as two transports collided in their haste to escape. A cargo vessel had its displacement engine sheared off when it got too close to a neighbor. In little more than three minutes, Martin had closed the odds to ten to three in carrier strength, but he was not done by a long shot. He gritted his teeth and pressed the advantage.

The Prescottians were beginning to firm up. Defense fields were activated, weapons became hot. A fifth carrier was put out of commission before a counter attack could be attempted. The capital ships that had flown past were receiving orders to return. The remaining Prescottian carriers tried to start launching fighters, but here a bold plan was hatched by Martin's commanding pilot.

Captain Alyssa Godfrey was a crafty veteran. She had seen many campaigns and had thirty seven victories to her credit. She put her canny mind to work and evened the odds further. The captain took her squadron and maneuvered them to the mouths of the enemy's fighter launch tubes. She began strafing these, putting many out of commission. Other squadron leaders quickly picked up on her tactic and began the same maneuver. They greatly slowed the Prescottian's launch, but the good captain was not yet finished. Those tubes that were still active, for even her best efforts could not destroy them all, were guarded by a trio of her best pilots. As enemy fighters emerged, they were simply destroyed. Dozens were disposed of in this way before the tables began to turn.

The Prescottians had been completely surprised, but they too were veterans. Their admiral was experienced, and his men were good. They began to fight back. Anti-aircraft batteries took their toll on the brave Protectorate flyers. Some fighters did make it into space and Captain Godfrey's men now had something new to deal with. Martin's vessels began taking hits. Casualty reports were coming in. The battle was now fully joined.

After ten minutes the situation was like this: Martin's forces had destroyed or crippled six carriers with all their spacecraft on board. Another three had their launch tubes crushed by fighter weapons. A further forty five space fighters had been destroyed right out of the tubes. A good beginning to be sure, but as Martin started the assault on the seventh carrier he suffered his first major loss.

The battleship P.I.V. Hadrian began a turn that would take it back into the fray. As she began to maneuver, she was jumped by three Prescottian destroyers. The fast ships darted and danced around the behemoth. She was too far away to get help from any Protectorate forces. The big ship fought valiantly taking two of the enemy with her. The remaining destroyer stayed with her long enough for a Prescottian battleship to close the range. Already damaged by her struggle with the smaller ships, she was easy pickings for the unscathed monster. A plasma bolt caught her in the aft armor belt. Metal splintered and crumpled under the force of the hit. The Prescottian gunner targeted the weak spot and immediately fired an antimatter device. Finding no resistance by either energy or armor, the missile burrowed deep into the ship before exploding. The one thousand, six hundred beings knew no more as their ship was virtually disintegrated. Martin sent a silent thought out to them as something even more dangerous fought for his attention.

A Prescottian cruiser had made its way through Martin's thinning defense perimeter. The menacing vessel had the Hornet in her sights and let loose with a withering volley of fire. There was no way Jaspa's ship could escape. Martin watched in horror and impotence knowing there was nothing he could do, but another brave man saw and made one final selfless act.

Lt. Commander Jyka Calrondo watched as his ship fell apart around him. His little destroyer, the Starling, had suffered many hits. He had ordered his ship abandoned when he saw the drama unfolding before him on his damaged viewer. He saw the cruiser slip in and bracket the Hornet.

He knew the Hornet could not take evasive action, neither could her defense fields hold at such close range; she would be destroyed for certain. As the cruiser launched its death strike, Lt. Commander Calrondo shoved as much power as he could through his limping engines. The brave and battered destroyer got herself between the Hornet and her attacker and took the brunt of the assault. Energy crackled over her already scorched hull. There was no contest. The little ship blew itself to pieces. Lt. Commander Calrondo's sacrifice saved the lives of thousands and rallied the Protectorate forces.

Martin saw the amazing maneuver by the Starling. The Europa and another Protectorate destroyer jumped on the enemy cruiser reducing it to slag in a matter of moments. The admiral saw yet another carrier spew its guts into space as a surgical FAL beam, courtesy of Ryn, opened her like a sardine can. He also watched as one of his own cruisers spun out of control away from the fighting. Enemy fighters swooped down like vultures and finished the job.

The Kraken was fighting valiantly up front. She already had two carriers, a cruiser, and destroyer to her credit, but enemy fire was starting to take its toll. Her starboard stabilizer was out and she was in danger of overloading her main power coupling. Commodore Randolph Scott stood on his bridge and weathered the storm. He was a family man with a wife and four children. He was in the middle of a distinguished and still very promising career. He was ordering a flank speed turn when the deck flew out from under him. He smashed his head and would never know the fate of his vessel. It may have been just as well that he spent his final moments in peaceful darkness. A plasma bolt smashed into a fusion engine vent. The reactors blew and the aft section of the ship skittered off into space. The ship lurched one last time and went up in a titanic explosion. The P.I.V. Kraken entered the history books as a loss at the Battle of Dryad.

*   *   *

Lt. (j.g.) Charles Preston was in love. He caressed the controls of his fighter as if it were a living thing as he piloted his "Devastator" class ship through the battle. He weaved between vessels in a graceful dance, his ship alive around him. Ah! An enemy fighter. Preston patted his control board affectionately as he began an intercept vector. He lined up his prey and pulled the trigger on his FAL guns. The enemy fighter literally came apart engines to nose as it was reduced to metal confetti. This was Preston's third kill of the day. He loved his ship, the battle, and his life. He came around for a really good shot on one of those big bastard carriers. He dodged and weaved his way through anti-aircraft bursts that lit space around him. His multi-barreled gun spat fire that rainbowed across the carrier's defense fields. He followed up the "dimple" he had made in the field with a missile. He whooped as an explosion tore the enemy's hull open. Preston pulled up hard and came around for another pass.

As he flew through the blossoming fire around him, the young lieutenant felt a hard thump. Sirens began to blare; he had not even seen what had hit him. His fusion engine was jammed in full forward. He had maneuvering jets but he knew immediately that they would not be enough to save him from a collision. He was too close and moving too fast. He made a decision. He armed the remainder of his missiles and then saw what he wanted; an empty fighter launch tube. He used his thrusters to turn ever so slightly. He lined his doomed fighter up with the tube and started firing for all he was worth. He actually made it halfway down the opening before a wing tip brushed the wall. Lt. (j.g.) Charles Preston and his one true love, a "Devastator" fighter, annihilated themselves. The tiny ship's fuel and weapons exploded. A huge gash was blown in the enemy's side. The fuel and ammunition in the launch bay went up in a fatal chain reaction. The Prescottian carrier blew its insides into space becoming the first capital ship to be destroyed by a single fighter.

Another fighter in a different part of the battle was destined for something else. The "Perseus" class ship was a sleek two man job. It was designed for speed and maneuverability; thus it carried little ordinance. It really did not need much apart from its powerful twin FAL cannons, but these fighters did possess four anti-aircraft missiles.

Ensign Donald Pultrain had never been in battle before. As he nervously glided his ship from the Yorktown, he began to sweat. This was not a normal launch, but the young man pulled it off well. Petty Officer Dwight Vanderlear complimented Donald from his seat behind the pilot. The command was given and off they went!

Donald spent the early part of the battle harassing the huge carriers and trying to avoid anti-aircraft hits. It was later, when the enemy carriers were able to launch fighters of their own that Donald became one of the best pilots of all time.

"Here they come sir, two from above." The petty officer's warning turned out to be superfluous as Donald had the enemy on his scope. He throttled down on his small craft bleeding speed and confusing his pursuers. He pushed his nose up and hit the reverse thrust. The befuddled foe flew right past Donald and into the open; just like in simulation! Donald opened up with his cannon. The first fighter blew into a million pieces and Donald kept pouring it on. He grazed the second fighter and sent it into a spin causing it to slam into a destroyer close by. The flight computer unemotionally recorded the two kills. Petty officer Vanderlear hollered, "That got 'em sir! Let's go get that bastard up front!"

Donald punched his afterburners and went after his next victim. This Prescottian was a wily one and led Donald a merry chase, dodging and weaving through the fleet. Donald squinted and finally lined up his adversary. He squeezed off a shot that blew a wing from the enemy's fuselage. It spun for awhile before exploding. That made three.

"We've got one on our tail!" exclaimed Donald's navigator. Dwight quickly put his shields on double aft, this split second decision saved both their lives. As soon as the young enlisted man fortified their defense fields, the Prescottian fighter caught Donald with a blast of plasma. The fighter shook and swayed but held together. Donald quickly dodged to the right and the enemy over committed. Donald wasted no time; he came hard over and peppered the Prescottian fuselage. Donald flew through the explosion. As his vision cleared he saw another fighter in his field. He opened up on this luckless victim too. It exploded in spectacular fashion. Five kills! In barely two minutes Donald had become an ace!

As the space around him cleared, Donald saw a large shape looming before him. Dwight yelled, "Donny, that there's a Prescottian battleship, better break off!"

Donald nodded, "Not until we give them a little present." He toggled the arming switches on his missiles. He danced and swooped through blistering anti-aircraft fire. Finally he saw what he was looking for. The enemy bridge filled his scope. He fired. The first two missiles crippled the bridge defense field; the second two obliterated the bridge itself. Brain dead, the immense ship drifted as the Prescottians desperately scrambled to their auxiliary control stations. They were too late. A squadron of heavier fighters off the Enterprise saw Donald's maneuver and began to pump energy and antimatter into the blinded monster. When it was all over, the enemy vessel had been pulverized. Ensign Donald Pultrain won the Protectorate Cross for his deeds at the Battle of Dryad and is still remembered as one of the greatest fighter pilots of all time.

Aboard the Europa things were starting to break down. Martin had had a good run of it for awhile, but the simple number of Prescottian ships was starting to win out. At this point in the battle, Martin's forces had destroyed or hopelessly crippled nine of the fourteen carriers, and heavily damaged a tenth. One hundred ninety seven enemy fighters had been destroyed apart from those taken out on the wrecked carriers. The admiral's ships had also wiped out three destroyers, two cruisers, and a battleship. In the mass confusion at the start of the battle, four transports and a cargo ship had the decency to destroy themselves, thus saving Martin the trouble later on.

These victories had not come free, however. Martin had lost about 40% of his fighters. Two battleships, a cruiser and a destroyer had also been eliminated. Many of the remainder of Martin's ships were also damaged. He was quickly running out of options. As Martin received a report from his sensor officer, he counted up the forces against his; five carriers, four battleships, thirteen cruisers, and seventeen destroyers. An inventory of his own ships yielded; three carriers, two battleships, five cruisers and eight destroyers. Martin had done what he set out to accomplish; he had greatly reduced the enemy carrier force, but if help did not arrive soon, Martin was bound to lose his entire task force.

Captain Vliah Barsh had come to the same conclusion. His cruiser, the Crimson Blade would not be leaving this battle. She was badly damaged. Her displacement drive was out, as were many of her other systems. There would be no escape, but Captain Barsh wanted to even the odds a bit more before his part in the drama was over. He ordered an attack run on the damaged Prescottian carrier. The captain had scanned the ship himself as his sensor officer was dead, and noticed that the enemy vessel's port side defense fields were all but gone. The valiant cruiser limped into weapons range. Captain Barsh gave the order and twin beams of light cut through the darkness. The hit was too much for the battered carrier. It swayed drunkenly before all the lights on board went out. Its engines went dead as all power leaked into space. The hulk would never fight again.

Captain Barsh figured he had enough power for one more strike. He carefully maneuvered his stubborn wounded vessel around the wreckage of the carrier. Apart from himself, there were only two crewmembers alive on the bridge. He channeled every ounce of power into his nova cannon. As the Crimson Blade emerged from cover, a Prescottian battleship filled the screen. The captain gave the noble cruiser the last command she would ever obey. The nova cannon belched out every erg of power the captain could give it. The deadly bolt struck the battleship in the starboard quarter. The once mighty vessel heaved and rocked as its starboard displacement engine and fusion pod sailed away into space. The ship did not explode, but it was plain to see that her day was through.

The shot was nearly as disastrous for the Crimson Blade. Consoles all over the bridge sparked with overloaded circuits. The nova cannon itself exploded, taking much of deck six with it. The lights went dead as every system on board shut down. Captain Barsh surveyed his handiwork. With a satisfied expression and a slight moistness in his eyes he said two words, "Abandon ship."

Martin watched the Prescottian battleship drift away into the void trailing debris and fuel. He stood in awe of the bravery and ability of the people under his command. No matter what happened, he made sure that this day would be remembered, and the super human actions of his force would not be in vain. Martin ordered the launch of several recorder drones. He hoped that at least one would be picked up by Admiral Beedle or some other Protectorate commander. He sat as his ship shook with a grazing hit and prepared for the end.

There was nothing else to do but inflict as much damage as he could before his ships could fight no more. A Protectorate destroyer careened across the viewer as it too succumbed to enemy blasts. Ryn was returning fire at a furious pace, but the Prescottians were finally closing in. Another destroyer had its guts blown out as enemy fighters tore into her. Anti-aircraft fire from the Europa blasted two more enemy ships as they dove at the command vessel. The Prescottian fighters were drawing ever closer to the carriers. As Martin's perimeter shrank, so did his chances of survival.

Martin listlessly punched several commands into his arm console. He waited as a comm link was established with the Hornet. Jaspa's face lit the screen just as her ship shuddered with a missile hit. The view behind her was not encouraging. Her soot smudged face was backlit by sparking consoles and smoke. Martin figured that he could not have looked much better.

Martin began, "I know this is against every rule in the book, but I had to see you one last time. You are the most remarkable, beautiful, and fascinating woman I have had the honor and privilege to be associated with. The time I spent with you was the best of my life. If you should survive me, please don't grieve. I will always be with you. I'll be there to warm you when you get cold, comfort you when you're frightened, walk with you when you're alone. Cherish the memories of me as I cherish mine of you, and I will never truly be gone. My Jaspa. You have completed me. You filled the empty spaces in my heart and I will forever be grateful to you. Live and remember me. I will always love you."

Jaspa's face was one of raw emotion. She brushed the image of Martin with her fingers and nodded, "I too love you with every fiber of my being, but we will be together after this battle, whether in life or death I do not know, but I feel . . . I know . . . that we were meant to be together." She let a small smile play across her mouth as she broke the circuit.

Martin sighed and leaned back in his chair overcome with emotion and nearly exhausted. The Europa rocked with a hit. The sensor officer looked up from his board and shouted, "Sir, I'm picking up several vessels closing fast!"

Martin stirred at the announcement. The officer continued, "I detect thirty seven ships of varying size."

Only thirty seven. Admiral Beedle had a force of at least ninety ships. This could mean only one thing; enemy reinforcements. The game was over.

"Time to intercept?"

"Ten minutes, eighteen seconds!"

They were that close then! The Europa's long range sensors must have been down to leave them that blind. Martin nodded his head. He had fought the good fight and could only hope the fleet arrived in time to follow up on his victory. Martin turned to Ryn, "Concentrate all remaining fire power on the closest carrier." As Ryn began to obey, the bridge canted to starboard in a nauseating twist. Debris fell from the ceiling, a piece of which landed on Martin's left arm, breaking it cleanly.

Ryn grunted in frustration and rage. He fired on the closest enemy ship. The carrier was buffeted and began to roll. Ryn was relentless in his pursuit of the enemy. He drained FAL power as he launched strike after strike. The carrier returned fire, but only one blast found its mark. The Prescottian seemed to stall in space before exploding in a kaleidoscope of color.

"Admiral, the lead vessel is hailing us."

Martin looked at his comm officer in confusion. They must be broadcasting terms of surrender. The admiral walked over to the young officer while cradling his wrecked arm. "Put them on speaker."

A voice that Martin never hoped to hear again came across the space waves. Admiral Beedle, a smile in his speech, came on, "Admiral Gammage, I think you've done enough for one day. Break off your attack and go after those troop transports. Sorry the whole fleet is not here to greet you, but they'll be along. I ordered all vessels to proceed at top speed so the slower ships are behind us. Well done, Marty. We'll take it from here. Admiral Beedle out."

Martin took in the sound of his deliverance. He slowly shook his head as if to clear it and said, "Recall our fighters to a safe distance. We'll take them on board when we clear the battle zone. Order all craft to retreat toward the incoming ships. Let's close the range. After we break off, all ships that are able will pursue the troop transports, they won't have gotten far."

No order was ever executed more cheerfully. Only a cruiser and destroyer were not fast enough to escape and became the last casualties Martin suffered. All three Protectorate carriers were intact while only three enemy counterparts were still under way. Some of the more lightly damaged ships sailed happily away to destroy the lightly armed troop carriers. Martin slumped into his command chair. A sense of overwhelming peace and contentment warred with his exhaustion. He had won a great victory.

*   *   *

The following is an excerpt from Admiral Beedle's battle report of the Battle of Dryad:

We owe our complete victory to the herculean effort of Rear Admiral Martin Gammage. He not only foresaw the Prescottian incursion into the Dryad system; he fought a truly inspired battle against impossible odds. His small force inflicted so much damage on the enemy that when the fleet arrived there was little left to do but mop up. Not a single enemy carrier or troop transport escaped our guns.

Before the battle, Rear Admiral Gammage remarked to me that his carriers bore the names of those the United States used at the battle of Midway. And like that battle 583 years ago, the Dryad victory is a turning point in this war. I recommend the promotion of Martin Gammage to Vice Admiral. I further recommend he be given a fleet of his own.

If he manages an entire fleet like he did T.F. 92, I have no doubt that this war will soon be over.

Chapter IX: VICE ADMIRAL
November 6, 2526
Sector 374a P.I.V. Triumph

The two beasts walked the busy corridors of the ship. They were magnificent animals, both Sanarian hounds. The woman strode behind them nodding at the respectful glances cast her way by officers and crew. The female hound, Teddi, was jet black and stood three feet at the shoulder. One could easily see the intelligence in her eyes. Indy, her mate, was slightly larger and heavier. He scanned the passageway with his yellow irises, taking everything in. His snow white body rippled with muscular flesh. Sanarian hounds were difficult to tame, but once domesticated, they remained fiercely loyal to their masters their entire lives, usually some fifty five years.

The woman stopped at a door right behind the animals. She stroked each in turn; she loved them very much, as did the occupant of the quarters they were about to enter. The woman opened the door and stepped inside. She removed her uniform jacket that displayed two silver stars on each shoulder cap. A man entered the room from the bathing chamber and gathered the woman into a tender embrace. The two dogs watched their masters and almost . . . almost smiled.

"Take them for their walk?"

"Yes" replied the woman; "They do enjoy it so. I also stopped at the practice range. Indy is getting so much better." The woman was referring to the Sanarian hounds ability to throw energy from their bodies. The animals were capable of stunning a humanoid at long range and killing one up to twelve feet away.

"Any news I should be aware of?" inquired the man as he began to dress.

"Not that I know of. The fleet is still on course for the Aldonian System. The Triumph is still flying like a dream."

The ship they were on was the first and only of its kind, although Protectorate shipyards were scrambling to build four more. The Triumph class command ship was an engineering masterpiece from a martial point of view. As a warship she had no equal. At 4,267 feet in length, she was the longest in the fleet. She carried ninety six fighters and six shuttlecrafts. She also embarked a Stinger class attack ship that had the punch of a small destroyer. The Triumph came equipped with the most advanced armament package ever incorporated into a Protectorate vessel. A two layered defense grid protected her heavily armored hull. Two nova cannon were fire linked to provide devastating offensive power. Ten antimatter missile launchers (6 forward, 4 aft) were experimental models to accommodate the new Mark VII antimatter device. These weapons were 80% more powerful than their predecessors were. Forty two FAL emplacements provided surgical precision in the hands of an experienced gunner. The Triumph was a marvelous ship and Martin felt privileged to fly his flag aboard her.

The vice admiral finished dressing and embraced Jaspa once again. Now a rear admiral herself, Jaspa acted as Martin's top aide. They had decided, after their close call at Dryad, to never be separated again, and at such high rank, they had the ability to see their wishes carried out. The lovers shared these spacious, and there was no other word for it, luxurious quarters. Martin had sent for Indy and Teddy when he became Deputy Commander of the 11th Fleet. The dogs had been with Martin for twelve years, and when he joined the military, he entrusted them to his father's care. Admiral Beedle was still in charge, but he commanded from afar at New Freemantle. Both he and Martin knew who truly ran the fleet and this situation agreed with both of them.

Another friend made the trip with Jaspa and Martin. Ryn had eschewed a command of his own to stay on Martin's staff. Ryn, now a commodore, was senior tactical advisor to Vice Admiral Gammage.

The war had finally taken a turn in the Protectorate's favor. The crippling losses at Dryad had opened the Prescottian's lines and Martin was quick to take advantage. The 11th Fleet moved its advance bases into the Dryad System. The surrounding sectors quickly fell as Martin blitzed through only light resistance. The Prescottians had to give up territory for time as they tried to consolidate their remaining forces.

Martin kept the pressure on and destroyed a Prescottian shipyard at Lyngol IX. He then leveled Halrunion I, an extremely important source of Prescottian ores and other resources. At the Nule System, Martin met and crushed another Prescottian fleet. His forces destroyed forty six ships while only losing nine. Martin's victories were beginning to be noticed by the admiralty. In this year's voting, Martin received 61% of the ballots. Admiral Morta got only 20%. Martin's old nemesis was finished in the race for Fleet Admiral after the debacle at Finian VI. Morta's fleet was badly mauled by a smaller force. Elements of the 20th and 21st fleets had to bail him out. The last Martin had heard, the aging admiral was on Earth trying to regain his badly cracked power base. Martin put the old man in the correct perspective. Morta was disgraced, but not yet ruined. There was still a war to win, and Martin found he could strike back at Morta by doing what he did best, command. Martin had his cake and ate it too.

The 11th fleet was now headed for the Aldonian System deep within Prescottian territory. This would be the first real strike at the vitals of the enemy. If Aldonia could be taken, the next stop could very well be Prescottia itself. Martin had lost much sleep preparing for the upcoming contest. His fleet was the spearhead of the Protectorate campaign. All other fleets were engaged in holding actions along the front. The 12th fleet had been moved to back up Martin's thrust. The vice admiral had a great deal to gain . . . or lose depending on the outcome of the mission.

"Ready?" asked Martin.

"Just one minute," came the reply. Jaspa threw her uniform jacket over one shoulder and nodded.

The two made their way to the bridge. Captain Jason Briggs was in command. An able officer, Briggs was hand picked by Jaspa to command the Triumph. He had proven himself as a frigate captain in the fleet's other battles.

"Now approaching the Aldonian System," announced the captain as the two admirals took their places. As soon as they were seated, Ryn appeared as the lift doors parted. He smiled at his friends and relieved a junior officer at the tactical post. Martin shook his head. Even at the high rank of commodore, Ryn just could not keep his hands off the weapons controls.

"Long range scan," ordered the captain.

A junior lieutenant adjusted her controls. She looked puzzled for a moment and finally said, "No contacts."

"Nothing?" inquired Martin as he stood and walked over to the sensor position. Aldonia was a vital Prescottian system. Martin could not believe they would leave it unguarded.

"I do not detect any vessels sir, not so much as a scout ship, however . . ."

"Yes, lieutenant?"

"However, there is a strange reading coming from a hydrogen cloud near the system."

"Analysis," ordered Martin.

"I can't really make anything of it sir. It is simply an anomalous reading. Like something solid in a gaseous cloud."

"I see." Martin turned toward Ryn who rewarded the admiral with a sardonic twist of his mouth.

The big man spoke, "Our friends are hiding in there." He said it with such conviction that Martin immediately nodded his head in agreement.

"They'll wait until we start landing troops with our defense fields down, then they'll jump us. That's what I would do. The problem is, we have no way of knowing their strength."

Ryn frowned, "We can launch the Stinger on a recon mission."

Jaspa chose this moment to speak out, "True, but she might get detected and force the Prescottians to jump. We want to trap the trappers.

Martin nodded, "I agree with you admiral, however, I want to know their strength. Captain, launch the Stinger with full sensor countermeasures."

"Aye sir." Captain Briggs said before giving the proper orders.

About ten minutes passed. The huge hanger doors of the massive ship parted and the sleek destroyer escort shot into space. It ducked and weaved around other ships in the fleet trying to confuse anyone that might be watching. It was the sensor officer's opinion that the hydrogen cloud would befoul the Prescottian sensors, but Martin was taking no chances.

As the Stinger closed the range, Martin and his ships waited. Finally, after what seemed an eternity, a garbled message came through " . . . definitely Prescottian . . . six . . . one carrier . . . standard formation . . ."

The communications officer looked up, "I'm sorry sir, the hydrogen cloud is interfering with their signal."

An irritated Admiral Gammage replied, "I gathered that, ensign. Ask them to repeat their message. If we cannot get a clear transmission, tell them to return to base."

The embarrassed young man sent the message. Again an incomprehensible reply reached the Triumph. Martin began to pace as he waited for the Stinger to return. He could not move until he knew the enemy strength. Thirty minutes passed, then an hour, and still no word since the second garbled transmission. The sensor officer reported no movement in the immediate vicinity and no explosions to indicate that the Stinger had come to a bad end. What could be keeping her?

Finally a blip appeared on the scanners, close aboard. Weapons turrets locked on but were not needed. The Stinger requested docking instructions and was granted immediate clearance. "Get her commanding officer up here as soon as she's in!" shouted Martin.

Soon thereafter, a young officer appeared on the bridge, "Lt. Commander Syth Palagrun reporting as ordered sir."

"What the hell happened?" Martin exclaimed as he took in the officer's disheveled appearance. He was blackened on one side of his body. Purple blood oozed down one shoulder and off his fingers.

"We encountered a scout vessel on the backside of the cloud as we circled to make it back to the fleet. We crippled her; she will not . . ." His words were labored, " . . . not report to the Prescottians. We counted . . . counted forty two ships . . . four carriers . . . many heavy vessels . . . did not see us . . ." the young Dranian's eyes rolled back as he fainted.

"Get a medic up here and put this guy in for a medal." Martin was smiling as he put pressure on the commander's shoulder. He looked up from the deck, "Now we've got them. Tell Major General DeGrasse to prepare for a ground assault on the fourth planet. They'll go in unescorted. Meanwhile, prepare a long range probe with an antimatter warhead. The Prescottians may have picked a hydrogen cloud to obscure our sensors, but if I remember my chemistry, hydrogen makes a big boom when ignited. We'll use our attack ships to pick up the pieces after the explosion. Go now!"

Officers scattered to do Martin's bidding. Ryn personally oversaw the arming of the "Seeker" probe with a Class V antimatter warhead. The thing was rigged to blow in the exact center of the cloud. Sixteen drop ships broke off from the main body of the fleet on their way to the undefended fourth planet. The remainder of the vessels, all warships, wheeled around and started for the hydrogen cloud. A single launch tube glowed on the bow of the Triumph as the probe was sent on its way. The 11th fleet closed on the cloud but slowed significantly outside the predicted range of the explosion.

"I'm detecting movement within the cloud boundary!" Exclaimed the sensor officer just as the probe burrowed into the volatile hydrogen.

Ryn and Martin both grinned, and as if they shared the same brain, both muttered, "Too late."

A titanic explosion ripped through space. Martin was grateful that sound could not be heard through the vacuum. He could only imagine what this powerful a blast would sound like. A halo of stunning violet surrounded a mantle of umber and brighter red. Greens and blues tinged the outer cove of the turbulent mass. The center was a blinding white. Martin could only guess at the temperature in the middle of the cloud. The shockwave reached the fleet. Many ships swayed a bit before their internal stabilizers could catch up with the ripples in space.

The blinding light started to recede. The sensor technicians worked frantically to see the results of the cunning move by their leader. Any vessels near the center of the cloud had been simply obliterated. All that was left were some free floating molecules. Farther out, the damage was less extensive and many ships could still fight. Martin prepared his ships for battle. He quickly took stock of the situation and ordered a snap census of the remaining Prescottians.

Of the forty two ships the valiant Lt. Commander Palagrun had reported, only thirty four remained. Of those, only twenty five could maneuver. The other six were drifting aimlessly, their hulls blackened and charred by the devastating holocaust.

"Let's tighten up. Formation 6C. Send to all ships: Set battle formation. Battle lines may attack at will." Martin's order went out to his seventy nine ships of the line. He decided not to risk the lives of his brave fighter pilots in such a lopsided engagement. They were far too valuable a resource to waste.

A magnificent sight unfolded on the main viewer. Martin's ships lined up in nine rows of eight. His seven carriers took up the rear position, as they would likely not be needed. The battle wagons were in the center of the lines while lighter, faster ships took up positions on the flanks. It was a truly awe-inspiring display and Martin felt pride in his men, his ships, and the Protectorate. When the lines were set, he released the hounds.

The first wave, which included the Triumph, broke off and made their attack run. The smaller ships strafed a damaged cruiser. Their quick precision bursts struck home. Chunks of metal flew from the stricken vessel. She keeled over as a missile caught a support strut. A blocky fusion engine broke away and exploded close aboard. The Prescottian lamely returned fire, but the fresh defense fields of the needle like destroyers easily absorbed the impacts. The battered cruiser finally succumbed to the harassing fire. Her lights went out. She drifted helplessly; dead.

The destroyers peeled off, leaving the way open for bigger guns. Ryn lightly worked his controls aboard the Triumph. He brought the double barreled nova cannon around to bear on a damaged battleship. Ryn was about to use the massive weapon for the first time in battle. The Triumph rolled as her defense fields were pummeled by fire from the big ship. Martin looked on as one of his cruisers to starboard engaged another enemy. The range was closing.

At the optimum moment, Ryn loosed a bolt of coruscating death upon the doomed Prescottian. The twin balls of energy crackled over the short distance they traveled. The burst struck the enemy. For a tiny fraction of a second, the view on the screen seemed to freeze. A bright shimmer effect engulfed the battleship as its defense fields were used up and burnt out in a flash. The remaining destructive force met bare hull. The metal just melted away. Molten material seemed to bleed into the space around the dying craft. Huge chunks of superstructure tore loose and careened into another luckless Prescottian ship aft of the crippled monster. Finally, another horrendous flash filled the screen. When everyone's eye adjusted, the battleship was gone. Ryn simply nodded and said, "Good gun."

The Triumph completed its run and came about to return to her formation. The nova cannon was recharging but this did not stop Ryn from using the aft weapons package to annihilate a destroyer that got too close.

"Admiral! Detecting fighter launches from the lone Prescottian carrier."

"Shit. I was hoping we would not have to use our fighters. Have the Hornet, Yorktown, Independence and Pongee launch immediately. We should have a five to one superiority. That should make quick work of the enemy fighters."

Martin had issued the orders just as another Prescottian ship, a frigate this time, shattered like a piece of glass struck with a hammer.

Martin turned to Ryn, "Was that the experimental molecular degrader weapon aboard the Calysto?"

Ryn nodded, "Yes. Very impressive. The ship just broke into a thousand pieces when its hull material was destabilized. Chalk one up for the boys in R and D."

Martin focused his attention back on the task at hand. His fleet was easily carving up the badly outmatched and decimated enemy contingent. His fighters were blasting the foe from the stars. Things could not be better.

"Report coming in from Brigadier General Salsettia." The female Tipinian was second in command of the ground forces.

"Let's hear what she has to say," intoned Martin.

The amazingly delicate voice of the general could barely be heard above the cacophony of battle around her. "We have landed all sixteen drop ships with only one loss. The Paul Revere was shot down by a surface to air missile. She was pretty close to the ground so many of her contingent survived. Resistance thus far has been spirited but scattered. We are ahead of schedule. Colonel Green has broken through their primary defense line and Colonel Dyane has flanked the enemy. We are continuing to attack from two sides. Casualties are light. I estimate only 620 so far and this figure includes the losses on the Paul Revere. I hope things are going well for you Admiral. Standby for further reports. Out."

All was proceeding according to Martin's design. This system would soon be in the hands of the Protectorate. A truly glorious victory was at hand with a minimum of casualties. Martin reveled at being in command of a sparkling fleet.

"Admiral. I am receiving a message on the surrender/ parlay band. It is coming from the Prescottian carrier."

Sure enough, the enemy fighters were breaking off and the capital ships were trying to gain space to fall back.

"Order all vessels to cease fire. Fighters will return to base. Put me on screen."

Within seconds, the crested head of the Prescottian commander filled the viewer, "I am Draaken Daala." A Draaken was roughly equivalent in rank to a rear admiral.

Martin nodded at the image on the screen. "Vice Admiral Martin Gammage."

"Vice Admiral," the enemy rolled the "r" slightly as he spoke, "We are clearly outmatched and I have no desire to see the blood of my men run for no good cause." The Prescottian closed his eyes. This was clearly difficult for him and Martin hoped the tables would never be turned. "I request your terms for our surrender."

Martin again nodded but inside he was surprised. This Prescottian Draaken was truly honorable and Martin was prepared to offer generous terms, "You will immediately power down all your vessel's systems with the exception of life support. Then, one at a time, your ships will launch their life craft to the third moon of the sixth planet in this system. The moon can support you until a Protectorate occupation force arrives to move your men to a prisoner camp. You will be a guest aboard this vessel. You will be given accommodations, however, you will be under house arrest and shall not be permitted to leave your quarters. Once all of your ships have been evacuated, they will be destroyed."

"Your terms are generous and accepted Vice Admiral. I see that your reputation for fairness is well deserved. I salute you. I will begin preparations immediately. Even as an enemy, I must thank you for sparing my men and not killing needlessly."

The signal was cut. Martin was truly impressed by this particular officer. Perhaps Prescottians would be a valuable addition to the Protectorate when the war came to an end. Martin finally believed that the end was drawing near. With the capture of this system, the final campaign could begin, and the killing could end.

An operations officer came onto the bridge and walked over to Jaspa, "I have our casualty reports, Ma'am."

"Very well."

"The destroyer Palma has been lost with all hands. The Hatchet was also destroyed but many of her crew escaped. The Argo is now engaged in picking up survivors. The Neil Armstrong is hopelessly crippled. I have made arrangements to have the survivors taken off, we will then destroy her. A number of ships have minor to moderate damage but all are reparable. In total, our losses are two destroyers and a light cruiser. We have also lost seven fighters. Total casualties are nine hundred sixteen dead and five hundred thirteen wounded."

Jaspa closed her eyes. The losses were light, but the war had been going on so long that she felt the pain of each casualty. "Very well commander. Send the more heavily damaged ships back to New Freemantle. The 12th Fleet can replace the vessels we lost. Send a message immediately to replace the two destroyers and cruiser." She looked over at Martin who nodded his agreement.

Two hours passed as the fleet took on the tedious job of scuttling the enemy ships and the Neil Armstrong. The prisoners were made as comfortable as possible. Martin had been informed that an occupation force was leaving immediately from New Freemantle. The ground assault had also been brought to a successful conclusion at the cost of

1,063 marines. Martin sat stoically in his chair for a moment as he said a silent farewell to all the good beings that had lost their lives in the performance of their duty. They had made possible the victory that was the stepping stone to Prescottia itself, and the end of the war.

*   *   *

Martin walked down to the shuttle bay with Ryn to greet their prisoner. They shared some empty pleasantries as they escorted the Draaken to his quarters. Martin did not expect to get information from him and did not intend to try. The Prescottian expressed his surprise when he was led into his VIP accommodations. Martin said that the Draaken had earned special consideration for his ingenuity in trying to use the hydrogen cloud for camouflage, his valor in combat, and his willingness to sacrifice his pride in surrender for the sake of his men. Following Martin's lead, Ryn told the Draaken that he would be at his disposal if he had any questions, wants, or needs.

The two left the VIP section and started for the senior officer's quarters. Ryn broke the companionable silence, "I wish more Prescottians were like that one."

Martin was forced to agree, "Yes. If they were, we would probably not be involved in this war in the first place. Our casualties were light, but like after any battle, I wonder if I could have done more to save additional lives."

"Oh please," intoned Martin's friend, "What you did at Dryad was damn near miraculous. You always do what's best for your men. I must admit though, even I am growing tired of the carnage. Our campaigns have been glorious and satisfying, but the killing must come to an end. I was reading the total casualty reports last night. We've lost two hundred and ninety three ships and over sixteen million lives, military and civilian. The Prescottians, I don't know how they still fight, have lost six hundred seven vessels and forty millions dead. I admire their tenacity but surely they must realize that the end is near. They only hold their internal lines and most central systems. The loss of Aldonia eliminates an important supply base. From here we can strike at Prescottia itself. They must see that."

Martin clapped Ryn on the back, "I'll tell you my friend that logically you are quite correct, but logic seldom enters the theater of war. The Japanese on my home planet were beaten in our second world war. They had virtually no shipping left and no territory other than their home islands. They were a proud people and would have fought to the end had it not been for the invention of atomic weapons. So you see, we may be fighting for quite some time. In my homeland's Civil War, the Southern forces fought until their men were eating only a handful of parched corn a day. I hope the Prescottians will see that their situation is hopeless, but this may only spur them on. I think there may be several battles yet to come. We can only do our jobs, inflict as many casualties as we can to bring them to their knees. Only then will they accept terms. You saw it in the Draaken's eyes. He was beaten, but still proud. We can only hope the Prescottian High Command will want to save Prescottian lives."

The two men turned a corner and came to a lift. As Ryn toggled the button, he turned to Martin, "On more mundane matters, the chief engineer informs me that we will be 100% in about two hours. I was pleased with the performance of the twin nova cannon."

"I figured you would be. The recharge time is a bit of a pain, but its sheer destructive power more than makes up for it."

The big man nodded, "Indeed. The battleship had full defenses and it was still annihilated." He reflected for a moment. "If just seemed to melt."

Martin nodded as he said, "It is a superior weapon. We'll really have something going when the Triumph's sister ships are built."

"Yes," replied the commodore, "I'll see you later, I have some business with the tactical officer."

"I'll see you at dinner." Martin watched his friend depart. He looked at the door controls in front of his quarters. The occupancy indicator reported that no one was inside. Jaspa must have taken the dogs out again. She loved to walk them and they could certainly use the exercise. It was more difficult to care for the creatures aboard ship, but Martin wanted them with him.

Martin opened the door and walked inside. The empty room was dimly lit. Martin ordered the lights on full, he intended to read before retiring. He had had a very busy day and he wanted to enjoy the fruits of victory. As he prepared to retrieve a book screen from his library, all hell broke loose.

Martin heard the bathroom door open behind him. This was odd as the quarters were supposed to be unoccupied. The slim woman was in uniform. Her rank badge indicated a second class petty officer assigned to cargo. Martin was surprised but not terribly concerned with this until he noticed the rather lethal FAL pistol she brandished in his direction.

Time seemed to telescope for Martin. He knew his life was about to end. There was absolutely no way he could avoid the woman's imminent shot, but he was damned if he was simply going to provide the assassin with a stationary target.

The woman smiled, "Good-bye Admiral." A number of things happened at once. The door to the quarters opened to reveal Jaspa, Teddy, and Indy. The male hound knew that the strange woman should not be in his home. He also had an instinctual reaction to the weapon. "This female plans to do my master harm!" the dog thought in his small yet astute mind.

Martin began to jump out of the way. Indy looked directly at the woman. Twin beams of light speared the intruder in the side. Her weapon went off, but her aim was spoiled by Indy's timely shot. Her bolt went down and wide. Instead of a direct hit, Martin was caught in the left shin by the crimson beam.

Time resumed normal speed. The woman screamed in pain and collapsed on the deck. Martin grimaced as his face twisted in agony. Jaspa rushed to the bulkhead comm unit and screamed, "Security and a medical team to Admiral Gammage's quarters now!"

Martin's pant leg was smoldering. The skin beneath was an ugly blistered mess. The woman was still breathing, but it was obvious that her wounds were quite serious. Indy had been a mere eight feet away when he shot her. Jaspa disarmed the unconscious woman and knelt at Martin's side.

"Are you all right?"

"I've . . . I've been better" Martin replied through clenched teeth.

The door opened to admit four security officers and Dr. Costantino, the ship's chief medical officer. Two medics brought up the rear. One of these began to treat Martin while the doctor tried to stabilize the intruder.

Jaspa ordered the security men to get a fingerprint and DNA identification of the woman. One security man took her print and pulled a hair from her head and slipped it into a portable analyzer. He left, promising to inform Jaspa as soon as he had anything.

Both Martin and the intruder were placed on stretchers and taken to sick bay. The woman would require immediate surgery. Doctor Costantino began work on her right away. Another doctor operated on Martin's leg. The burnt flesh and bone were quickly regenerated. Martin would have to wear a regeno-cast for a week however.

As the surgery on the woman continued, Martin and Jaspa received the security men in recovery. The security lieutenant began, "Our mystery woman came aboard listed as Petty Officer Second Class Mary Ann Koestner. She had been assigned to cargo bay five. DNA analysis reveals that she is really Lt. Commander Charlotte Little, a field operative for Admiral Cyrus Morta."

Jaspa slammed her fist against the wall, "Morta! I am going to deal with that bastard personally!"

Martin looked stricken for a moment before his face hardened to a stony expression, "He couldn't get rid of me by having me killed in battle, and he couldn't do it in the political arena. That 'Fleet Captain' crap backfired on him too. I look at this as the last gasp of a very desperate man." He looked over at the security officer, "I trust the locator panel on my door had been tampered with."

"Yes sir."

Martin shook his head and sighed. Jaspa spoke through clenched teeth, "Now we can ring up that worthless piece of dung. We'll have him court martialed and thrown out, or, preferably, shot."

Martin took her hand, "We can't. We have no real proof that the agent was sent by Morta to assassinate me. Just because she's one of his operatives does not mean he gave the order. We know he did, but he can simply deny everything. I'm sure he wasn't stupid enough to give his orders in front of witnesses. I'm also certain that there will be no "paper" trail either. Unless this would be assassin lives and is willing or can be coerced to testify, we have nothing."

Jaspa knew he was right. If this woman was a fanatic, and it was likely this was the case, she might very well take the fall for Morta by saying she was acting alone.

Martin continued, "I really think this was Morta's last card. He knew that if this attempt failed that I would make it impossible for anyone to get close enough again. It was a close thing anyway, far too close."

Doctor Costantino emerged from the operating suite. He got down to business immediately, "I can't save her. Her liver is gone along with her right kidney. She's in a coma and I doubt she'll regain consciousness. You, on the other hand, can leave sick bay tomorrow with a regeno-cast for seven to ten days. I hope you have a speedy recovery, Admiral."

"Thank you, doctor." Costantino nodded and withdrew. Martin continued, "Well, there goes any chance of nailing Morta, small as it was to begin with. Let's move on to more immediate concerns. Jaspa, you will be in command for forty eight hours. I have one more day in sick bay and then I will take twenty four hours to recuperate. I want you to secure this system until we are relieved by the occupation force. We will stay in system until they arrive. I will also draft a request for fifty additional ships. We are going to take the war right to the enemy. I figure with one more solid push, we can infiltrate all the way to Prescottia and finish this thing once and for all. Take care of my fleet, Jaspa." She kissed him sweetly and, without a word, turned on her heel and left.

*　　*　　*

December 30, 2526
Aldonia System

Martin put a small pill in his mouth and swallowed. It was the last of the regentin he needed for his leg. The wound had been painful for a time, but it had finally healed adequately. It had not caused him significant pain for a week or so although Dr. Costantino told him that an intermittent ache would be with him for the rest of his life.

His would be assassin never regained consciousness and died sixty hours after the incident. Martin, Ryn, and Jaspa all blamed Morta for the attempt, but with no real proof, a court martial was out of the question. Martin had decided that they would bide their time.

The last several weeks had gone well. The Protectorate's hold on the system became more secure with the arrival of the occupation force. Martin's ships had time to repair their battle damage and four fresh vessels replaced their minimal losses almost immediately. What troubled Martin was the lack of orders to follow up on the victory. He had anticipated the arrival of some fifty ships, not four. Whenever he requested a status report or orders to move, he was met by bureaucratic nonsense and double talk. Martin could not understand what was going on.

For two weeks now, he had basically nothing to do. Rear Admiral Charles Sabo was in command of the occupying vessels and Major General Tywracha Coshin was the viceroy of the only inhabited planet in the system. The 11th Fleet sat and did nothing, and Martin really wanted to know why.

In the interim, he occupied himself with catching up on the news; both with the war and at home. The Protectorate was on the verge of wrapping things up. The Aldonian thrust put a large bulge in the line pointing directly at Prescottia. The 17th Fleet had driven the enemy from Dreena IX creating another jumping off point for the invasion of the home system. The 18th Fleet suffered a minor set back when the Prescottians counter attacked. Admiral Slu Bya lost sixteen ships before he could rally to hold his position. Martin saw this incident as further proof that the Prescottians would fight on until their home planet could be taken; and still his forces sat.

At home a celebration took place to honor the 480th anniversary of the maiden voyage of the P.I.V. Wanderlust. She had been the first ship to use fusion engines. It had also been 400 years since the Protectorate fought its first interstellar war with the Nari. The first shot had been fired in July, 2126. Martin's favorite team, the New York Giants, won the Interstellar Pressball Championship. Pressball had evolved from the ancient game of football and was popular throughout the Protectorate. A cure had been found for Blotay Syndrome. The disease affected 30% of Protectorate species and the breakthrough was sure to win Dr. Clin'la'doum the Nobel Prize.

Martin was reading additional news items in his flag office when a junior aide arrived.

"Come in Lieutenant."

"Thank you sir. I thought you might want to know that the P.I.V. Whirlwind is on our outer scopes and should be here in about three hours."

This was strange. The Whirlwind was Admiral Beedle's flagship. The admiral had not radioed ahead or sent any message to announce his arrival. The situation was irregular to say the least, but perhaps Martin would get some of the answers he was looking for.

Martin invited Ryn and Jaspa to his office. He found that waiting was not quite so bad if he could pass the time with his friends. It took the pair about eighty minutes to finish their duties and join him. In the meantime, Martin caught up on some overdue paperwork. There was no paper in this day and age, but the archaic name for the odious and tedious task was still in use.

With about ninety minutes to go until Admiral Beedle's ship arrived, Jaspa and Ryn entered Martin's sanctum. Ryn did not know it, but Martin had a fantastic surprise for him. Martin had been able to keep it a secret from Jaspa lest she spill the beans. Promotion for officers in the Protectorate forces were accomplished through a review board. Up until the rank of captain, a candidate would be nominated by a senior officer at least two grades higher in rank. A board of three officers, one of which was at least a commodore, would then review the candidate's record. In peacetime, an officer had to hold rank for a minimum of six months in the case of an ensign or junior lieutenant, one year for senior lieutenants, two for lt. commanders and commanders, and three for captains. In wartime, the time restrictions were removed so promotions could occur rapidly. If the officer had minimum time in grade, the board would vote. A unanimous ballot would advance the officer.

This process was a bit different for admirals. Another admiral would submit a name for consideration to a rotating advancement board. The board consisted of two commodores, two rear admirals, one vice admiral and one admiral. The vice admiral's vote counted twice and the admiral's vote counted three times. This board would vote on the advancement of the nominee. Six votes out of nine would be sufficient to advance the candidate. Martin had put Ryn in for promotion after the battle for Aldonia. He had just heard back yesterday. Ryn had received a unanimous vote and was now a rear admiral. Martin could not wait to tell him.

The two friends stood in the entryway. Martin waved them over as he looked up from his desk, "Come in, come in. How are things going?"

Ryn replied first, "Same as usual. We sit and do nothing in an already occupied system. I hope Admiral Beedle plans to give us orders when he arrives."

Jaspa took an offered chair. "What else could it be? What I don't understand is why he's coming all this way. He could just as easily have radioed our orders from New Freemantle."

Ryn offered this suggestion, "Maybe he's moving his base of operations here. After all, New Freemantle is pretty far from the front now that Aldonia is in our hands. It must be something like that."

Martin and Jaspa both nodded. Nothing else made sense. With an advance base at Aldonia, two fleets could move up and advance the front. An attack on Prescottia was the next logical step.

Martin opened a drawer in his desk and pulled out a tan envelope. There was a slight bulge in the package. He placed it in front of him and took a sonic opener to it. He began, "At the conclusion of the Battle of Aldonia I sent a communication to Earth. I just received word a short time ago to my request. Ryn, for sterling performance in every facet of your duty, it is my pleasure and honor to promote you to rear admiral with all the privileges and responsibilities of that rank." Martin pulled two stars from the package. He gave the bits of metal and promotion papers to his old friend.

The big man's smile lit the room; "I don't know what to say. Thank you for your confidence in me. You know that I have been honored to serve under you . . ."

Martin raised a hand to stop Ryn; "There is one other thing. With your increase in rank, I am removing you from my staff. I already have a rear admiral serving as my senior advisor." Martin indicated to Jaspa as he said this. "As of right now, you are in command of Task Force 32. I know it's what you have always wanted. You have been an invaluable asset, but it is time you had a command of your own. I have no doubt that T.F. 32 will soon be alive and full of your own command style. Do me proud."

Jaspa kissed the Pologian and congratulated him. Ryn pumped Martin's hand and swore he would be the best commander in Martin's fleet. The three friends left for the docking bay to await the arrival of Admiral Beedle.

*   *   *

The admiral's shuttle touched down on the deck. The nearly silent engines purred and then grew quiet as they were turned off. A minute passed before the door opened and Admiral Beedle was piped aboard.

The senior officer met Martin and his staff. He immediately dispensed with the pleasantries and told Martin he wanted to speak with him alone. Martin dismissed the gathering and escorted the older officer to his quarters.

As soon as the doors shut behind him, Admiral Beedle got down to business, "I have to deny your request for reinforcements. Fifty ships is simply impossible at this point."

Martin was stunned; "I don't understand Admiral. The 12th fleet is sitting doing nothing. Surely a task force can be created from that group to strengthen my forces for the attack on Prescottia."

Beedle took on an angry visage, "Are you questioning my orders? I said it was impossible at this time! Something has happened that is going to change our plans in this area."

Martin was undaunted by the chewing out, "May I ask what has happened?"

"I am returning to Earth to assist with the strategic planning of the final assault. As such, I require a replacement. Admiral Bengarian, Commander 12th Fleet is also being reassigned."

Martin was becoming more confused. "Why is such a major command change occurring at such a critical juncture?"

"Are you now questioning the decisions of your superiors?" Beedle seemed truly angry now.

"No sir, I just want to know what is going on."

The old admiral's face softened and he even cracked a smile, "I'll tell you Marty. By the powers vested in me by the Protectorate Advancement Board of Admirals, I hereby promote you to the rank of admiral. You will be given command of the 11th and 12th Fleets. If you can finish this mess by September, you will have my support, and everyone else's I can talk to, for Fleet Admiral."

Martin sat down. Full admiral, and the command of two fleets. With so many ships at his disposal, Martin had no doubt he would finally bring this war to a successful conclusion. Admiral Beedle congratulated the new four star and dismissed him. Martin hurried to find Jaspa and Ryn. There would be a celebration tonight, and hopefully, in a few months, a toast could be drunk to the peace treaty.

Chapter X: ADMIRAL
June 1, 2527
System 163a, 42 light years from Prescottia

Admiral Martin Gammage was alone in the primary conference chamber aboard the Triumph. Within minutes, the room would be filled with admirals and their aides. Their task was to discuss how best to take Prescottia and what would be the disposition of the conquered system. The enemy was fighting with the dregs now. The last engagement fought at System 163a could hardly be called a battle. Martin's two hundred six ships outnumbered the Prescottian force three to one. Most of the enemy's ships were damaged and below par before the fighting started. The combined 11th and 12th fleets destroyed all but ten of the Prescottian ships and lost only six of their number. Martin was ready for the war to end and the killing to stop.

Rear Admiral Ryndock Calplygian was the first to arrive. The big Pologian was in his dress finery. Medals studded his barrel chest. He came alone. Ryn usually eschewed staff members at these conferences and briefed them later. Ryn smiled at his friend and took a seat without a word.

Vice Admiral Jaspa Shindessa arrived next. Technically, her flagship was the Theodore Roosevelt, but she spent most of her time in Martin's cabin. Since her promotion to three stars, Martin had put her in nominal command of the 11th Fleet. Ryn was the heavy ship commander in that fleet and reported directly to Jaspa. The vice admiral, seeing that only Ryn was in the room with them, kissed Martin lightly before taking her seat, Jaspa's staff contingent, a commodore and two commanders, entered seconds later.

The last major player in the fleet, Vice Admiral Keena Slopac, entered with a massive staff. The Colarian was an able officer, both as an administrator and battle commander, but like other members of his race, insisted on a huge staff. High ranking Colarians were known to have assistants numbering in the hundreds. For this conference alone, Martin made out twenty seven before he stopped counting. The vice admiral himself was in fastidious uniform. Every button was polished to a gleaming shine. His stars shone from decorated epaulets. Instead of ribbons, Slopac wore the actual decorations. Dozens of medals were pinned to his narrow physique. The vice admiral nodded respectfully to Martin as he and his entourage took seats. Martin overlooked the vice admiral's eccentricities. The Colarian was respectful at all times, and what was more, he handled the 12th Fleet expertly.

Another rear admiral, three commodores, and a myriad of staff officers entered and sat down. The final being to enter was an unobtrusive female wearing the rank insignia of a Lt. Commander. She did not sit with the others. Instead, she sat on the stage to the left of the podium. Admiral Gammage nodded to her and she smiled in return. Many decisions that were to be made today depended on the report of this woman.

Martin stood and made his way to the podium. The murmur of conversation ceased as the admiral gazed out into the audience. He spoke, "We are here to finally discuss the, hopefully, last campaign of this war. Without further ado, I present to you Lt. Commander Jessica Stone, our operative on Prescottia for the last two years. Her information will be extremely valuable in helping us decide what to do with the enemy when we engage them in battle, and after we have beaten them. Lt. Commander . . ." Martin gestured toward the young lady. A smattering of applause greeted her. Undercover work for such a long time was dangerous to say the least, and the senior officers were showing their respect.

"Thank you Admiral. As you know, I have been an undercover operative on and around Prescottia for the last two years. I must tell you that it was a wonderful feeling to have my face back after so long. I would like to thank everyone here representing the combined fleets for their support and welcome home." More enthusiastic applause met these remarks. "Now, down to particulars. The Prescottians are an extremely determined race. They are wounded and cornered and we all know how dangerous a cornered animal can be. It is my opinion that only the complete destruction of the Prescottian home fleet will force them to sue for peace."

Vice Admiral Slopac interrupted her at this point; "Do you believe that we will be forced to bombard their home planet into submission?"

The spy thought for a moment, "I do not think that will be necessary, although it remains a possibility. There are several small groups on the planet that know they're beaten. The high command is pretty hard core, however. We cannot rule out a surface attack. I have some numbers that might clear up the picture."

The commander consulted some notes, "As an office worker in the central military authority, I had access to many government statistics. The information ministry has been lying to the populace for quite some time, however, most Prescottians are becoming aware just how bad things are. The Prescottians have lost 79% of their territory since the war began. Additionally, some 70% of their fleet has been destroyed. Their casualty rate is horrifying." She paused. "They have lost nearly seventy five million lives."

Gasps filled the room. The admiral looked stricken, "That is much greater than we thought."

"You will notice admiral, that Prescottians are not easy to capture. In fact the surrender of that Draaken some time ago was an anomaly, correct?" Martin had to agree. "At home, that Draaken has been vilified, his family disgraced, all because he did not want to spill blood needlessly. When Venari II was taken, almost 100,000 Prescottians had themselves disintegrated rather than be placed under Protectorate rule. The officer in charge of our ground forces could not understand why so few surrendered. I do not know what kinds of problems this . . . foolhardy stance of theirs will cause when Prescottia is taken. We may be facing mass suicide."

The gathering chewed on this for a moment before Jaspa asked, "Do you know what we will face when we enter the Prescottian system?"

"The Prescottian Navy will throw everything they have left at us. They are scraping the bottom now, but they should have about one hundred fifty ships waiting for us. About forty of those will be the elite Tar' nor' sloat, the Prescottian Special Guard Force. This task force is roughly the equivalent of our First Fleet."

Martin ruminated on this fact. He would still outnumber the Prescottians two hundred six to one hundred fifty and he was expecting more vessels shortly. He listened as the briefing continued.

" . . . some of our officers are famous among the Prescottians, or perhaps I should say infamous. The admiral is wanted for war crimes and is portrayed as single handedly starting the war." There were some snickers at this statement.

"Rear Admiral Calplygian is often cartooned as a devil like figure and is wanted for atrocities committed on Prescottian women and children." Ryn did not take kindly to this at all. The big man turned purple and vowed to crush all Prescottian ships in battle.

"Vice Admiral Shindessa is a kind of "angel of death" figure in Prescottian news media. She is drawn as a beautiful woman with a sickle slicing through fields of Prescottian 'grain'."

Hoots and catcalls at this one. Vice admiral Slopac spoke up, "I feel left out. Is nothing said about me?" It was hard to tell if the egotistical man was serious or not.

"Thank you commander," said Martin. "You all have copies of the commander's full report that you may read at your leisure. Our plan for taking Prescottia will be a simple one. The 17th Fleet will attack here . . . at Jylna Prime. The Prescottians will think that we are trying to take their system from the flank. The 20th Fleet will conduct harrying tactics in their rear. Hopefully, these actions will draw off some Prescottian ships. Even if they do not, we will still substantially outnumber them. Are there any questions?"

Ryn immediately spoke up. It was obvious he was still incensed by the Prescottian slander at his expense, "What do you plan to do if and when they surrender . . . sir?"

Martin paused for a moment. He had thought about this for a long time. The Prescottians had started the war, but he had been able to find honor among some of them; the Draaken being the best example. He thought for another moment and said without flinching, "I will ask for unconditional surrender. We will be the ones to dictate terms." His words brought some grumbles from the more liberal officers, but by and large, the audience agreed with him. At any rate, his tone offered no room for compromise. Ryn sat down satisfied.

"This is it ladies and gentlemen. We will depart for Prescottian space in seventy two hours. Let's end this . . . and go home. Dismissed."

June 5, 2527
Outskirts of the Prescottian System

Two hundred seventeen ships of the line dotted the inky blackness of space. The 11th and 12th Protectorate Fleets were on a course with destiny. Over twenty three hundred embarked craft were being fueled and readied. Two hundred twenty five thousand beings awaited the orders of one man. The combined fleets carried enough firepower to shatter an entire star system. They were backed up by sixty five drop ships carrying some one hundred sixty five thousand marines. The supply convoy that serviced the fleet and drop ships spread out to cover an entire parsec of space. Five hundred three supply ships, fuel and ammunition ships, tenders, cargo vessels, couriers, scouts, and a plethora of others stood ready to assist the fleets and the occupation forces. This was the might of the Protectorate. This is what the men and women who had served so long and suffered so much were waiting for, and one man stood over all. Martin was awestruck at the raw power at his command. This was it . . . the final showdown with the Prescottians.

The Triumph was in the vanguard; Martin would have it no other way. The Theodore Roosevelt was close at hand as was the Unicorn, Admiral Slopac's ship, and the

Vorpellian, Ryn's majestic battleship. The fleet was cruising at a modest 1750c and decelerating slowly. The Prescottian sun was growing on screen. A modest white star fueled the Prescottian system. Martin had thought it would be something sinister, that perhaps a red giant had spawned the aggressive race that had fought so long. Yet, there it was, a system of five planets orbiting a dwarf star.

"Admiral!" yelled a young communications officer. In her excitement she forgot protocol and simply announced, "Jylna Prime has fallen!" A hurrah spread through the bridge. Jylna was to be taken by the 17th Fleet in the hope that some of the Prescottian forces would be drawn off to defend that sector of space.

"Does Admiral Neeber report any casualties on either side?" demanded Martin.

"Yes sir. The admiral faced forty two ships. He destroyed thirty seven at a loss of twenty three. Stiff resistance was reported. The other five broke off when it seemed hopeless and were reported headed in this direction."

"Very good. Have this news dispersed to all ships on an open band." It was Martin's hope that the enemy would be listening in, and that this news would demoralize them further.

The fleet was now below 500c and was finishing their breaking maneuver. Sensor officers were working madly over their screens to determine opposition. One young man was the first to speak up, "Admiral, I am detecting numerous vessels just outside the Prescottian system in battle formation. A preliminary count shows one hundred twenty two craft of varying sizes. I can have types for you as we close in."

That was good to hear. It seemed that the feint by the 17th Fleet had drawn off some of the expected Prescottian strength. Martin had thought to face some one hundred fifty ships. The admiral would be fighting from nearly a two to one advantage. He reigned his thoughts in however. It would not do to become over confident and over estimate his position. The Prescottians had nothing to lose and would fight to the last man. If Martin wanted to avoid a bloodbath, he had to stick to military principles.

"Order the drop ships to hold position. Their escorts should be near enough to protect them. I don't want them risking themselves unnecessarily. They will go in only after the entire system has been secured. Order all vessels to general quarters. All fighters will be readied to launch. All ships of the line will do battle with enemy vessels only. I do not want my ships conducting planetary raids until every last Prescottian ship is destroyed or surrenders. We will keep our forces unified and intact. General Stonewall Jackson said that if a small force can throw itself on part of a large one and destroy it, a less numerous army can defeat a larger one. This will not happen to us. Your targets are enemy vessels. This order is not open to interpretation. All carriers will keep two fighter squadrons in reserve to protect the capital ships. All others will penetrate enemy fighter screens to destroy large enemy vessels. Have the carriers move to the rear of the formation to launch their fighters. Heavy ships up front. Frigates, cruisers, and destroyers on the flanks. Formation nine delta. Go now."

The orders went out to every ship in the fleet. The Prescottians were lining up their ships as Martin's carriers fell back. Ryn's heavy ships formed the vanguard. Rear admiral Charlotte Carrington's cruisers took up position on either side and above and below the battle wagons. Commodores James Blyleven and Karen Jones dispersed their frigates among the cruisers. The various destroyer commanders placed their ships on the flanks for quick hitting forays into the enemy fleet. A multi-colored formation of dots lit up the tactical display. Just then, the carriers launched their fighters. Space was alive with ships of every shape and size buzzing about one another. The larger capital ships launched their fighter craft as well to add to the tightly choreographed dance that was about to unfold.

Martin sat in the eye of the storm, giving orders to his fleet commanders. The "three stars" in turn set their rear admirals in motion. The battleship, cruiser, carrier, frigate, and destroyer admirals set their pieces on the board under the control of task force commodores. Finally the captain of each ship placed his or her vessel on the board in space. A three dimensional ballet took place as ships flew, retreated, wheeled, or held station. Interlaced with all these ships, one or two man fighters took their place on the stage. Some orbited the larger ships, but most were confirming attack vectors. The Protectorate cloud was much larger than that of the Prescottians, but the enemy was impressive in its own right.

The thirty some ships of the Tar' nor' sloat were in the van, and all were battle cruisers or heavier. The Prescottians had a respectable carrier force of some sixteen vessels. They were presently disgorging their complement of fighters. These enemy pilots were the final reserve and were reported to be in excellent spirits. The Prescottians had a high degree of training and battle experience. The Protectorate flyers could not afford to take the enemy pilots lightly. Prescottian cruisers and frigates dotted the formation here and there. Enemy destroyers were clustered in groups of six each. Apparently the enemy would try the old "wolf pack" mentality. One destroyer alone was not much of a threat, but six could bring down the largest battleship when they acted in concert. Yes, the Prescottians were ready for this and they would give it all they had. Martin was conscious of all these facts and knew full well that victory was anything but assured.

Martin wanted to give the Prescottians one last chance. He turned to his comm. officer, "Broadcast this to the Prescottian Fleet: This is Admiral Martin Gammage, Commander 11th and 12th Protectorate Fleets. I beg you to power down your weapons and end this contest peaceably. So many have died on both sides and I see no need to continue the slaughter. You are outnumbered with your backs to your home worlds. Please reconsider your actions. If you capitulate now my terms will be generous. If there is any more blood shed, let it be on your hands. Let us end this now." The com officer confirmed that the message had been received.

For a minute nothing happened. A flicker of hope grew in the hearts of the Protectorate forces. Perhaps the enemy admiral wanted to stop the suffering. The hope died as soon as it began when an ensign at a short range scanner scope cried out, "Here they come!"

Sure enough, the Prescottians were advancing. A phalanx of fighters flew away from the enemy position and came barreling for the Triumph. "Damn it!" cried Martin; "Here we go." The captain of the Triumph opened up with a vicious anti-aircraft barrage. Four enemy fighters went up before they could fire a shot. Support from a nearby cruiser took out three more. The five remaining squadron members over flew their target in confusion. The battle was now joined.

"All ships, fire at will!" bellowed Martin as he strapped himself into his command chair. The Triumph wasted no time. The weapons officer lined up a Tar' nor' sloat battle cruiser with the nova cannon and fired. The lights dimmed briefly as a burst of massive energies were loosed in that one double barreled shot. The stricken cruiser tumbled out of control and exploded in a cloud of super heated gases. The weapons officer fired through the cloud and scored several FAL hits on another battle cruiser. There were so many targets, it was hard to miss. Martin hoped to remedy that situation promptly.

The fighters were slugging it out toe-to-toe. The Prescottians seemed to have the upper hand for a while. A whole Protectorate squadron was wiped out. The enemy strafed the Triumph. Martin had to hold onto his chair lest he lose his seat. Sparks flew from a burnt out console behind him. Protectorate fighters rallied and chased off the marauding bandits. Familiar smells and sounds of battle reached Martin's senses: burnt insulation, and worse still, burnt flesh; screams of the injured, muffled explosions below decks; orders being screamed from the center seat; bright flashes on the view screen as metal and men were reduced to flotsam. Martin hung on, riding it out.

The Triumph sliced through the enemy formation. A Prescottian frigate made a run at her. The enemy scored an antimatter missile hit in the big ship's flank, but the Triumph was a thick skinned lady. Most of the energy was absorbed by the defense fields. The noble girl struck back. The frigate was shredded by repeated FAL hits. Two antimatter missiles nailed the doomed ship as she tried to turn away. The hulk swerved on her one remaining engine to no avail. A final FAL hit finished her.

A Protectorate cruiser lit up space to the right of the Triumph as she came around for another pass. The cruiser, Martin could make out the name "Glory," spilled her guts behind her as she fell far away from the fleet.

"Damage report!" cried the captain from the center seat. Martin could tell something was wrong with his flagship. She was slow, sluggish. She was not handling well at all. The answer was quick in coming. A voice from the engine room said, "Port defense fields down 26%, starboard down 31%. Our primary stabilizer gyro is out. I should have the auxiliary patched in . . . now." Immediately the ship felt better to Martin. The captain had a gleam in his eye as he brought the valiant lady around and back into the fray. The crew had suffered six dead on the first pass and nineteen wounded. Martin just caught sight of the Theodore Roosevelt. Plasma sparks were jetting from her port side fusion engine number two, but other than that, she looked unscathed.

The helmsman lined up an enemy battleship. The weapons officer squinted and held her finger just above the firing switches. She was waiting for the critical moment. The Triumph completed her turn. The lieutenant fired. She pumped huge quantities of fusion laser energy into the battleship's overburdened defense fields. She launched missile after missile, there being no point in saving ammunition at this point. Flowers of fire bloomed on the enemy ship reaping a crop of destruction. The starboard weapons pod exploded, tearing the starboard displacement drive engine free of its moorings. Hull breaches opened all along her bulky flank. Streamers of atmosphere, equipment, and men trailed out, but she stubbornly refused to explode. The Triumph left her there, dead in space.

A destroyer pack watched helplessly as their battleship was dismembered by the Protectorate Flagship. They could do nothing to stop the destruction, but when the Triumph flew free of the debris field, the C.O. of the wolf pack saw his chance. The destroyers let loose with a withering volley of FAL fire. The Triumph took the hits well and rolled with them, but the strain was beginning to show. The defense fields turned an ugly scarlet as they began to overload. A direct hit on the bridge sent scaffolding crashing to the deck. The weapons officer was killed along with the communications crewman. Martin immediately rerouted the weapons control through his console and sought revenge on the Prescottian wolf pack.

The nova cannon was not fully charged, but for Martin's purposes it had enough energy. He primed the gun for a proximity blast. He found a point in the wolf pack and fired. The energy bolt reached that point and exploded. Three of the destroyers were extremely close to the blast point as Martin had planned. One was vaporized. The other two exploded in spectacular fashion. The other three were caught in the nimbus of the detonation. One shuddered and drifted. All of her lights went out and her engines went cold; she was out of the picture. The other two righted themselves, but were badly damaged. Martin fired with deadly pinpoint accuracy. The closest enemy destroyer tipped precariously upward as an antimatter missile caught her on the chin. With no defense fields remaining, the bow blew off, taking the bridge with it. The other destroyer limped away as fast as it could. Martin smiled grimly.

The captain of the Triumph was wounded. A shard of metal had torn through the man's arm. Blood streamed freely from the wound, but the captain refused to be relieved.

A med-tech with a portable cauterizer stanched the flow of blood. The captain's voice was thick with pain as he croaked, "Damage report!"

The news was worse this time around, "Starboard defense fields down 50%, port 48%. Main stabilizer gyro is out once again. Port side number one fusion engine down 35%. Displacement drive down 15%. Structural damage on decks one, six, eight, twelve, and twenty two."

The captain asked, "Any damage to weapons?"

"No sir."

"Then we fight on."

Martin admired the captain's spirit, however his X.O., Gail Hutchinson spoke out, "Sir, we have already destroyed a battleship, battle cruiser, and five destroyers. We have also damaged a sixth destroyer and a cruiser. You are wounded. We have fifty three dead and scores injured. Perhaps we should retire."

"No commander. We will not retire unless I am ordered to do so." He looked back at Martin. His gaze said that the admiral had better not disagree. Martin simply nodded.

"Bring us around for another pass."

The Triumph came about. She was spewing plasma and other debris, but she was still in one piece. Martin clutched his fists as he saw two Prescottian ships coming in fast. He opened up on the closest one. The enemy cruiser withstood the pounding and returned fire. The Triumph bucked nauseatingly as she was hit repeatedly. The cruiser flew by and Martin turned his attention to the bigger ship. She was a battle cruiser and Martin knew he had to do significant damage to it before it could return fire. The Triumph was badly hit, and if the enemy could put a volley together, it might finish them.

Martin rerouted unnecessary systems and slammed the power through the nova cannon. He fired the huge weapon. Sparks erupted from the control console as it, and the cannon, overloaded and burned out. Martin was badly burned and his uniform caught fire. He swatted at the flames and tried to see through his stinging and tear filled eyes. The shot had the desired effect. The battle cruiser went up like a super nova. The crew let out a ragged cheer as the Triumph flew out into the clear again. She would not be going back, as two things happened simultaneously.

The damage report this time was a death knell. The Triumph was still space worthy to be sure, but she could not continue in battle. The starboard defense fields were down 80% and the port side was burned out. The fusion engines were only pulling at one third capacity. Martin's stint with the nova cannon had fried most of the FAL control circuits. The ship flew drunkenly on damaged stabilizers. The captain had finally succumbed to his wounds and passed out. The Triumph had over one hundred ninety dead and three hundred wounded. A hull breach had opened on decks twenty two and twenty three. Martin was just about to order the ship back to the safety of the carriers when the second thing happened.

Martin's forces had destroyed sixty of the one hundred twenty two Prescottian ships. Many of the remainder were damaged. Every single Tar' nor' sloat ship was destroyed. With that tough nut of resistance gone, the Prescottian admiral had had enough. "Admiral, I'm picking up a transmission on an open band."

"Let's hear it."

"This is Conphir Noak. All fighters will break off and return to base. Protectorate Commander, we surrender . . ."

Pandemonium drowned out the rest. Even on the battered bridge of the Triumph, peals of laughter could be heard. Many shed tears, but however they expressed it, victory was at hand. Admiral Martin Gammage, veteran of so many battles, simply placed his burnt hands on his lap and closed his eyes.

Five minutes later.

A medic had been ordered to the bridge to see to Martin's injuries. As the young woman treated the burns on his hands and face, Martin ordered a channel opened to the Prescottian flagship.

The battle cruiser Peneer answered moments later. A high ranking Prescottian appeared on the screen. He seemed in no better shape than Martin. His head crest was bleeding and one eye was covered by a medical patch. The Prescottian officer gathered himself and said, "This is Conphir Noak speaking for the Zyldonian High Command. Martin took this in. Martin knew from his operative's report that "Zyldonian" was the Prescottians' name for themselves. Noak continued, "As Bar-Conphir Yarnalian has been killed, I have been empowered by the Zyldonian Prilate to ask for your terms."

Martin sized up his enemy. He took in a lung full of air and said, "Neither of us seems to be in the best of shape. I would be honored to receive you on board this vessel in two hours. This should give us both time to be medically checked. I warn you, however, that my vessels are even now surrounding the remainder of your fleet. I also have ships headed for your home planet. Any treachery will be met with immediate and devastating reprisals."

The Prescottian nodded his head in a diagonal gesture; "I thank you for the time to tend to my wounds. I assure you that there will be no moves on my part. I am empowered to negotiate treaty stipulations. I will see you in twenty five calnors."

Martin cut the transmission and ordered his vice admirals to come aboard. He wanted Ryn at the negotiations as well. All of them had fought long and hard for this moment. He also gave orders that if any Prescottian ship so much as moved, the fleet would obliterate the remaining Prescottian forces and begin a bombardment of the surface of Prescottia. That accomplished, he finished his treatment with the med-tech and left for his quarters to change into his dress uniform. History was about to be made.

*   *   *

One hour, forty five minutes later.
Hangar bay of the P.I.V. Triumph.

A nervous young ensign stood at the entrance to the cavernous hangar. She had been asked to announce all the senior officers as they came aboard, even the enemy admiral and his staff! This ceremony was to be recorded and sent to the four corners of the Protectorate. She checked her dress uniform for the umpteenth time and waited.

The first to arrive of course was the architect of the victory. As host, Martin made sure everything was in order. It was not everyday that one welcomed aboard a vanquished foe to negotiate a war ending treaty. He took a deep breath as the hangar bay doors parted to allow him entry.

The ensign saw the hero of the hour enter. She closed her eyes and thought, please don't let my voice squeak. She took a breath, "Admiral Martin Gammage. Commander of the combined 11th and 12th Fleets."

A huge cheer drowned out the Protectorate anthem playing in the background. Martin smiled and waved to the gathered officers. Some of his senior commanders were already there, but all of the major players had yet to arrive. Martin decided he was going to enjoy this to the fullest. He strode to the raised platform and took his seat. Around his neck were the two Protectorate Medals of Honor. He was also decorated with two Protectorate Crosses, several silver and bronze stars, and more Purple Hearts than he cared to acknowledge. With one more glance at the crowd, he turned his attention to the first arriving shuttle.

The small craft lightly touched down. The ensign consulted her arrival pad, "Commodore Harold Barnes. Commodore Milna Kreen, Commodore Lindail Posta, Commodore Jackarya Lodash."

Martin nodded at each of his frigate and destroyer commanders. He felt the absence of Commodore Jill Sayers; she had been killed in the battle. The shuttle taxied off the landing pad to make room for the next arrival.

A slightly larger craft made a smooth landing. Higher ranking officers would be arriving now and they would be coming individually. The door opened to admit a debonair human. The grey haired admiral looked about as the ensign said, "Rear Admiral Robert Pelletier." The cruiser admiral saluted Admiral Gammage and found his seat. The taxiing process was repeated with his shuttle. The space had been cleared for only seconds before the next arrival touched down.

"Rear Admiral Blytar Simsensola." The appearance of the battleship commander of the 12th Fleet was incongruous with her tongue twister of a name, and the huge ships she commanded. The three foot tall Pondar found her place. Martin was very interested in the next scheduled arrival.

A medical shuttle whispered into the bay. The over large doors opened and two men appeared supporting a third between them, Rear Admiral Ryndock Calplygian.

Thunderous applause met Ryn as he shrugged off the assistance of the medical orderlies. Ryn's ship had been destroyed in the battle. The big man had a broken arm, thirteen broken ribs, a bruised kidney, a broken wrist, a concussion, and the universe only knew how many lacerations and bruises. He had told Martin in no uncertain terms that he would be here for the ceremony and that he would come aboard under his own power. He seemed to be making good on that promise.

The entire gathering watched Ryn's trek across the bay in agonizing silence. A gasp went up as he slipped and nearly collapsed, but he righted himself and continued on. A collective sigh of relief went up as he folded himself into a special chair. Only then would he accept pain medication. He looked up at Martin and smiled an "I told you so" grin. Martin could only shake his head and return the glance. He added a jaunty salute for good measure.

The next shuttle bore the emblem of the 11th Fleet. Its occupant could be only one person. The ensign consulted the board just to be sure and announced, "Vice Admiral Jaspa Shindessa." A cheer greeted the well liked and respected commander. Martin flashed a look just for her. Volumes were spoken in that one glance. The love of his life found her seat near his own.

Only two more shuttles would touch down. The first deposited Vice Admiral Keena Slopac onto the deck. The commander of the 12th Fleet had outdone even himself in his victory regalia. The ribbon encrusted admiral nodded respectfully to Martin and took his seat as well.

The moment everyone had been waiting for finally arrived. The alien shuttle looked just that, alien. Its unorthodox lines seemed to defile the pristine docking bay. A hush fell over the crowd as the doors opened. An honor guard of Prescottians filed out, all unarmed at Martin's insistence. An FAL toting security force lined up behind them. Several Prescottian officers walked off the shuttle before the ensign finally announced, "Acting Bar-Conphir Noak." Dead silence greeted his arrival. Martin stood and met the enemy. The two looked at each other for a long moment before Martin said simply, "Shall we?" The two admirals and their respective staffs departed for the negotiations. The gathering was dismissed.

Main conference room, P.I.V. Triumph.

A couple of very long tables were laid out in the center of the room. Behind one stood the banner of the Protectorate. Behind the other was placed the symbol of the Prescottian governing body. Martin made a mental note to congratulate his quartermaster for coming up with the enemy flag so quickly.

The Prescottians entered first. Noak took the center seat as his various staff officers sat to the right or left. Martin took his place. To his right sat Slopac; to his left Jaspa. Ryn was assisted to a reclining chair on the end. When all were seated, yeomen entered to arrange water and drinking glasses for both parties. Martin asked Noak if he required anything further. The Prescottian simply said he wanted to conclude this business as soon as possible. Martin could not help but agree.

Martin flipped a switch on the recording device in front of him and began, "The following is the treaty negotiation between the Protectorate and Prescottian . . ." that was as far as he got.

Bar-Confir Noak interrupted, "We strongly resent the term 'Prescottian'! That is the name you have chosen for us. We demand to be referred to as the Zyldonian people." Anger and the pain of defeat dripped from his words. The Bar-Confir was trying to salvage some dignity for himself and his race.

Ryn leaned over and said to a rear admiral sitting next to him, "Pretty damn cocky for someone who's just been whipped, but I've got to give him the nod." The admiral smiled but did not reply.

"Very well," continued Martin, "Make a note," he said to the recording specialist, "The term Zyldonian will replace Prescottian in all treaty matters and will be the nomenclature employed from this day forward."

"Thank you . . . Admiral" conceded Noak.

Martin decided to take some of the wind out of Noak's sails and remind him exactly who was in charge regardless of the face saving tactics being employed by the Zyldonian, "For the record Bar-Confir, the Zyldonian forces have surrendered to the Protectorate unconditionally."

"Yes," spat Noak.

"Further, you understand that you will have little or no say over peace conditions, lest your home planet be opened to surface bombardment and destruction."

Noak could only muster an affirmative grunt this time.

"Good. That settled, let us get down to cases." Despite Noak's attitude, or perhaps because of it, Martin very much wanted to give the Prescottian's somewhat favorable terms. After all, he was certain that the civilian population had to have suffered greatly in this war. Making harsh terms against women and children was not Martin's style, however, the costs of ruling an empire were great. The Protectorate had no choice but come down hard on the Prescottians. An example must be made of these people to quash rebellion among new acquisitions.

Martin took a sip of water and began, "Article I: The Disposition of the Zyldonian Armed Forces. All remaining Zyldonian ships of war shall be examined by Protectorate scientists. After said examination, all valuable technological features shall be removed, and if possible, shall be incorporated into the Protectorate fleet. After this process all Zyldonian ships of war will be scrapped; their metals to be used to Protectorate ends."

The Zyldonians exploded, "How shall we protect ourselves? This is preposterous!"

Martin calmly explained, "You will be an occupied Protectorate Territory. We will bear the responsibility of your protection."

The Bar-Conphir was outraged, "Oh, so we're to depend on your military for protection? Laughable."

Ryn had had just about enough. He tried to contain himself but at this comment burst out, "We beat you easily enough!"

A round of "Hear, hear!" went up from the Protectorate brass. Martin had to reign this in, no matter how insufferable the Prescottians were, "Admiral Calplygian, you will control yourself or I will have you removed. The rest of you will maintain proper decorum at all times!" The Protectorate side of the room fell silent. Martin glared at his officers in turn. Inside he chuckled and applauded Ryn's comments. Who did these little shits think they were anyway? Dignity aside, they were a conquered people, in no position to bargain or make demands.

Martin continued as calmly as before, "I assure you that Zyldonia shall be protected. Article I continued: All Zyldonian ground forces shall surrender their small arms and all other military hardware and equipment. A Protectorate occupation force shall decide the disposition of this equipment. No Zyldonian citizen shall be permitted to own or be in possession of any firearm or directed energy device for any reason. The Protectorate occupation forces shall provide police for the civilian population. This ban on weapons will be in effect for forty years, at which time this section of Article I shall be re-evaluated."

Noak tried to bore holes in Martin with his eyes. The admiral for his part was unperturbed.

"Article II: Zyldonian Territories. All space claimed by the Zyldonian Prilate shall now be considered Protectorate territories. All planets that were claimed, captured, or annexed by Zyldonian forces shall be under Protectorate martial law for a period of ten years. At the end of this time, those worlds shall be evaluated and, if conditions are met, shall become Protectorate Worlds with all the rights and privileges thereof. All worlds allied with Zyldonia shall be under Protectorate martial law for a period of thirty years. The same process shall be repeated for those worlds at the end of that time. Zyldonia itself shall be subject to Protectorate martial law for a period of seventy five years with the same stipulations at the end of that time."

"This is outrageous!" bellowed Noak. "We will not subject ourselves to this tyranny, we will not . . ."

Martin stood, cutting off the tirade, " What you will not do is make demands on my flagship! Place these men under arrest. Order the fleet to destroy what is left of the Prescottian ships and order a bombardment of Prescottia itself. I want the planet bombed until the rubble jumps!"

"Wait! Wait!" cried Noak in desperation, "We can be reasonable! Please!"

Martin sat, "I wanted to make you aware that total destruction is your only alternative. I trust I have made my point."

Noak looked suitably embarrassed, "Yes."

"Good. Shall we continue? Article III: Compensation of War Debt. A complete inventory shall be done of the Zyldonian financial system. All metals, gems, ores, and like materials shall be catalogued. The Protectorate shall compare what it holds valuable with what Zyldonia holds valuable. When this is completed, 85% of all goods, presently in Zyldonia's possession shall be seized by the Protectorate to help pay for this debacle. For ten years, Zyldonia shall pay 75% of its mined products as a war tax. For twelve years after that, 50% shall be paid. After that time the amount will be reduced to the standard 15% tribute that all Protectorate worlds are responsible for.

Article IV: Prisoners of War. The Protectorate agrees to a 100% exchange of all prisoners. We understand that it is your custom to take prisoners, but not to become prisoners yourselves. As such you have many more prisoners than we do, however, a complete exchange will be made. Do you agree?"

Noak looked at the table as he said, "We agree, as we appear to have no choice."

Martin did not like the sound of that, "Be advised that if you were to do something foolish, all Zyldonians in our custody will be killed, and for each Protectorate citizen in your custody harmed, we would kill one thousand of your citizens by orbital bombardment."

"Understood" was all Noak could muster.

"Said exchange shall occur within fifteen Earth days. We will have transports on hand to retrieve our people. We shall also launch a prisoner convoy immediately to return your people to you."

"Very well."

"Article V: Disposition of Zyldonian officers and men. All enlisted personnel of the Zyldonian armed forces shall be granted a full pardon and are hereby paroled. All officers of the Protectorate equivalent rank of ensign to captain shall be required to sign an Oath of Loyalty within sixty Earth days of the ratification of this treaty. Any officer not complying with this clause shall be imprisoned until the oath is secured. If the imprisonment lasts longer than four hundred Earth days, said officer shall be executed. All officers having the equivalent rank of commodore to fleet admiral will be required to sign an Oath of Loyalty to the Protectorate within thirty days of ratification. Any officer who is not in compliance after that time shall be executed. I will have oaths drawn up for you and your men should you wish to sign today."

Noak looked like he wanted to die, "How very gracious of you."

"Article VI: Occupying Forces. As has been stated above, Zyldonia shall be under Protectorate martial law for a period of seventy five years. A special occupation fleet shall be assigned to this system consisting of no less than sixty ships of the line. Further, a full army of Protectorate Marines shall be stationed on Zyldonia. Said army shall consist of no fewer than 210,000 marines. The general in charge of said troops shall be the military governor of Zyldonia and all of his decisions are law. Only the Council of Admirals shall be able to review his actions and make any necessary changes. Another marine corps consisting of no fewer than 50,000 marines shall be stationed on the fifth planet of this system. A pressure dome base shall be built there and a Protectorate training facility and weapons depot shall occupy the planet. All Zyldonians already on . . ." Martin consulted a pad for the name of the planet, " . . . Anceph, shall be relocated to Zyldonia. No Zyldonian citizen will be permitted on or near Anceph. A no fly zone shall be established in a sphere 1,000,000 miles around Anceph. Any unauthorized vessel in that area will be destroyed."

Noak did not like this at all, "We'll have to evacuate fourteen million people! They have lived there for over one hundred fifty years. You can't expect for them to just pick up and leave! They won't stand for it!"

"Be that as it may, you will have four Earth months to clear the planet. Anyone left on it after that time will be eliminated."

"That's not enough time. These terms are ridiculous. I beg you to reconsider."

Martin shrugged and said without much sympathy, "To the victor go the spoils. I very much doubt that if the situation were reversed, we'd be getting much consideration from you. We want the world for its metal rich crust, good farmland, and to set up training facilities." Martin's voice softened a bit, "However, I can be reasonable. The Protectorate will provide troop transports and cargo carriers to assist with the evacuation. That's the best I can do.

Noak looked a bit mollified, "Thank you. That's something at least."

"Article VII: Ceding of Zyldonian property and territory. Beginning immediately, all Zyldonian government and military offices and lands shall belong to the Protectorate occupation forces. Said buildings and lands shall be used as military headquarters, barracks, and residences for high ranking officers and the like. In addition, the island continent of Palaboa and three hundred square miles of Klyla, as indicated on this map, shall be cleared of Zyldonian citizens so that Protectorate military and their families may use it."

The Zyldonian contingent erupted, "Those are our finest lands . . . we won't stand for this . . . that's nearly 20% of our habitable land . . . these are not peace treaty terms, this is extortion!"

Martin let them babble for a while before bellowing, "Silence! You know the alternative. If and when the occupation ends, and Zyldonia takes its place in the Protectorate, those facilities and lands shall revert back to you."

Noak was incensed, "Are we to believe that you will simply give our land back to us after you have a foothold on our territory? After your families have lived there? After two or three generations have been born there? I think not."

Martin gave Noak a level stare; "The Protectorate has never reneged on a treaty. If I say the land will be returned, it will be."

"I don't believe you."

"That is your prerogative."

"Are you done?"

"I'm fairly certain that the Council of Admirals will add a great deal more to this document, but I believe I have presented the main points. My final stipulation is for me alone."

"And that is?"

"First everyone will leave the room. Admiral Shindessa, please have our guests escorted back to their shuttle. They may depart."

One of Noak's aides protested, "We will not leave without the Bar-Conphir. You will not use him as a hostage."

Martin looked put out as he said, "I have no intention of doing so. In addition, you must be fully aware that I have no need for hostages as you are in a position to do absolutely nothing. I simply want the Bar-Conphir as a witness." He turned to Jaspa, "After our guests are on their way, have all senior officers report to the bridge."

Jaspa opened the door and had the Zyldonians file out. A security contingent met them and led the party to the hangar bay. Noak turned to Martin, "Now what is this all about?"

The bridge was crowded with all the admirals standing around in addition to the normal complement. No one had any idea what was going on. Even Noak had only the slightest hint, and even that did not help much.

"Admiral on the bridge." Martin's presence was announced by the ship's captain.

"As you were. Helmsman, take us into Zyldonian orbit."

The confused lieutenant broke formation and headed for the second planet in the system. "Speed?" inquired the officer.

Martin replied, "Maximum sublight. The sooner we get this done, the sooner I will feel like this war is actually over." This comment only served to befuddle the personnel on the bridge further.

The Triumph glided out of the battle zone with its lifeless hulks and various ships conducting rescue operations. Fortunately, Zyldonia was on the same side of the star as the battle, so the trip would be a relatively short one.

Martin moved to the tactical position, "I will relieve you, ensign." The young man looked at the admiral then at his captain and said simply, "Yes sir."

After a short twelve minute cruise, the Triumph arrived at its destination. Martin called down to the helmsman, "Put us in a geosynchronous orbit above 36°, 17', 56" N latitude and 105°, 6', 7" E longitude." The helmsman did as he was told. Noak now knew why Martin had asked him about these coordinates in the conference chamber, but he still had no idea what Martin intended to do. 'Maybe he's cracked' thought Noak with glee, 'but alas, I do not have that kind of luck!'

The next thing Martin did alarmed the crew and downright frightened Noak. The admiral was bringing the weapons system on line! Power indicators on the forward FAL banks pegged at 100%.

"What are you doing?" cried Noak.

"Calm yourself Bar-Confir. If you remember, I asked you for an uninhabited, desolate section of your world."

"I still don't understand!"

"You will." With that Martin targeted his controls and put a picture of the target area on the main viewer. A piece of land appeared on the screen as barren as the dark side of the moon. A grey, parched landscape stretched from horizon to horizon. Martin liked what he saw, aimed, and fired. A red beam shot from the Triumph. Air was ionized as the FAL burst ripped through the atmosphere. The land exploded forming a large crater that was bordered by a glassy surface where the silicone rich sand had melted.

"There" said Martin, "The circle is closed. I fired the first shot in this war for the Protectorate, and now I have fired the last. Helmsman, you may take us back to where we came from." With that, the war ended for Martin. The history books record that the last shot of the Prescottian War was fired by Admiral Martin Gammage at 1619 hours on June 5, 2527.

Chapter XI: THE END OF THE BEGINNING
September 23, 2527
Just outside the Sol System aboard P.I.V. Triumph

The yellow light of Sol could just barely be seen this far out. The Triumph had just completed her deceleration maneuver. Her fusion engines thundered to life to take the gallant lady on the last leg of a very long trip. Martin had waited twelve days for elements of the 20th Fleet to arrive and relieve him. Most of the 11th and 12th Fleets were on their way back to various home bases for much deserved R and R and of course, the inevitable repair of battle damage and refits. Martin, however, had the Triumph buttoned up in system so that he could make the voyage back to the Sol System and home.

The Triumph had been cruising at 2750c and had only slowed to tune her engines periodically. Even at that great speed, it had still taken 95 days to cover the 712 light years of the voyage. The strain had been great, but Martin had wanted to return before the end of September so that he could be a part of the voting. Just about everyone believed that the vote was a mere formality, but Martin wanted to be there to see it. He had been through so much, and had sacrificed much. He felt he had to be present to honor Marcus' memory and the memories of all that had died.

As the Triumph skirted the Oort cloud of Martin's home, another vessel came along side. The P.I.V. Maximus had just been finished twenty days ago. The Triumph's sister ship had not been completed in time to see any action, but she was a welcome addition to the depleted navy. The Maximus was just the first of many vessels that would join Martin's victory parade home to Earth.

"Admiral, the Maximus is signaling."

Martin nodded to the young lady at communications. A familiar face lit up the screen. Admiral Beedle smiled upon seeing Martin, "Welcome home Admiral. I speak for the entire Protectorate when I congratulate you on your historic victory. I have been given the honor of being the first to escort you to Pluto where the procession will begin. Shall we?"

Martin nodded, "Lead on Admiral, and thank you for the welcome. It's good to be home."

The lift doors opened and Ryn and Jaspa stepped out. Jaspa walked over to Martin and put a hand lightly on his shoulder. Martin reached up and clasped the proffered hand. Jaspa was now a full admiral at Martin's urging to the Council. Slopac had also been promoted. There had been other changes as well. Ryn, now sporting a third star, was engaged to be married. While convalescing, he had rekindled the romance with Sarah Blaithe, former X.O. of Martin's battleship command. Captain Blaithe had been at the final battle in command of the Battleship Heroic. Ryn had taken great pleasure in personally promoting her to commodore. Sarah was expected to join them on the bridge shortly. Ryn had all but recovered from his wounds. It was good to see the big man hale and healthy once again.

The two mighty vessels approached Pluto. The tiny ball of ice floated lazily in its orbit around a distant star.

Martin could not wait to feel the warmth of that sun on his face. He squeezed Jaspa's hand tighter at the thought.

Three vessels of the 1st Fleet were waiting for them in orbit. The plan was to make the "Grand Tour" of the Solar System to act as a victory parade. More and more ships would be joining them as they passed by each planet in turn. At least one vessel representing the planet would join the group at each stop. In this case, the Pluto survey ship, Cerebus, took up a position in the parade. The five ships joined up and headed for their next stop, Neptune.

Sarah joined the gathering in the flag alcove on the bridge. It was becoming crowded, but no one seemed to mind. Each was occupied by his or her own thoughts on this momentous occasion. The trip in was scheduled to take twenty hours, so the heroes had plenty of time to talk, relax, and unwind before the real festivities on Earth began.

The stops at Neptune and Uranus increased the Triumph's following to over twenty vessels. The ships made good time, and soon the magnificent rings of Saturn came into view. No matter how many times Martin saw that gorgeous sight, it never failed to amaze and awe him. The rings were more beautiful than he had ever seen them. Perhaps the sweetness of victory was shading his vision. Whatever the reason, the sight was breathtaking. Martin ordered a thirty minute halt. Jaspa, Martin, Ryn, and Sarah made their way to the observation deck. The couples held each other and shared a moment in silence. Martin doused the lights. The only illumination in the room was sunlight reflected off the rings. Martin wished that moment could last forever, but the thirty minutes flew by. It was time to continue on their way.

The Jovian System added fifty vessels to the gathering. Jupiter's many moons were the homes of millions of

Protectorate citizens. Jupiter's satellites were rich in valuable ores. The king of the planets was in all its glory. Martin watched as the great red spot slipped by still intact after all these centuries. His own system was replete with wonders uncountable. He was so happy to be alive. The love of his life was by his side and he was returning a conqueror. Good friends had seen him through, and thank the universe, most had survived. The growing parade shot away from Jupiter on their way to Ceres.

The largest of Sol's asteroids grew larger on the screen. Six thousand hardy souls had chosen to make their homes there. They subsisted by trading Cere's valuable ore resources for foodstuffs, money, and even luxury goods. Several mining ships joined up for the trip to the red planet.

Mars had always fascinated Martin for as far back as he could remember. Mars had changed so much since the Viking probes of centuries ago. Now, over 850,000,000 souls called the red planet home! Terraforming of the world had started in 2052. The day was rapidly approaching when a man could step outside into the Martian air without a respirator or pressure suit. Martin thought of all the monumental things the Protectorate had done for all its citizens, and soon, Martin would be the ruler of this vast empire. The thought was almost overwhelming. He would do everything in his power to be certain that he ruled well and continued to do the "greatest good for the greatest number of people." This had been the Protectorate creed for centuries. Earth was by-passed as the procession made its way to the inner planets. Venus and Mercury, the two inner gems of the Sol System, yielded their participants. The fleet looped around the sun on its way to the moon. Earth's lone satellite was now a crowded, bustling megopolis. Mines dotted the surface and bored their way deep into the moon's crust. Vital ores were extracted with care and were sent back to the mother planet or used right there in the numerous Lunar shipyards. A plethora of vessels of all shapes, sizes, and classes joined the gathering. The final leg of the journey took seven minutes. Martin thought back to man's first lunar mission. His mighty ships had just accomplished in seven minutes what it would have taken their primitive rockets three days. The ironic part was that Martin's ships could have easily gone much faster. The Triumph slipped into high Earth orbit. The other vessels took up positions and began firing FALs and special missiles. The pyrotechnic display was dazzling. Martin took a deep breath and smiled. His eyes were moist. Again he clasped Jaspa's hand and then though better of it. "What the hell," he said, and took her into his arms and kissed her passionately. The crew cheered. Martin was home.

September 26, 2527
Grand Chambers of the Council of Admirals
Phoenix, North American Continent, Earth

The last three days had been one giant celebration. From the moment his shuttle touched down, until now, Martin had been shuffled from parties, to receptions, to ceremonies, to meetings with dignitaries from various Protectorate worlds, to just about anything imaginable. Everyone wanted to catch a glimpse of Martin Gammage.

He had been able to squeeze in a two hour visit with his father. Ryn, Sarah, Jaspa, and Martin had barricaded themselves in the elder Mr. Gammage's home to avoid the media. The five had talked about any number of things until Martin became very serious. He stood, walked over to Jaspa and got down on one knee, "I realize that this is a very old fashioned way of doing this, but what I am about to say is so important to me that I want to give the occasion all the respect it deserves." Being human, Martin's father and Sarah knew what was coming next, but Jaspa was in the dark, although she did have some ideas. Ryn was completely mystified.

"My dearest Jaspa, I love you so deeply that I am ashamed that I must use cumbersome words to express such a profound and forceful feeling. There are many types of love, and people are fortunate to feel perhaps a small sample in their lifetimes. In you I have found them all. You are my lover and my friend. You are a confidant, a protector, an angel, a joker, a lover, a child, a trickster, and a caring woman. I do not know how I became so fortunate to have you enter my life. You have seen me through the bad times; picked me up when I was down. We have shared everything and we complete one another. Without you my triumphs are meaningless, my life . . . empty. I want to be with you forever. I want to continue to share myself with you. Please complete me and make my life whole forever. Will you be my wife?"

Sarah was in tears and Ryn placed a strong arm around her shoulders. Martin's father simply nodded to Martin, but that simple gesture spoke volumes to the admiral. Martin's father had been extremely impressed and moved by the amount of emotion his son had displayed. Jaspa sat for a while unmoving. A single tear traced down her cheek. Finally, the spell was broken. She looked into Martin's brown eyes with her purple ones, "Yes" was all she said, and all Martin needed to hear. They kissed. The date was set for the first of October. It was hoped that they could celebrate their marriage on the day that Martin got his fifth star.

The celebrations continued right up to the vote. At exactly 1300 hours, the Grand Room was sealed. Those admirals unable to attend had already sent their ballots by F.T.L. Communications. Those votes had been tallied and would be added to the results of today's polling.

Admiral Bue-Sing Fong stepped to the podium, "If you will all take your seats we can begin. There are but two nominees this year. The first is Admiral Martin Gammage . . ."

Pandemonium. The hall erupted with cheers of support. To say that behavior was unusual for such high ranking officials would be the understatement of the millennium. When all was quiet once more, Admiral Fong continued " . . . nominated by Admiral Beedle, Admiral Shindessa, and Vice admiral Calplygian, among a host of others. The second nominee is Admiral Cyrus Morta, nominated by himself."

Dead silence at this announcement. Morta was dead and he knew it. All his campaigning, all his schemes, all his plans were about to be blown away like chaff on the wind. The only saving grace was that Admiral Gammage could not take any action against him without looking ridiculous. After all, there was no proof of any wrong doing on his part.

The vote commenced and was soon concluded. Each admiral placed his or her thumb on the ID plate and pushed the appropriate button for his or her choice. The computers took it from there. After about forty five minutes, the results were announced.

A computer specialist mounted the stage and removed the result card from a force field box. The computer room was heavily guarded day and night all year round to prevent tampering. The nervous technician began, "This year there were 2,840 possible votes." He paused for a moment to make sure his information was correct. He could not quite believe the results; "I am surprised, but pleased to inform you that there were no abstentions this year." A murmur of surprise swept through the hall. Every year there were at least a few who did not vote for whatever reason. It seemed that everyone wanted a piece of this action. The tech continued, "The results are: nine votes for Admiral Morta . . ."

Chaos erupted outside. The vote was being simulcast all over the planet. The Protectorate now knew they had a new Fleet Admiral after the longest drought in history. They needed to calm themselves, however. By law the results had to be read into the record in toto or the vote was not considered official.

Hushes swept through the crowd, of course, this only served to make the problem worse. Eventually things calmed down from within and without. The tech continued, "Admiral Gammage received 2,831 votes. This translates to 99.7%. Congratulations, we have a new Fleet Admiral!"

The din that took place before was only a warm up for what happened now. Martin had been elected by the largest margin ever. Everyone was trying to be the first to congratulate him. Ryn caught him in a huge bear hug. Jaspa kissed him sweetly. The news ran around the world faster than Hermes could have carried it. The Protectorate had been headless for twenty years. The war split power among many of the fleet commanders and other well liked officers, but no one had been able to secure a large enough power base, until now. The Protectorate had desperately needed a leader to consolidate its war winnings. The end of the war was going to bring huge amounts of territory, most explored, but some not. Several new races would be entering the Protectorate. Fleet Admiral Gammage had his work cut out for him.

There was one being in the hall that was not sharing in the exuberant antics of his peers. Admiral Cyrus Morta sat with his head in his hands staring into nothingness. He would undoubtedly be shipped to the hind end of space if Gammage could not come up with a way to cashier him outright. That might be preferable. Morta's desperation was short lived, however. He was resilient and nothing could curb his greed and lust for power. He still had his four stars. He would find a way yet to do away with Gammage and his sycophants. He would . . . something was wrong. He was getting another one of his headaches. He had been having them for several weeks. He had not seen a physician, as he was too busy preparing contingency plans should Gammage be elected.

His black skin had turned a sickly gray. Red began to frame his eyes. He was having trouble seeing. A young aide of one of the other admirals approached him, "Are you all right sir? You seem . . ."

"Mind your own business boy! Get away from . . . from me." The admiral pitched forward onto the table, unconscious.

October 1, 2527
Grand Phoenician Amphitheater

Jaspa Gammage looked at her husband of three hours. He was resplendent in his dress uniform. The epaulets still contained four stars as did her own. Soon, however, one little star would elevate Martin above all others until his death or retirement. Jaspa was so pleased for Martin she could burst.

The wedding ceremony had been marvelous. As a retired admiral, Martin's father had obtained permission to conduct the ceremony. Protectorate weddings were short affairs as all religious overtones had been done away with centuries before. The bride and groom, by custom, simply said whatever was in their hearts. Jaspa professed her undying devotion to Martin, and Martin, oddly enough, thanked Jaspa for the honor she was bestowing upon him. Jaspa thought that the loveliest sentiment she had ever heard.

"Ready?" she asked her husband.

"I don't know, what do you guys think?"

The "guys" wagged their tails at Martin. Teddi and Indy had stood with the couple all through the Battle of Prescottia and Martin had not forgotten that he owed Indy his life.

Suddenly, trumpets sounded, "This is it" said Martin, "you had better get in your place."

"Yes sir Fleet Admiral."

Martin smiled, loving Jaspa very much, "Don't make me bust you for insubordination, ensign."

Jaspa giggled lightly and found her place in the processional. A lone drummer began a march. By custom, Martin was to select one representative of each grade of admiral on active duty to serve in the processional. He could also invite up to four guests at his discretion. The first man to enter and make his way to the reviewing stand was his father. The elder Gammage was wearing a slightly out of date uniform from his time in service. He walked down the isle and sat in the chair with his name on it.

Next, walking side by side, were Indy and Teddy. One might think that animals in the processional would be strange, but a great many Fleet Admirals had chosen their pets to be with them on their special day. Fleet Admiral Cooper had brought a huge Hyacinth Macaw. Fleet Admiral Lesniak rode his horse. There were many other examples.

The drum beat changed to the "March of the Commodore." Sarah Blaithe walked down the isle. She had been overwhelmed when Martin had asked her to do this; she felt it was a great honor.

The music changed once again to the theme of the rear admirals. Edward Longly strode down the center isle, head held high. He was the highest ranking engineer in the entire Protectorate. His argument with Martin in the galley of the Vasco de Gamma felt so long ago. He was happy they couldn't come to a decision then. Edward was extremely proud to serve Martin.

The cadence changed to the appropriate bent for a vice admiral. Ryndock Calplygian was bedecked in his greatest finery. He was so proud that he puffed up beyond his already impressive bulk. The mountain of a man caught the eye of his fiancée, already seated. He smiled at her as he took his seat.

A trumpet now accompanied the drum as Admiral Jaspa Shindessa-Gammage made her way to the reviewing stand. Her eyes glistened. She was so proud of her husband. She was awash in love, pride, and devotion for that man. She did not think it possible to hold so much emotion for one person. She accepted the salutes of all present, being the highest ranked person in attendance thus far. She found her seat.

The Protectorate National Anthem boomed from the band as several more full admirals made their way into the room. Admiral Beedle was last. There were but two more people to enter now.

Martin was permitted to select anyone he wished to conduct the promotion ceremony as long as the nominee was presently serving or had served in the Protectorate Armed Forces. He felt it only fitting that this man should be the one to promote him. Without his help, he probably would be a retired Fleet Captain by now. Admiral Donald Higgins (retired) made his way to the stand. In his hands, on a satin pillow for all to see were two rank insignia pins for a fleet admiral. Five stars were surrounded by a half wreath on either side. In the middle of the stars were a silver eagle holding a ribbon. Upon the ribbon was written, "Fleet Admiral of the Protectorate." The aged admiral stood behind the podium.

A hush fell over the crowd. The band began the "March of the Fleet Admiral" and Martin Gammage strode into the isle. The hall erupted, drowning out even the loud music. Martin kept his eyes forward as he became aware of the awesome responsibility he was about to take on. He knew that he would have advisors and very gifted, capable, and loyal subordinates, but when it came down to it, Martin was ultimately the man in charge. He took a deep breath and mounted the stage.

Quiet fell across the room. Over nineteen billion pairs of eyes were watching as this took place. The remainder of the Protectorate would see it when the F.T.L. beam reached their sector. Admiral Higgins began, "We are gathered to witness a very rare, very auspicious event. An event that has only taken place a handful of times since the dawn of the Protectorate: The promotion of a being to the rank of Fleet Admiral. I cannot begin to convey the singular honor I feel to be the presenter at this ceremony. Martin Gammage has fought bravely, cunningly, and with honor to bring us a great victory. I am in possession of a double honor as I was the great man's teacher as well. It is the dream of every educator that someday a student shall surpass his or her station to a higher level. I am blessed to have this happen to me. Admiral Martin Gammage, do you accept the judgment of the Council that you be promoted to the rank of Fleet Admiral?"

"I do."

"Do you swear that all of your actions will be geared to the philosophy of our first Fleet Admiral, Alexander Kinkaid, that is, to do the greatest good for the greatest number of people?"

"I do."

"I have waited a long time for this, sir. I knew even when you sat in my classes that you were destined for great things. If I have assisted you in any small way, I must tell you that it was an honor to be of service. May you rule well. May your reign be a long and fruitful one. At this time I will remove your rank insignia.

This was the beginning of a ritual that dated back to the second Fleet Admiral. Martin's four stars were practically ripped from his shoulders. They were then unceremoniously destroyed as Donald Higgins crushed them under his feet.

"You are now nothing" Higgins continued, "You now know what it is like for someone to have absolute power over you. You must remember to be kind and just to everyone under your command from the highest admiral to the lowest crewman. Do you swear to respect all beings under your command?"

"I do."

"In that case, having agreed to all terms, and having been duly elected by the Council of Admirals by a 75% or greater margin, it is my profound honor to promote you to the rank of Fleet Admiral." Donald pinned the elaborate rank insignia to Martin's shoulders. A standing ovation ensued. Tears were rolling down Martin's face. Ryn, Jaspa, Eddie, and Sarah were crying as well. So much had been faced: Friends were killed, injuries were sustained, ships were lost, and blood was shed by their hands, so much had happened that this ceremony was acting as a catharsis. Emotion broke through the dams the friends had built to protect their own sanity. They all found each other and embraced.

*   *   *

One day later
Admiral's Hospital

Before Martin took command for good, he had one more thing he had to settle before he could put the war behind him, before Marcus could rest in peace.

The Fleet Admiral was greeted at the door by a young nurse. She congratulated him on his promotion and directed him to where he wanted to go.

The door to room 414 was closed. Martin opened it, stepped inside, and locked it.

"Wake up you bastard!"

Admiral Cyrus Morta awoke from a nap. When he saw who it was, he immediately adopted a sarcastic and condescending demeanor, "Well sir, here to tell me personally about my assignment to a backwater nowhere? I'll save you the time sir and simply read the orders when I get out of here."

"Oh, you'll be leaving before you know it."

This comment took Morta back a bit. He had suffered his race's version of a mild stroke. The doctor said it would be eight to ten days before he could leave. That was all right though since he was treated like a king in the Admiral's Hospital. "What do you mean? I'll be here for another ten days . . . sir."

Martin smiled a dangerous grin. "Let's reminisce, shall we? Do you remember an aide by the name of Calvor Joor?" Morta turned an interesting shade of ash gray.

"I can see by your reaction that you do. You see, I simply bribed him with the star you held back from him for so long. He was so grateful, he wanted to know if there was anything he could do for me."

Morta was badly shaken now but he tried one last card, "That means nothing. All you have is his word against mine."

"Wrong again! Joor wasn't as stupid as you thought. You should have known that the way you treated people would come back to bite you in the ass someday. He recorded everything Morta, everything. He made copies of all your orders. He made audio records of your conversations. There is an old phrase on my world that I think applies here: You're fucked! I have already distributed copies of everything to every admiral in all twenty three fleets."

For once in his life Morta was speechless. Martin jumped all over him, "Nothing to say? You're going to pay you miserable bastard. It seems I'm not the only officer you tried to bump off. You were successful with four others. FOUR! Four good men and women plus the crews of two of them. You cowardly little shit! Well now's the time to pay the penalty."

Martin calmed himself before continuing, "As of now, you are stripped of your rank and privileges. You will no longer disgrace this place of honor with your filthy presence. You will be moved to a prison hospital where you will be placed in one long ward with no privacy. I'm not going to kill you, oh no, that would be too easy. You are going to suffer as you have made others suffer. After you recover, I sentence you to hard labor until death. You are going to sit and rot in the sun with a pick in your dried, shriveled hands. How do you like that, you disgusting piece of filth? For what you've done, you should be put to death, but I think this is better. I'm going to make certain that every man, woman, and child in the Protectorate knows what you have done. I'm going to make you a public spectacle. And it won't stop there. I'm having this entire incident placed in the history books so that the name 'Morta' is vilified for all eternity. Good bye Mister Morta."

Martin walked out of the room feeling vindicated. The war had caused so much suffering, and Morta had the audacity to add to it for his own personal gain! Well now he would pay, and the ghosts of the past could be put to rest.

One month later
Office of the Fleet Admiral

Martin sat in his huge office reflecting on recent events. Ryn and Sarah had been married two days ago. Martin had happily granted them leave. They were presently on Duriac II for their honeymoon. As a wedding present, Martin had given Ryn a fourth star and placed him in charge of everything having to do with weapons and defense systems for the entire Protectorate. The promotion did have to go through the Board of Admirals, but this was a mere formality when the nomination came from the Fleet Admiral himself. He had also made Sarah a rear admiral and placed her on Ryn's staff.

Martin had bumped Eddie up to vice admiral and gave him the title of Chief Engineer of the Galaxy. It would be his job to improve repair times, refit procedures, new constructions, etc. An extremely important job indeed, as many vessels had been damaged and lost in the war. Subsequently, Martin had ordered a vigorous rebuilding project. By the time he was done, the Protectorate Fleet would be the largest ever with state of the art vessels and technologies. When confronted by the enormous cost this building project would incur, Martin exclaimed, "What the hell, the Prescottians are paying for it!"

Jaspa was made Martin's Chief of Staff. For all intents and purposes, she was the second highest ranking officer in the Protectorate.

Martin was firmly in place now. He had hand picked officers in all key positions. His advisors were set. He shuffled around Fleet commands. Most importantly, he set in motion the wheels that would be needed to govern all his new territory. He planned to increase the number of fleets from twenty three to twenty five. He wanted to add fifty new vessels to the 14th Fleet, the Protectorate's exploratory arm, to search the uncharted territory won in the war. At the beginning of the conflict, the Protectorate had some 6700 ships all told. That number was down to around 6000 now. In addition, scores of vessels still had damage of some kind. Many more were nearing the end of their operational lives. The Protectorate had lost many ships of the line in addition to countless cargo carriers, support vessels, and merchant ships. Martin wanted a 7000 ship navy by 2555. An ambitious goal to say the least, but if anyone could do it, it would be Ryn and Eddie.

Some parts of his new job were not as pleasant. The final casualty numbers were appalling. The Prescottians, (Zyldonians now, Martin reminded himself) had lost a total of six hundred fifty six ships of the line and nine hundred eighteen support craft and merchant ships. The Zyldonians had lost one hundred and six million lives; Martin still could not bring himself to believe that number. A further twenty three million had been wounded. The Protectorate had lost three hundred and ten ships of the line and countless auxiliary ships. Their loss of life had been much less; about thirty eight million dead and wounded, but over four hundred thirteen thousand prisoners had been taken and treated horribly. There would be emotional wounds to heal as well.

In that vein, Martin had passed judgment on his first war crimes case. A Zyldonian Raheem (the equivalent of a commander) had worked 10,000 Protectorate marines to death in baltonium mines. Baltonium is very unstable, and no safety precautions were ever put into place. Hundreds died every month in massive explosions. They were the lucky ones. The rest died slowly by overwork, exposure, and slow starvation. Martin had sentenced Raheem Blont to death.

Another case involved one Sholet Cuam (sergeant in Protectorate terms) who enjoyed beating Protectorate citizens to death for his own amusement. He also set up gladiatorial contests among the inmates. This one was also put to death.

Martin was also kept busy with the massive rebuilding projects in the Protectorate and former Zyldonian territories. Eddie had put a very capable man in charge of this project; one Rear Admiral Gary Doyle. He and his staff, including

Commodore Keith Proehl, had already gotten Tyla V up and running again. That world had been all but devastated by a Zyldonian orbital bombardment. The planet's valiant inhabitants had put up resistance for eighteen hellish hours before a Protectorate task force could arrive.

The Protectorate worlds were not the only ones receiving benefits from this program. Adena VIII was in the process of being rebuilt. Martin looked on this as helping himself. As a world conquered by Zyldonia, Adena VIII would become a Protectorate world in ten years if all went well. It only stood to reason that these planets should be assisted. Martin wanted working, viable planets when they were taken over by Protectorate rule.

As for the Zyldonians themselves, they were getting settled into occupation rule. Only two former admirals refused to sign the loyalty oath and were put to death. Thirty five former officers were languishing in prison. That number was down from the original five hundred seven. Martial law did not look too bad after a few months in a Protectorate prison.

There had been no major incidents on Zyldonia, and the military governor, General Joseph Terlaje, had not had to order one execution. A few imprisonments had been made. By and large, Martin was extremely pleased at the occupation thus far. Nearly all fourteen million inhabitants of Anceph had been relocated to Zyldonia. Some fanatics chose to stay, and Martin had even granted them an extra three days. Some left, but many clung to their home, hoping the Protectorate had been bluffing. Martin had no choice; five hundred forty three Zyldonians were executed to make way for the Protectorate.

The occupation forces were all in place. Elements of the 11th, 12th, 20th, and 21st Fleets were detached to form Special Occupation 1. Sixty ships of the line patrolled Zyldonian space at all times. All new constructions were being sent to relieve Occupation Force ships so that they could return to their respective fleets. Two hundred fifty thousand marines were stationed on Zyldonia. Their presence was tolerated if not embraced. Another fifty thousand were on Anceph. Some idiot tested the enforcement of the forbidden zone around Anceph. His ship, along with the eighteen aboard were destroyed. No one else had tried that stunt to date.

Yes, everything was going well. The occupation was proceeding to plan. Martin had sent the 14th Fleet on its way to chart and examine the Protectorate's new unexplored territory. He smiled a bit at that thought. He simply could not believe it had been eight years since he was a part of the 14th Fleet. He wondered if there was an ensign out there with a similar date with destiny. Martin hoped not. It would be some time before the Protectorate was back up to full strength. That was why he was only sending the 14th Fleet out about fifty light years. Martin simply wanted to firm up the borders. After that, he planned on consolidating his gains and rebuilding.

In the spirit of rebuilding in another fashion, Martin and Jaspa had been to see a geneticist. With a little help from the doctor, Jaspa was now three weeks pregnant. The child would be a boy. Surprisingly, it was Jaspa who insisted on having a son. She was quite pragmatic when she said, "If we have to go through all this trouble to get our DNA sequenced properly, we should be allowed to choose the sex of our child, and I want our daughter to have a big brother."

So a boy it was. Martin could only wonder at Jaspa's plans for their number of offspring.

Martin was content. He was so proud of everyone who had served under him. He took his vow seriously, and planned to do the greatest good for the greatest number. He had put the ghosts of his past behind him and had accepted the role of a leader. Thoughts like 'I should have done more to save lives', or 'If I had done this differently . . .' no longer haunted him. Martin casually lit a pipe and checked his appointment calendar. He was to interview one Lieutenant (j.g.) Andrew Gabbert for the last junior aide post on his staff. He took a couple more puffs from his pipe. The war was over, but Martin's reign as Fleet Admiral was just beginning.